THE YEAR THAT CHANGED US

HELEN ROLFE

Boldwood

First published in Great Britain in 2024 by Boldwood Books Ltd.

Copyright © Helen Rolfe, 2024

Cover Design by Alexandra Allden

Cover Illustration: Shutterstock

A CIP catalogue record for this book is available from the British Library.

Paperback ISBN 978-1-80415-556-1

Large Print ISBN 978-1-80415-557-8

Hardback ISBN 978-1-80415-555-4

Ebook ISBN 978-1-80415-559-2

Kindle ISBN 978-1-80415-558-5

Audio CD ISBN 978-1-80415-550-9

MP3 CD ISBN 978-1-80415-551-6

Digital audio download ISBN 978-1-80415-552-3

Boldwood Books Ltd
23 Bowerdean Street
London SW6 3TN
www.boldwoodbooks.com

To Jo, for the memories of primary school, my first true friendship and all of the letter writing when we were separated by the miles at the tender age of eleven; to Amanda for the college memories – Amanda, you will definitely recognise at least one particular scene (names have been changed to protect the innocent, or is that the guilty?); and to Amara for all the grown-up adventures we've had along the way, especially the Sunday drives around Dorset with ABBA as our soundtrack.

All of you are such wonderful friends – forever.

1

NOW: 2023

Emma

Emma felt like she could finally take a breath. The gathering in the café had whittled down to just a small group. Everyone had been here for a few hours now. But when she heard the group become a bit more lively, following the sound of the front door opening despite the *Closed* sign – which had been that way all day – she knew exactly who must have come inside. And she knew she couldn't hide in the kitchen forever.

She emerged to find Annalise standing just inside the doorway to the café, smiling over at the group, accepting their well wishes.

Memories washed over Emma, making this confrontation even harder than she'd always imagined it would be. Annalise still wore her trademark red lipstick, stunning against her dark hair. She'd aged of course, hadn't they all, but she was still beautiful and it conjured up the bubbly girls who'd once sat in this very café after school or at weekends, who'd walked arm in arm along the pavement outside. The girls who'd had their whole lives ahead of them.

Annalise. Her best friend. Or at least she had been. Once upon a time. But that hadn't been the case for almost two decades. Annalise and Emma hadn't seen or spoken to each other in eighteen years – she could almost define the duration to the day, which she supposed was what happened when you lost someone who had once meant so much.

Emma could hear murmurings, Annalise's name whispered on the air, which suddenly felt stifling in the confines of the café. The people here were mostly neighbours from Honeybee Place. A lot of them had lived in the street for as long as Emma's family had. Some of them could remember this very café twenty years ago when it was a greasy spoon, before her parents took it on and made it welcoming, cosy, friendly. And plenty of them knew Annalise Baker, who'd once lived at number twelve.

'What are you doing here?' Emma's sharp words stopped Annalise, who had taken a few tentative steps towards where Emma stood near the counter. Her bluntness had some of the other neighbours and friends occupying the café's tables looking across at the women, who had at one time been inseparable, who'd gone off on the adventure of a lifetime. Now, they stood metres apart in a showdown Emma had suspected might come one day, but she hadn't expected it to come without any warning.

Annalise rebutted the question by offering her condolences. 'I was really sorry to hear about Mrs Griffin. I came because I wanted to pay my respects.'

Today had been Mrs Griffin's funeral. Mrs Griffin had lived at number seven Honeybee Place since she was married in her twenties. When her husband Len died, Emma's family, the Millers, had taken Mrs Griffin under their wing somewhat, as an extension of their family. It was something they were good at doing. They'd done it with Annalise, although these days that was easy to forget. Two years ago – when things got too much despite the Millers' help – Mrs Griffin had gone to live with her son in Bristol and had stayed there right up until the day she died last month. At Mrs Griffin's request, the wake to follow the funeral was to be held here at the café she'd visited so many times over the years. It was a nod of appreciation to the closeness of the Miller family she'd been able to rely on a great deal before she left Honeybee Place.

Today's arrangements had gone smoothly. Neighbours had pitched in to lay out the food the second Emma opened the doors to the café. Regulars who didn't know Mrs Griffin had respected the café's closure and passed on their condolences. The only thing that had set Emma on edge was the funeral service itself. Not that anything had gone wrong specifically, but when she'd taken her dad's arm to escort him out of the chapel, she caught sight of the woman who'd lingered at the back as though she was afraid to come any closer. And a few more steps towards the chapel entrance had revealed her identity to Emma, a discovery that almost made her legs buckle beneath her right there and then.

Part of her was angry Annalise had shown up; the other part of her wanted to run to her one-time best friend and hug her and hold on tight and never let go again. Instead, she'd looked away, put one foot in front of the other to leave the service and hadn't seen Annalise's face again until now.

'She was really kind, wasn't she?' Annalise ventured.

'She'll be missed,' said Emma as though she was talking to anyone else who'd come to the funeral or the wake. Emma wanted to shriek, *Why come back here after all this time?* But she settled for a polite reply if only so she didn't get furious at a sombre occasion that deserved better. She tried to squash down her frustration that Annalise had shown up and was acting as though nothing had ever come between them and drawn a line beneath their friendship forever.

'I kept sending the postcards from Paris.' Annalise smiled

tentatively. 'To Mrs Griffin,' she clarified. 'She sent me postcards back from Bath and then Bristol.'

If Annalise was expecting her to smile in return, then she was going to have a bit of a wait. She picked up a stray napkin from the floor and took it over to the bin. She knew about the postcards – Mrs Griffin had told her – but she'd always been mindful not to interfere in what was going on with the girls. She hadn't asked questions. All she'd done was expressed her sadness that they were no longer friends and promised never to share the details of Emma's life if she was in contact with Annalise, and because Emma never heard about Annalise, she could only assume Mrs Griffin had done the same for her. Emma had needed the complete separation, the distance, an end after what happened, and information fed across the miles wasn't going to help her.

Annalise took another step closer. 'Can we talk? Please, Emma?'

'How did you hear about Mrs Griffin?'

'What?' Unsettled by Emma's avoidance of her question, she garbled, 'My mum told me.'

Emma nodded. But while she'd never planned to take on the Café on the Corner, the Millers' family business, she had learned to be a good hostess. And so she faked a smile and told Annalise, 'Help yourself to food, plenty left.' She gestured to the buffet that had been laid out on the pushed-together tables positioned against the side wall. The dishes no longer looked the way they had when they were served – sandwich arrangements were in disarray, slices of quiche were missing, ruining the perfect circular shape the pastry had been before. There were crumbs on the edge of the tables, a few little spills of tea here and there from the urn at the end.

Emma disappeared into the kitchen at the back, leaving people to flock to the former resident of number twelve. Hands resting on the counter in the kitchen, she looked out of the small back window that was open most of the year round, given how stuffy it could get with all the cooking going on. Emma closed her eyes. Allowed a moment to pull herself together. She would have thought it was losing dear Mrs Griffin who'd been so special to them, the service, the wake that might tip her emotions over the edge but she was wrong. It was Annalise's presence that had done that. After all this time, Annalise was back in Bath in England's south-west, the city she hadn't looked back on for years.

She jumped when someone pushed open the door to the kitchen and asked if they could get some more water. She put on a faux jolliness she didn't feel and turned to take the empty glass jug from one of her neighbours, assuring them she'd sort it in a jiffy. She robotically set down the jug, filled it with ice cubes, added slices of lemon and held it beneath the tap, waiting for the water to fill the vessel.

With a deep breath, she went back to the gathering, eyes down-cast wherever possible to avoid meeting Annalise's gaze, and set down the water jug. She went to open another window. Was it just her feeling the heat in here?

She swore beneath her breath when the window wouldn't budge but it gave up the battle with a good shove. She fixed the latch in place so it wouldn't blow wide open on the September evening breeze and looked out at the narrow, cobblestone street, wishing it was just another regular day at the Café on the Corner – the café that got its name from its location in Honeybee Place. The café was a stone's throw from the green square surrounded by iron railings – the square with trees and small pathways that led to patches of lawn exclusively for residents' use.

'You okay, dear?' Mr Cavendish from number nine put a hand on Emma's shoulder.

'I am, just a little sad – that's all.'

'Of course, as we all are.'

With a sigh, Emma thought about the flip of the seasons, how the leaves would soon turn, the sun would lose its warmth and gradually, the city would wrap itself up ready for another Christmas. Mrs Griffin had always been the first to comment on the seasons, the first to welcome the joy and the heat in the summer, the first to give out warnings about slippery pavements come winter. She'd been a delight to spend time with and Mr Cavendish was right: they were all sad at her passing.

Her neighbour patted her once more on the shoulder and left her in quiet contemplation, her mind back to Annalise's presence. Not all the neighbours would know of the big falling-out. Some would just assume the girls had drifted apart, that today's melancholy was only for Mrs Griffin.

When she felt the presence of someone else behind her, Emma knew it wasn't her neighbour this time.

'Can we talk?' Annalise repeated her earlier suggestion.

Emma turned. Her limbs felt heavy, her head foggy. 'Why now, Annalise?' She noted Annalise start at her use of her full name. Emma hadn't called her Annalise in years, not since Annalise turned eighteen and settled on the name Lise; she'd felt it suited her much better, as though trying to break out of a mould that up until that point had constricted her more than she could bear. The only person who had insisted on calling her by her full name, aside from her parents, was Xavier, the man she'd met and the man who'd ruined it all. It wound Emma up then that he wouldn't call her Lise and it still did now, even though it had nothing to do with her any more.

'What do you mean, "why now"?'

'Why come back for Mrs Griffin's funeral?'

'She was special to me.' Annalise gulped. 'So was your mum. I'm sorry she died. I sent a card, some flowers.'

'To my dad.'

'I thought that best. I would've come when I heard but... well, I didn't want to upset you, or anyone.'

'It was a long time ago.' Emma shrugged as though it was of no consequence but of course it was. Annalise had been a part of her life for so long. Her parents had welcomed her into their home as often as she needed, and no matter what had gone between them, Emma was touched when, following her mother's death, she took delivery of the flowers for her dad. Emma had been too wrapped up in grief to feel much that day but even now, ten years on, she remembered the gesture and how it had made her wish things had worked out differently with her best friend. She'd thought about Annalise in the middle of the funeral too, wishing she was at her side.

Keely – Emma's mum – had been sick for a while and had planned her funeral down to the last detail. She'd chosen a humanist service and the celebrant spoke eloquently using all the information he'd been given by the family, plenty of stories of Toby and Emma growing up, occasional memories incorporating Annalise and Emma, because they'd both been a big part of Keely's life, especially during their teenage years. That day, there'd been laughter, tears, togetherness, but there'd been no Annalise.

The words were out, the accusation, before Emma could stop herself. 'Is that why you didn't come to Toby's funeral? Because you thought it would upset me, or anyone else? Or was it that you were too busy with your new life to even care?' Arms crossed in front of her, Emma got ready to shove past and get out of Annalise's orbit.

Annalise's mouth fell open. 'I... I...'

She choked back a sob. 'My brother died and you weren't there for me.' And it hurt just as much now as it had done almost eighteen years ago. Annalise not showing up to Toby's funeral – no matter whether they were on speaking terms or not – had been a huge slap in the face for Emma. As well as everything else that had gone on, Annalise's absence that day and in the days after had been something Emma had never been able to come back from.

'I sent you emails, I sent letters.' Annalise hooked her dark, wavy, bobbed hair behind her ear, causing the sapphire and diamond teardrop earring on that side to wobble. 'There was good reason for me not coming to the funeral, Emma.'

But Emma held up a hand. 'I'm not listening to excuses. You weren't there, for me, for my parents, for Toby. And you coming back here now was a bad idea, full stop. So please, just go away and leave me alone.'

She stalked into the kitchen and promptly burst into tears. Annalise had been her best friend and she'd never ever thought that would change. She'd never thought her friend would hurt her or not be on her side.

And Emma didn't intend to make the mistake of ever letting Annalise get close again.

2

NOW: 2023

Lise

Lise stared at the closed door to the kitchen. She'd known coming here to face Emma after all this time would be hard. Mrs Griffin's funeral wasn't the only reason she'd come back to Honeybee Place; neither was the fact that her mother had transferred number twelve into her name. She had other reasons, and facing the past was always going to happen eventually.

Hearing Emma address her as Annalise had been surprisingly hurtful. She'd been Lise to her best friend for as long as she could remember. Was Emma going to try to hold her at arm's length until she upped and left? It would be easy for her to turn around and walk out of the café once and for all. But she couldn't. Being here was too important, and not just to her. She thought about the photograph in her purse, the love of her life. The person she most wanted to share with Emma. And she knew she had to persevere no matter how awful this was.

Lise was upset that her once best friend wouldn't hear her out, and she was frustrated, annoyed even. Emma was acting like she hadn't ignored every attempt Lise had made to get in touch. Lise had sent emails, then letters in case Emma had her emails going direct to spam if they were from her. She'd written time and time again until she realised she needed to accept that Emma wasn't ever going to reply. Emma knew her address; she knew where she lived. There was no excuse. The ball was well and truly in her court. But Lise had never once heard from her friend again. And admittedly part of her had dug her heels in at that. It wasn't only up to her to make the effort – they'd both made mistakes, both played a part – but Emma seemed to have forgotten.

After Lise was quizzed by Jenny Fairbrother from number fifteen, a newcomer to Honeybee Place long after Lise's time here, she spotted a pile of empty dishes and saw her chance. She scooped them up and walked away from the gathering that was diminishing as people peeled off to go home in quiet contemplation. The natural light in the café had dimmed, and someone switched on a light as she walked away. The nights were already beginning to draw in on the approach to autumn, and it struck Lise with a moment of nostalgia. She thought about the days she and Emma would hang out in the city or in the square for as long as they could, how they'd swap the outdoors for cosying up at the Millers' in the colder months to talk about school, friendships, boys, life.

As soon as she saw Emma's face when she walked into the kitchen, Lise knew she'd been crying. 'Where do you want these?' Probably best not to ask whether she was all right, if there was anything she could do. It was like teetering over eggshells – most of them were broken already but she had to believe some of them were still intact and worth saving.

Emma pointed to the counter next to the big sink. 'Leave them there. Thank you.'

The dishes clattered against one another as Lise clumsily set them down, almost losing the top two. She separated the pile into a couple of stacks so they had no danger of crashing to the floor.

She knew Emma was waiting for her to leave the kitchen but she had to stand her ground. 'Emma, I needed to come – to Bath, I mean. It wasn't just for Mrs Griffin. Number twelve is mine now. It's a bit of a mess from the tenants according to the agent.'

'They were noisy sometimes.'

'I apologise about that. But not too noisy I hope?'

Emma shook her head, her back still turned. 'Pleasant enough.'

'Untidy though.' Lise felt like she was wading through treacle trying to get a conversation going. 'Emma, please will you hear me out?'

Emma had a scrunched-up tissue in her fist, one that didn't look like it would stand up to the task of any more tears. 'Who told you my mum died?' Her hands didn't leave the edge of the sink.

Lise had noticed her friend looking out of a lot of windows since her arrival in the café – she felt like blacking them all out so she'd be forced to turn around and face her properly. 'Mum heard from Mrs Griffin and called me.'

Emma went quiet again and Lise looked around the kitchen. It was almost the same as it had always been, which was comforting. The only difference was the new cooker, stainless steel and with a much wider oven than before, and – she thought – extra rings on the top. Lise had worked here for a time with her best friend and it had been busy, chaotic, but fun. She warmed at the memory until the thought of her dad putting a stop to it crept in. It was a memory she'd rather quash than revisit.

'Emma, I tried to keep my distance today so you weren't uncomfortable at the funeral. I wasn't going to come to the wake but I really want, and need, to talk to you. I've been hovering outside for a couple of hours.'

Emma turned, reached past to grab the dishes and dumped

them into the soapy water, all of them rattling together unceremoniously. She plunged her hands into the suds without washing-up gloves and they soon turned red in the temperature of the water. The first dish survived its journey from the sink to the drainer despite the force behind it. Splashes rained down from the edge of the sink to the floor. Bubbles ran scared off the next dish to make its way from the water to the drainer.

Lise tried again by shifting focus to something that wasn't to do with their friendship. 'The group out there were just talking about Mrs Griffin's job as a dinner lady. One of them worked with her and has a few stories to tell.' No reaction from Emma. 'Imagine if we'd done that at school – thrown a Brussels sprout at a teacher when they walked past. Wonder if it was firm or soggy.'

Emma's smile was weak at best. 'Mrs Griffin would've kept the kids in order, I bet.'

'They were most likely scared of her.'

'Probably.'

'It was a nice service today,' she prompted again when Emma gave her nothing more. She supposed this was the difference between being the person who showed up unexpectedly and the one who'd been caught off guard. Lise had had time to prepare for this moment; Emma hadn't had a heads-up and it showed.

Dumping another soapy dish onto the drainer, Emma muttered, 'Let me get on; there's a lot to do. I'll be better if I'm left alone to do it.'

'Emma—'

But she cut her off. 'Not now.'

And that was it, Emma locked her out the way she'd done for the last eighteen years. She was on autopilot in her kitchen in the café she'd once talked about taking on before she saw her dream of teaching and went for that instead. Lise wondered what had happened to change her mind or whether it was simply because her parents needed her to be here as they got older.

Lise had no choice but to go back to the wake, although it was all but over now. Well-meaning neighbours wanted to catch up with her, ask her all about her life, and she kept her replies positive, devoid of any details of the dramas since she'd last seen them such a long time ago. To them, she was the girl who had gone to Paris, had lived and was still living the dream. In reality, it couldn't be further from the truth.

As she made small talk and shifted the focus to others whenever she could, preferring to talk about them, which let her zone out too, all she wanted was for Emma to give her time, to talk about everything that happened. They'd laughed and talked as teenagers, as young adults, vowing to be friends forever, to be the sort of women you saw still laughing together in their eighties with most of their years behind them. And yet here they were, both forty-four years old, and almost strangers.

What happened to those two girls? Those young women with their lives in front of them?

An hour later, when Emma came out of the kitchen, Lise was about ready to leave. Perhaps giving up for today wasn't a bad idea. She could go back to the townhouse that had once belonged to her parents and was now hers, the place she'd come to give a facelift ready for the next stage, whatever that was. All she knew right now was that it was a place to stay, the walls she'd grown up in, the house where she'd dumped the luggage a few hours before the funeral.

But Lise stayed put. She couldn't walk away. That's what Emma had done all those years ago and they hadn't spoken since. As far as Lise was concerned, walking away just made things worse.

Darkness cloaked the café and Honeybee Place, and it was almost another half an hour before Lise got Emma's attention.

Emma thanked the last two people remaining for coming as they collected their personal effects and made for the door, and instead of closing it, she held it open for Lise.

Deflated, Lise picked up her bag from the chair she'd left it on. She weaved between two tables but before she stepped out onto the street, she turned. 'Sooner or later, you're going to have to talk to me.'

'I don't have anything to say.' Emma walked back towards the counter.

Lise stopped in the doorway, her hand on the door handle, ready to pull it closed behind her. 'Is that it for us? Is that it for good?'

Emma stayed silent.

'If you say we are done, I'll get the townhouse ready for sale and you won't ever have to see me again.'

Her friend's shoulders tensed and she turned, came back over to where Lise was standing.

For a minute, Lise thought finally her friend was going to give in to the battle to hold her at arm's length.

But Emma merely pushed the door closed on Lise without another word.

It seemed the bonds of their friendship were gone forever. And that left Lise in an impossible situation, because she had to talk to Emma. She had to tell her the whole truth.

3

THEN: 1995

Annalise

Annalise threw herself onto her bed and let the noise carry on around her. She'd just arrived home from boarding school for the summer and her mother, with impeccable timing, had insisted on getting her new bedroom furniture. Today, the final stage – construction of the new desk – was happening. Still, at least the guy putting it together had a seriously cute butt – it made the noise and inconvenience far easier to bear.

She hooked her headphones over her head and pressed play on her Walkman. She'd drown out the noise, the bashing around, and go to a happier place. This morning, she'd been collected from boarding school in Yorkshire not by her parents – her dad was busy with work and Shelly didn't like to drive on the motorway any more, especially if she was going some distance – but by a car service. The sleek, black vehicle looked seriously impressive when it pulled up but Annalise would've much rather been one of those guys or girls whose parents had turned up, arms outstretched, welcoming their offspring into the bosom of their family for an entire summer. Perhaps she should be grateful. At least she hadn't had to lug a duvet, bedding, books and desk supplies, heaps of clothes and everything else on a train. Her parents had a heart, kind of.

The sound of Take That's 'Back For Good' had Annalise huffing and puffing. Not the best track to start with. She was only back in Honeybee Place for the summer, as per usual, and it appeared her best friend, despite the letters they'd sent back and forth, had a whole other life without her.

Emma and Annalise had been best friends since primary school, since Annalise had felt sorry for the six-year-old Emma who'd been tasked – like the rest of the class – with painting an opened-out egg box in bright colours. Some had painted theirs bright green to create a crocodile; others had used psychedelic colours just for the sake of it. Annalise was going to make hers orange and blue because those were her favourite. She had looked to the end of the table at the little girl with bright-red hair who was quieter than everyone else and had tears forming in her eyes. Nobody else seemed to have noticed but Annalise could see straight away what the problem was. The girl had been given an egg box to paint all right, but it was one of those plastic boxes and the paint slid right off every time she tried to put some on it. Annalise had promptly torn hers in half and given the unpainted half to the little girl with red hair and they'd been friends ever since.

The girls had seen each other through primary school, transitioning to middle school along with their high ponytails and big hoop earrings, which were all the rage, inseparable until Annalise's father decided that it would be in his daughter's best interests to send her to boarding school. She hadn't been interested in hearing about the standard of education she'd be getting, the opportunities it might well present. She was ten years old and all she knew was that she was being ripped away from her very best friend in the whole world.

The day her parents told her, Annalise sobbed her heart out, ran straight to Emma's house and cried all over her. There had been tears, from both of them, right up until the day she left. Over time, as Annalise and Emma kept in touch by letter, the days got easier and their friendship remained as tight as it had always been. But what really kept Annalise going was coming home for the holidays. She'd run straight to the Millers and she and Emma would hug and squeal, both talking over one another as they fought to catch up on the time they'd missed.

But that hadn't happened today. Annalise was sure she'd given Emma the right date for her homecoming but with end-of-year exams, it was quite possible that she'd missed the detail out of her letters, which had tailed off with so much study to do. An hour ago, after Annalise had got her bed straight – her mother had insisted she do that before she go anywhere – she'd shot off to number four and her best friend. She'd received a warm welcome from Emma's parents, Brendan and Keely, and Emma's brother Toby did a double take as he came down the stairs given their paths hadn't crossed in over a year.

She'd glowed inwardly at his reaction. It made her feel beautiful and a tiny bit powerful with her femininity, as he clearly hadn't expected this version of Annalise that came with curves and breasts. But as for Emma, she had no luck. Emma was at a sleepover party and wouldn't be home until tomorrow. And despite the smile Annalise had plastered on her face in front of the Millers, she was gutted. She should be the one having a sleepover with Emma, gossiping late into the night, in the same city again at long last.

Instead, Annalise had returned to number twelve, grabbed a

can of warm 7Up from the shopping bags in the kitchen and headed up to her room in a sulk and a panic that she no longer had the one friend she'd thought she could always depend on and vice versa. What kind of summer was it going to be if she didn't have Emma? Her boarding-school friends were scattered around the country. Some were even from Europe, and she didn't share the same bonds with any of them as she did with Emma Miller.

A knock at Annalise's door was swiftly followed by her mum Shelly poking her head around the door frame. You wouldn't think she was doing household chores today given the way she was dressed. No sign of a creased old shirt or pair of dusty jeans – she had an elegant, formal, summer dress with a stiffened collar, manicured nails and hair styled in an updo as usual. She'd soon be seeing to things around the house whether they needed attention or not – positioning the cushions on the downstairs furniture just so, making sure the rug in the sitting room was in the perfect place, polishing the glass-topped coffee table so you could see your face in it, dusting the ornaments here there and everywhere to within an inch of their lives.

Annalise tugged her headphones off when her mum lingered. 'What?'

'Don't say it in that tone. And lying there isn't going to sort your bedroom out, Annalise.'

'I'm tired. And the desk isn't even built yet.' She admired the desk-builder's butt again in black cargo trousers. 'I'll put everything in it and on it once it's done, but I'm staying out of the way for now.'

Her mum sighed. 'I suppose not getting in the way is best.' This earned her a look from butt-guy as he reversed out from beneath the desk with a screwdriver and moved to one side of it before crouching down there instead. 'I thought you were going to see Emma.'

'She's not there.'

For a moment, Annalise wondered whether her mum wanted to say something else but she simply picked up a vacuum storage bag of clothes and put it on the end of the bed, presumably as a hint to get everything hung up now, and left. Annalise might be away for big chunks of the year but she never forgot how her mum became nervous when anything was out of place. The untidiness in here must be her idea of hell, but that thought hardly gave Annalise any impetus to make it better until she had to. And why should she? It wasn't like her parents cared about her that much; they hadn't even come to collect her from school.

Annalise turned onto her back, headphones on again, and looked up at the ceiling with its light fitting that was far too fancy for her taste. She hummed along to 'Never Forget', tapping out the beat with her foot against the wall at the head of her bed, but she was interrupted again by butt-guy and hooked her headphones around her neck.

She flipped over rather than looking at him upside down. It seemed he was finished. 'Could you move it to the other wall for me? Please...'

'But your mum said—'

'Take no notice of what she said. I won't tell her that you moved it. I'll tell her I dragged it there myself but I probably shouldn't actually do that as I might damage the carpet. And then she'd hit the roof.'

'Right you are.' He was grinning as he said it and confided, 'I'm a bit scared of her to be honest.'

'Her bark is worse than her bite. And you haven't met my dad yet. He'll go ape if he knows you put the desk in the wrong place.'

His face fell and he cursed, unsure whether to honour her request now.

'I'm kidding. Don't worry, he's hardly around and when he is, he probably won't notice you unless you do something awful to get his attention. And putting the desk on a different wall to where my mother told you to put it doesn't really fall into that category.'

Annalise wondered how old this guy was – twenty maybe? And very cute. But too old for her when she was only fifteen. She looked older though, especially out of school uniform and wearing make-up. And in another month or so, she'd be sixteen like Emma – far more respectable to have an older boyfriend like some of the girls at her school. Sometimes, she hated being the youngest in her year. It meant she was the last to be able to do things like dating someone older – not that her parents would ever be happy with her doing that, or dating anyone for that matter. She'd be the last to be able to learn to drive, the last one to be able to buy a drink at the pub.

The desk guy finished up and Annalise had no idea whether he was really worried about her dad showing his face, but he packed up his tools and headed downstairs quick enough.

Annalise didn't have much inclination to get her desk sorted but for the sake of peace if her mum came back up here, she made a half-hearted attempt and put everything that had been on the old desk onto the new one, unpacked her school paraphernalia and then turned her attention to the box she'd ensured came upstairs with her first, for fear it might be left out for someone else to see. She pulled out a stack of hardcover notebooks and put all but one of them in the deepest of the new desk drawers before picking up a pen and the most recent of her diaries, the one that was only half filled with entries.

With her headphones on again she lay down on the bed and titled today's entry: *Summer 1995 – Honeybee Place.*

So many things about being here felt the same as they always had, except it was the first time she'd come home and hadn't seen

Emma within the first hour or two. Emma had made other friends and the thought of her best friend moving on without her terrified Annalise. Now, in the pages of her diary, there was no judgement. She put her whole self onto the pages including her worries, her insecurities, and her joys. The whole truth.

4

THEN: 1995

Emma

Emma took her overnight bag from the boot of her friend's mother's car when they dropped her back at Honeybee Place. It was only just after 9 a.m. but Sasha's parents had needed the gang all gone by nine so she could get to work.

Her head heavy from being up most of the night talking with her friends, Emma wrestled her bag through the front door to the Café on the Corner. Her throat was dry, her tummy grumbling and one of her dad's cooked breakfasts would go down a treat.

'Hello, lovie.' Keely came over and wrapped her daughter in a hug. 'How was it? Tell me everything.'

As if.

Emma dumped her bag out of the way at the foot of the coat rack in the hallway separating the kitchen from the café.

'Sasha got a karaoke machine for her birthday. We put it to good use last night.' She'd followed her mother into the kitchen where her dad was at the cooker and beckoned her over for a welcome-home hug even though it had only been a single night she'd been gone. She didn't know how they did it sometimes, the hours they put in here, but they appeared to love it. *Half the battle with a job*, her father always said.

'Those poor parents.' Keely buttered wholemeal toast and added on the poached eggs when Brendan passed the pan her way. They were a well-versed team. And Emma was often roped in. 'Table three.'

'Mum...' she groaned. 'Where's Toby? I thought he was working in here today.'

'Your brother is late, again. Go on, do that and your dad will whip you up your favourite – scrambled eggs with mushrooms and grilled tomatoes.'

'On it,' Brendan called out.

Emma couldn't complain at the deal being offered. She picked up the plate and smiled at her mum, the woman she resembled not only in her medium height but with her red hair and blue eyes and her organisational skills. But Emma didn't plan on using hers for a kitchen; she had her heart set on using her skills in a class-room and becoming a teacher.

Emma helped out in the café on Saturdays and sometimes for a few hours after school during the week if her parents needed her and if her school workload allowed, so she was familiar with the way the place ran, as well as some of the regulars given a lot of them were neighbours. She had a short chat with Mrs Griffin who was sitting at table three waiting for her poached eggs on whole-meal toast.

'You flew in the door so fast, you're lucky nobody was going the other way,' Mrs Griffin said and laughed as she picked up the black pepper pot and ground some of the seasoning over her eggs.

'I just came home from a sleepover and I need some of Dad's food.'

'I understand completely. Go get your sustenance or you'll

waste away.' She tilted her head in the direction of Emma's
exposed midriff. It was summer and plenty warm enough for crop
tops. 'I had a waist like that once upon a time.' Mrs Griffin sighed
as Emma left her to enjoy her food.

Toby came barrelling into the café next. 'You're late,' Emma
chided.

While Emma was a lot like their mum, Toby was very much
like their dad, as though characteristics passed through gender
alone. Toby had Brendan Miller's dark hair and smile full of
mischief. What he didn't have was Brendan's joy of the kitchen,
the café life, and instead had his sights set on flying planes.
Emma couldn't decide whether he was dreaming and needed to
get back to reality or whether he would one day be able to make it
happen.

'You're not the boss of me.' Toby was about to race past the
counter and towards the kitchen when he looked over at his sister
again. 'You seen Annalise yet?'

'She's not back until the end of next week.'

He shook his head. 'Nope, she's back already; came to the
house yesterday. I told her you'd dumped her as a mate, moved on
and sent her packing.'

'Mum,' she groaned when Keely came into the café and
ushered her son through to the kitchen with a message he keep his
clever remarks to himself.

Keely took the two orange juices in tall glasses she'd been
carrying over to the table in the middle. And when she was back
with her daughter, she told her that Toby was right: Annalise had
come to see her yesterday. 'She's looking really well. It's lovely to
have her back for another summer.'

'Mum, I need to go.' Filled with urgency, Emma suddenly
wasn't hungry any more.

Keely put a hand on her arm before she could move off

anywhere. 'Not yet, eggs are almost ready. Eat first, then go home and unpack. Another half an hour won't hurt.'

Her mum clearly didn't understand best friends and how much they needed to catch up when they'd been apart for so long.

Emma sat out in the kitchen on the stool by the back door and burnt her tongue as well as the roof of her mouth by shovelling her eggs in at a rate that would give even the hardiest eater indigestion. She didn't unpack her bag at home either – she opened the front door to the Millers' townhouse and slung the bag into the hallway. It had barely hit the floor before she closed the door and ran back down the short path and turned to go to Annalise's place.

It was Annalise's mother Shelly who opened the steel-blue front door with its rectangular glass panel at the very top, but Emma didn't get any words out before Annalise came flying down the stairs behind her, skidding along the wooden floorboards in stripy slouch socks. There was enough shrieking to make Shelly retreat, and Annalise took Emma's hand and ran back up the stairs with her, narrowly missing knocking the ornaments off the period shelf in the hallway.

They ran along the first-floor landing with its ivory and blue runner, up the next flight of stairs where there was a similar runner stretched out, and into Annalise's room. Annalise's bedroom hadn't changed much over the years. She had a new desk by the looks of things but the same wrought-iron bedstead on the double bed – she was so lucky; nobody their age had a double! – and the same tallboy were in situ. The rosettes from gymkhanas she'd taken part in as a kid weren't there any more, nor was the collection of Judy Blume and Enid Blyton books on the single shelf behind her bed or the giant poster with Bananarama on the biggest wall. Instead, there was an enormous print of Oasis, books by Virginia Andrews and Stephen King, and rather than rosettes, there was a jewellery box and a china tree, which held rings, necklaces and earrings on its branches. Annalise knew fashion. She always knew what to choose for herself and for Emma too.

'Have you turned all dark?' Emma plucked a copy of the first Stephen King book, *Misery* – which was alongside *The Shining* – from the bookshelf.

'No way.' Annalise bounced down on the bed next to Emma. 'I just like to read different things.'

They were facing each other the same way they'd done ever since they were little girls, knees clasped up against their chests, gossiping. They'd never had to worry about being overheard at Annalise's; her parents rarely came up to see her in her bedroom. Not like at Emma's house where her parents seemed to pop in every five minutes despite having a café to run full-time. Annalise's mum didn't work outside of the house and yet they had always seen less of her than Keely or Brendan. And as for Mr Baker, Emma had always been wary of him. He was so serious and didn't smile much, not like her dad who often laughed and kidded around. Mr Baker was tall, imposing and she tended to feel like she was in the way and should make herself really, really small when she came over so perhaps he wouldn't even notice her.

When Annalise had first come to number four with the devastating news that she was being sent away to boarding school, Emma had comforted her friend. She'd tried to think of the positives, the adventure, to make Annalise feel better. 'It'll be like *Malory Towers*,' she'd told Annalise, 'or the twins at *St Clare's*.' But it hadn't worked. Annalise had told her that it wasn't a fairy tale; it was her life. And she didn't want to go.

Now, there was interrupting, squealing, tripping over their words in the enthusiasm to get them all out at once. It didn't matter that they'd stayed in touch as much as they could; there was nothing quite like seeing one another in person.

'Your hair is *gorgeous*,' Annalise reached out to the very-red tresses that weren't cut in such a boring style any more. Emma's blunt-cut fringe had gone, the length of her hair was three times what it had been, and she'd been allowed to have a loose perm for her sixteenth birthday last November. 'Curls look so good on you. I always told you they would.'

'You have great hair without trying.'

'You have to say that. You're my best friend.' Annalise lay on her front, her knees bent so her feet were waving in the air behind her. 'So these new friends of yours... the friends you were with rather than here with me. Will I like them?'

'I'm not sure you'll get to meet – Sasha is moving to Oxford; the others have jobs and holidays lined up. The sleepover was a bit of a farewell as we're not even all going to the same sixth form.'

'Can't say I'm sorry that I get you all to myself for the summer.'

Emma could tell Annalise was testing the waters, testing whether they still had that solid friendship that had been in place or whether anyone else might have filled the void.

They gossiped right up until lunchtime when Emma and Annalise finally gave in to their hunger, ate a hastily made sandwich in the kitchen and snatched a couple of cans of lemonade from the fridge to take upstairs with them. Emma would much rather have eaten upstairs too but house rules were such that no food was consumed outside of the kitchen. They'd scarfed their food down without much chit-chat and as they ate, it had all come back to Emma. After a term apart, the tension in her friend's house, the rules that made it feel less of a home, were exactly the same.

As they left the kitchen, they bumped into Mr Baker coming along the hallway. He nodded a hello, the merest hint of a polite smile buried somewhere in that expression.

Another memory came back to Emma as they took the stairs back up to Annalise's bedroom: the recollection of having to endure breakfast with the Bakers after a sleepover here one night. It hadn't been anything like the chaotic scene played out at the Millers' every morning with conversations overlapping one another, an open milk bottle passed to the next person to appear, cereal bowls stacked haphazardly awaiting washing up, the sound of toast popping up before whoever made it hastily ate and got on with their plans for the day. At the Bakers' breakfast, there'd been perfectly laid place settings with napkins, a toast rack in the centre of the table, proper butter in its own glass dish rather than margarine scraped from a container, and barely any conversation.

'Your parents haven't changed,' said Emma as they flopped down on the bed and flipped the ring pulls on their cans. 'Your mum is so glamorous; she always dresses nicely.'

'I'd rather have your mum any day.' Annalise swigged from her can. 'Mum is like a wagging-tailed dog for Dad – takes his praise and attention as though it's the only thing in life. And he just keeps on putting on his suit and tie every day, works all the hours in the world, and barely takes notice of much else.' She shrugged but she wasn't fooling Emma when she said, 'It's fine. He can live his life; I'll live mine.'

'Annalise...'

'Emma, seriously. It's always been this way. I don't know why I ever expect it to change.'

Annalise's dad was a total contrast to Emma's. Brendan would hug her every day on his way out the door or when he came home – Emma couldn't remember Mr Baker ever hugging Annalise. Emma's mother, no matter how busy she was, always asked her daughter how her day was going, how school was, how her friends were. Emma heard similar questions from Shelly Baker but mostly, she was about keeping order to the house and the family, with requests for Annalise to be sure to put her laundry in the basket, to come down to dinner. And Emma had never heard laughter in this house either, something that struck her as odd and rather sad. And while Emma knew it wouldn't make up for the lack of interest or attention from her parents, Annalise would always be welcome at the Millers'.

In the written word, in the pieces of paper sent from one part of the country to another in their innocent pale-pink or cream envelopes, Annalise and Emma had kept their talk light, avoiding the topic of Annalise's parents and instead discussing what happened at school, friendships, boys, the latest bands and trends and how many days it would be until they saw each other again.

Emma leaned against her friend and put her head on her shoulder. 'I'm so glad you're home. I'm always there for you, you know.'

'You've got me too, Emma. I promise you.'

They linked their little fingers together the way they'd done as little girls. But it didn't feel silly; it felt as important now aged sixteen and almost-sixteen as it had back then.

They gossiped some more, finished their drinks and Annalise leaned over the bed to drag something from beneath it.

'What on earth are you doing?' Emma giggled and grabbed a hold of her friend's legs before she fell.

'Got it!' The triumphant victory was accompanied by a huff of exertion as Annalise pulled her body back up and properly onto the bed, a small bag in her hands. 'In here,' she said, 'is a bit of mischief for us both. Something I got from boarding school.'

'Show me!' Emma urged.

'Only if you promise not to tell anyone.'

Emma didn't want to do anything that would get them into trouble and her silence told her friend as much.

'Relax, it's not that bad, honestly. Boarding school is totally respectable, I swear. And I would say Guide's honour but I was never a Girl Guide – didn't even stick to the Brownies after I failed to make an acceptable bookmark using the appropriate stitching and then Brown Owl caught me sewing the bottom of my shorts to my friend's.'

'Just show me,' Emma begged.

But Annalise put a finger to her lips. 'Not here... your place. No arguments.'

* * *

Back at number four the girls, giggling away, ran up the stairs and into Emma's bedroom.

'Now show me.' Emma's impatience grew.

Annalise upturned the bag.

Emma peered closely at the alien item. 'What is it?'

'It's a gun.'

'It's not a gun.'

'An ear-piercing gun, an old one.'

'O-kay...' She dragged out the word, no idea where Annalise was going with this until the look on her friend's face said it all. 'No! You want to pierce your ears?'

'Shhhh... keep it down, Miller!' But she was grinning from ear to ear. 'I want to do a second piercing for me and for you. I don't even know where the gun came from originally, but I do know I bought the earrings myself from a reputable place so it's all hygienic. I've even got a bottle of surgical spirit and some cotton wool.'

Emma's hands went to both of her earlobes. 'I don't know.' But then Emma's sense of adventure kicked in. 'Is this one of those initiation things?'

Annalise rolled her eyes. 'Again, enough with the Enid Blyton references and the assumptions about boarding school.' And then a wicked smile beamed across her face. 'But in this case, yeah, totally like that. Four other girls did it already and passed the gun around. All I had to do was buy some piercing earrings, which was easy enough to do, all part of the initiation.'

'Wow.'

'So are you in?'

Emma leapt off her bed and had a quick check outside the bedroom door. She closed it again, making sure it clicked into place, and leaned against the wood. 'You bet I'm in. Cooper Billington from school says I'm too much of a wuss to do anything involving risk.'

Annalise shook her head. 'Who gives a flying fuck what that dickhead thinks?'

Cooper Billington was among the group who'd given Emma a hard time at school. She'd been teased about being too shy, too quiet, boring. She'd been called a Boring Fart enough times in her early teens and sent many a letter to Annalise saying how left out of groups she felt, ostracised – and all because she wasn't as mouthy or loud as they were, because she wasn't putting it about with the boys at school, or smoking and drinking. Annalise had told her then that it was their loss, that she should hold her head up high and know she was a hundred times better than they were. But Annalise also knew the pain the boy had inflicted on her when Emma had fallen for him. She'd had her first kiss with him too and then when Emma said she wasn't ready or willing to go all the way with him, he'd blown hot and cold and been messing around with another girl in one of Emma's classes.

'You're right: Cooper is a dickhead. Now show me the earrings,' said Emma.

Annalise unveiled the jewellery.

'You got two pairs,' said Emma. 'But we only want a single second one, right? That's way cooler.'

'Sure is. I just wanted us to have options.'

They both faced Emma's mirror on top of her tallboy and pulled back their hair to assess their single piercings, Emma with her gorgeous red hair and cheeks the same colour now she was getting excited about the prospect of updating their look, Annalise with her dark waves and olive skin back here for the summer and ready for whatever came their way.

When Mrs Miller called out from downstairs that there was Victoria sponge on offer, the girls left the bedroom with their secret intact and frustrated Toby and his mate Max in the kitchen as they whispered conspiratorially over what they were going to do and wouldn't share with either of them.

'What classes are you doing at school, Annalise?' Mrs Miller asked as the girls ate their cake.

'Mum,' Emma groaned.

Glasses perched on top of her head, her mum held her hands up in defence as she picked up the cake knife for washing. 'What? I'm just curious.'

'It's all right, Mrs Miller.' Annalise was always so polite with her parents when they drove Emma to distraction. She told Emma's mother all about school, the subjects she was taking, what she liked the most.

'I thought you'd never stop talking,' Emma whispered as they ran up the stairs and bundled back into her bedroom ready for Operation Ear Piercing. 'What are you doing?' She watched Annalise open her desk drawer and then move over to the tallboy.

'Please tell me you have some film in your camera?'

Emma went over and pulled open the very bottom drawer. 'Just put a new film in so we've got twenty-four chances to get the evidence.'

Jittery, Emma darted over to the door again and poked her head out. Once she'd closed it after she was reassured they were alone, she told Annalise, '*Corrie* starts soon and they'll never run up two flights during the ads, no matter how much they like talking to you.'

Annalise took the earrings out of the bag again. 'Only one pair is cubic zirconia; the others are plain.'

Emma noted the sharp points on the backs of them. 'We've both had our ears pierced already. It didn't hurt much then. Did it?'

'Can't remember.' They'd gone to get their ears pierced at the same time, both age ten. Emma's mum had taken them and they'd had hot chocolates and cookies afterwards, both of them unable to keep from looking in the aluminium serviette dispenser on the table at the café to check out their reflections.

Emma picked up the gun and suddenly, it felt heavy. 'How do you use it?'

'Easy.' Annalise showed her how the earrings were loaded and demonstrated the simple action to do the piercing. She'd lined up the cotton wool and surgical spirit on the desk and moved the chair to the middle of the room. 'Now, who's first?'

'You... you go first – you're way braver than I am.'

'Sure.' She sat down but not before she grabbed Emma's teddy bear from its position on her pillow and prompted Emma to pass her the camera. 'I'll do my best to take a picture and hope we're both in the frame. Although do you think I'll manage to do it? Shouldn't I be sitting still?'

'You're panicking.'

'I am not!' But she passed the camera to Emma. 'Take my photo before and after.'

Emma set down the gun and took the photo. While Annalise clutched her teddy bear tight, Emma wiped her earlobe with surgical spirit and then before either of them could change their mind, *clunk*.

'Shit!' Annalise yelped.

'Oh my God... sorry!' Emma flapped.

But now Annalise was in fits of laughter and it wasn't long
before Emma collapsed into the same, lying on her back on the
bed and clutching her tummy.

Annalise leapt up and looked in the mirror, smiling as she
admired her friend's handiwork before posing for the after photograph and declaring it was Emma's turn. Emma took a picture of
her loading the gun with the next set of earrings before Annalise
told her to stop stalling and to clean her ears with surgical spirit.

Emma cleaned her ears and then, clutching the teddy bear,
settled into the hot seat and squeezed her eyes tight shut. 'Just do
it.' She waited and when it came, it hurt so much she yelled, swore
out loud more than once.

'Shhhhhh…' Annalise snorted, she was giggling so much and
after she'd taken a picture, she lolled on the bed. They both did,
getting in the frame to take a photograph of them together with
any luck.

'That really hurt!' Emma had leapt up and was looking at her
ear in the mirror. The lobe was bright, bright red. 'I mean *really*
hurt.'

They stood side by side, admiring their reflections. 'We are the
coolest!' Annalise declared.

But their smiles disappeared when the door to the bedroom
flew open and made both girls jump. 'What's going on in here?' It
was Toby. Max had obviously gone home. 'I'm trying to study and
you both keep yelling.'

'Sorry, we'll try to keep it down.' Annalise tilted her head so
that her hair would fall over her ear.

But with Emma's ear almost as red as her hair, he didn't miss a
trick. 'What have you done to yourself?' And then he spotted the
debris on the bed. He rifled through it before either of them could
stop him. 'You pierced each other's ears?'

Emma dashed for the door and closed it. 'Tell the whole world why don't you?'

'Mum is going to go mental – you know that, don't you?'

'I'll tell her I had it done at a jeweller.'

'Can we even do that at our age?' Annalise wondered out loud.

Toby shook his head. 'You can't hide it, you know. What were you thinking?'

Annalise leapt in. 'The redness will go. Stop nagging her, Toby.'

'If you both yell again like that, they'll soon be up here.'

Annalise prodded his chest with her finger. 'Hey, for your information, it bloody well hurts.'

He laughed. 'Sure it does.' He turned to go but before he reached the door, Annalise put herself between him and the wood.

'Care to put your money where your mouth is?' she challenged.

'What?' His cheeky smile wasn't quite there now.

'I said put your money where your mouth is. We've got spare earrings – your turn.' She held out a hand and Emma passed her the gun and another stud.

'Thanks, but I'm not a girl; I don't need an earring. Now let me out.'

'Come on, Toby, I've seen plenty of guys your age with an earring,' Annalise told him, her voice softer now, an edge of flirt that Emma didn't want to think about where her brother was concerned. 'I think it's kind of sexy.'

He hesitated, looked closer at Annalise's ear. 'Too girly.'

She showed him the plain stud, different to the cubic zirconia choice the girls had opted for. 'Come on, do it, then you can prove your point that it doesn't hurt... you know, if you don't scream, that is.'

Annalise might not have a sibling let alone an annoying older brother but she certainly knew boys and their weaknesses. And being challenged by a girl to show his manhood and how brave he was worked on Emma's brother. He was such a sucker.

Toby sat down. 'Do your worst, Baker.'

'Okay, you asked for it.'

'He's scared,' Emma teased. 'Admit it, Toby.'

'No chance.'

'You can hold my teddy bear if you like.' Emma felt a bit sorry for him; maybe they shouldn't do this. He was obviously trying to prove himself in front of her friend. But before she could voice any concern, there it went, *clunk*. It was done.

Emma put a hand across her mouth as Toby's face turned pale but if it hurt, he didn't let it show. He simply stood up and checked out his reflection in the mirror and, with a look in Annalise's direction that told Emma her brother definitely had a crush on her best friend, he left them to it.

Annalise checked out her reflection again. 'I love it.'

Emma did the same. 'Me too. I hope the redness goes. It's like a beacon to Mum and Dad that I've done something bad.'

'It'll go, don't worry. And then you just say it was at the jeweller. Let's go to Bristol next week, say you got it done there and they won't be able to question it or go after who did it.'

'Do you think you'll get in trouble?'

Annalise let her hair go. 'I doubt either of my parents will even notice.'

5

NOW: 2023

Lise

Being back at number twelve Honeybee Place was surreal for Lise. The Georgian townhouse had been rented out for years since her mother moved to the south of France to be with her new husband Maurice, and since Lise's mother had put it into Lise's name, Lise had kept the same arrangement. It was an income. It wasn't much hassle, or at least that had been the case before the agent got in touch to say that the house was in a bit of a mess now the most recent tenants had left. He'd had the cleaning firm come in and deal with a lot of it, make minor repairs, but Lise had told him to hold off finding anyone new until she had been back to Honeybee Place to see it for herself. She intended to clean it up a bit and then either get it tenanted again, move in herself, or sell it. Right now, she had no idea which of those options she'd go for.

Lise hadn't intended to unpack much here until she was sure what she wanted her next step to be, but this morning, she opened up the box containing all her photographs, wanting to connect herself with her past life when she'd been in this house, before she'd left for the adventure that hadn't quite had the ending anyone envisaged.

She pulled out a photograph of her with Mrs Griffin, taken when Lise was twenty and home from university. She'd captured them well, given how hard it was to do selfies back then with no way of knowing for sure if you were in the shot. Both were smiling, laughing at something Lise couldn't remember, and freshly baked scones were lined up on a cooling rack in the background. They'd made those scones together, gossiped about the neighbourhood and they'd carried on chatting while they enjoyed the scones with a dollop of cream and a generous serving of raspberry jam from Mr Walker at number fourteen.

Lise had always been able to chat easily with Mrs Griffin and knew that if her former neighbour was still alive, she would have been at her kitchen table pretty soon after her arrival. The woman had been an unlikely friend to a young girl who was lost. Nothing much had changed it seemed. She still didn't know where her life was heading. The only difference was she was older, she had her own responsibilities, and she and Emma were no longer friends.

Lise continued rummaging in the box of photographs. There were so many of her and Emma covering summer after summer, every winter and Christmas season Lise was home from boarding school. She came across the photographs of the day they'd pierced each other's ears, smiling fondly at the shots capturing their proud faces, their red ears. There were pictures of the times they'd met up when they were separated across the miles again as they attended different universities, but when she pulled out another bundle from the very bottom of the box, she sat back on her heels.

In the bedroom at the very top of the house that had once belonged to her parents, Lise clutched the framed photograph of her and Emma on millennium eve. Bright flashes of the fireworks behind them illuminated their faces, their rosy cheeks full of cold and excitement. It had once been the photograph that sat on her bedside table and had become a part of the furniture until their friendship splintered. She ran her fingers across the glass frame with the picture beneath. It might have been a disposable camera they'd used that night but this shot had captured the moment perfectly, their friendship as it had once been – it was the photo Toby had taken, far better than any of their attempts, and Lise was immediately catapulted back to the crowds, the hugs, the kisses, the togetherness with Emma.

It was a world away from the reception she'd got today at the Café on the Corner. Emma had been cold, distant, unforgiving. And Lise had come home to this quiet, empty house and cried. Cried for the death of Mrs Griffin who'd been so kind to her, for the death of Toby who she'd never had the chance to say goodbye to, and for all the lost years where she'd tried to move on and forge herself a new life.

Lise had dreamed about Emma last night too, a weird dream where they'd been on opposite sides of the Millers' café, a glass partition between them, both of them trying but failing to find some way through it.

And today she'd woken up realising that that partition may as well be there right now.

The only thing that made Lise smile was the heavy knock at the front door that sent her galloping down three flights of stairs to the ground floor of the townhouse. She was under no illusions that this would be Emma here to make peace, to apologise for her part in what went on. She knew exactly who it would be and she flung the door open and launched herself at Maisie, wrapping her in a hug that had her daughter begging for mercy.

'Mum, seriously, too tight!' Maisie managed to squeal.

Lise pulled her inside. 'I can't believe you're here at long last.'

Lise had got back in time for Mrs Griffin's funeral but saw no reason to make Maisie tag along, and when Maisie's nanna suggested Maisie join her in London for a couple of weeks while she was there with her husband on business, Maisie had been filled with enthusiasm.

Lise was initially worried about disrupting Maisie's education by coming back to England and she never would've done it had Maisie not been the one to suggest it in the first place. Maisie had loved school as a little girl but as a teenager not so much, not where mean girls were all part of the package. She'd told Lise she could do with a fresh start. She wanted to see England, experience where her mum grew up. And so the plan had fallen into place. Lise had got a school place sorted in Bath for Maisie. They had the townhouse and while they'd definitely be in Bath for the two years Maisie completed sixth form, Lise had explained that it wouldn't necessarily be in Honeybee Place, that she still might very well sell the townhouse.

Maisie shrugged off her denim jacket. 'I only saw you a few weeks ago, Mum. You're being a drama queen.'

'My favourite role.' Lise smiled. 'Tell me all about it. How was London with Nanna? Was it fabulous?'

'Mum, nobody says fabulous.'

'Yes, they do.'

'Not anyone under forty,' she muttered. But Lise didn't care. Her daughter was here; they were together.

'So how was it?'

'Fabulous,' Maisie teased. 'Nanna enjoyed the company. We shopped, we ate brunch—'

'Fancy.'

'You know Nanna – she likes her luxuries. We even had pedicures and manicures.' Maisie shifted her holdall and her enormous rucksack to the side of the hallway and looked up at the stairs that could be seen from the hallway where they stood. 'This place is totally cool.'

'Believe me, it didn't feel *cool* growing up. I couldn't wait to get out.' And she wasn't in the least bit surprised that her daughter's time with her mother had involved pampering, shopping and brunch. Not that she minded. She loved that they had a good relationship. She didn't mind Maisie's nanna spoiling her, because it was Lise's job to keep her daughter grounded.

'You didn't think it was cool because you didn't get on with Nanna and Grandpa,' said Maisie.

She hugged her daughter again, inhaling the smell of the minty shampoo she used on her hair, which looked like it belonged in a shampoo advert with its glossy waves and the bounce that came with youth. 'You're probably right. And luckily, you and I don't have that problem.'

'No... we have the opposite problem. You are determined to smother me with your love and affection.' She scrunched her face up as Lise squeezed her affectionately again.

Maisie was sixteen and ever since she was old enough to understand, Lise had found herself telling her about her parents and her life with them. Some of it had been an adventure: going away to boarding school, posh holidays to see parts of the world, having anything she wanted, a hefty allowance that allowed her as much freedom as she liked. But she hadn't held back on telling Maisie that all she'd ever wanted was for her parents to notice her. And she also hadn't held back making sure that her daughter never felt that way.

'Where are all our boxes?' Maisie asked.

'A few of yours are in the room you'll have while we're here. The stuff we don't necessarily need is all shoved in the study.' The room she'd rarely been allowed in when she lived here, the room that had felt weird entering even though her dad's bureau was long gone. The filing cabinet had disappeared; even the mahogany shelves on the walls were bereft of reminders of that time.

Lise had taken the few boxes she wanted for her own room upstairs as soon as they'd arrived, before Mrs Griffin's funeral. She hadn't meant to time their move with saying goodbye to Mrs Griffin, but the delivery company had botched the date and instead of the day before, it had fallen on a day when actually, she'd been glad of something, anything, to distract her.

'Let me show you around,' Lise enthused. Already, it felt more like a home with her daughter here. The same walls, the same décor, and yet something had been added by the simple arrival of someone she loved.

They started with the downstairs. The kitchen had once been sleek with glossy white and swirled-grey countertops and gleaming white cabinetry, but after years of the house being rented out, changing hands and never having an update, it was tired. The surfaces in the kitchen were no longer highly reflective; stains and smudges were apparent and the cabinetry had nicks and scratches. The tiles behind the sink were cracked near the taps. The windowsill and surround were crying out for a repaint. The floor had marks on it. Out in the hallway, the runner was well worn and the one on the first-floor landing was threadbare, tired like the bannisters with chipped paint in several places.

'I thought perhaps I'd get the bannisters sanded back,' said Lise. 'They'd look good in their original state – varnished, traditional and old like the house.'

'I like that idea. I can find some magazines with ideas for you, if you like.'

Maisie had a good eye when it came to making a house a home. She might only be sixteen but Lise could already see her daughter wanting to go into interior design. Her bedroom before now had been designed by Maisie herself. Rather than the delicate pinks and whites of her childhood, she'd chosen lavender and dark grey as the colour scheme with bold print wallpaper on one wall, a huge poster of an enormous flower with the same shades on another, a statement chair in one corner, a rug rather than the same carpet as elsewhere in the apartment they'd called home.

Maisie had taken charge of their lounge room too and Lise had given her free rein. What they'd ended up with had reminded Lise of the pages of a stylish magazine featuring homes of a wacky designer – it was out there for Lise but she'd got used to it with its eclectic mix of pieces, from the reconditioned, stripy sofa and the mismatched side tables to the second-hand rug she'd rolled out proudly after finding it at an indoor market. Lise had thought it wouldn't look right but again, she was proven wrong, for it had felt as much a part of the room as everything else.

They made their way into one of the bedrooms on the second floor, the room Maisie would be using for the time being, with a good view of the street. 'Are you happy with this room? It was mine once, but there are other options.'

'Mum, this is fine. It's really bright. It gets the afternoon sun – I like that.'

'I'm on the top floor. Come on, let me show you.'

'Wow,' was all Maisie said when she got up there. In fact, she'd been making similar assertions ever since she'd arrived. 'I mean, it needs dusting.' She ran a finger along the mantelpiece of the decorative fireplace and promptly pulled a tissue from her pocket to wipe it on. 'But it's even brighter than the room I'm in. The light is great up here. Was this Nanna's room?'

'It was.' And she hadn't come in here much at all back then. She'd never sat on her mother's bed while she braided her hair. Lise had never played with her mother's make-up the way Maisie had done with hers, upending Lise's make-up bag to the command of *Go for it*. She'd not climbed into bed with her mother after a bad dream.

'Mum...'

'Sorry, Maisie. I was miles away.'

'What colour do you think would look good in here?' She looked around at the walls. 'You know, if you were going to paint it, that is.'

'Which I am. It needs it. I think a very pale lilac.'

'Isn't that the colour in my room downstairs?'

She nodded. 'Yep, it's faded a lot but I chose it back then and I might well choose it again.' She'd never been allowed to paint her own wall of course, but the professionals had been called in to redecorate and Lise had at least chosen the colour.

Maisie went into the en suite adjoining the bedroom and came out again, pulling a face. 'Do you think whoever rented this house knew how to clean a mirror or a bath?'

Lise laughed. 'They've had the professionals in to clean already. And I had a go myself.' There were stains around the sink, in the bath – marks that wouldn't budge.

As Maisie talked more about paint colours, for the walls, the mantel, the window frames and in the en suite, Lise spotted the old tea caddy storage tin in the corner shoved beside one of her boxes. She'd brought it up here for safekeeping.

Lise and Maisie's decision and plans to come to Bath for Maisie's sixth form education coincided with a call from the rental agent in England to say that he had a gardener on standby to sort the small garden at number twelve. The cleaners had already been in but when he'd inspected the place himself, he'd noticed the tenants had trashed the veggie patch outside. As soon as he said it, Lise had a sinking feeling. She'd buried something in the veggie patch, something she was planning to dig up when she moved in for a while, but had someone beaten her to it? The thought that someone might have unearthed it, quite literally, had her wishing she could go to Bath right there and then.

The veggie patch was the first thing she'd inspected when she got back here yesterday morning as the removalists unloaded all her boxes. She'd opened the doors into the garden, walked over to it and willed the tin box to still be in there.

It was – buried so deep that no matter that the tenants had upended planter pots and weeds were growing in amongst the earth, it still lay undiscovered. She'd got the spade from the shed, which had a busted lock and door so would need sorting with the deposit money that hadn't been returned to the tenants, and she dug in the centre before getting down on her hands and knees and pulling the old tea caddy storage tin from its resting place. She lay her hand on top of the plastic-covered note she'd written and folded over before fixing it to the tin prior to its burial. She knew what it said without looking, that the contents of this box shouldn't be looked at unless Emma was at her side and not until they were at least forty, which back then had seemed like eons away.

She wasn't going to do much with the contents right now, but after the tin box had almost been disturbed and was now seeing the light of day for the first time in years, she at least wanted to know whether the contents had survived. She took a quick peek and sure enough, the same bag filled with her diaries was in there. She put her hand inside and ran a finger up the spines and counted. She knew exactly how many she'd written and sure enough, they were all there.

If the removal man who had called out of the back door to ask which room was Maisie's thought she was crazy, he didn't mention it as she stood, tin in her arms, her jeans covered in dirt. She'd gathered herself, gone inside and helped the removal men out by showing them which rooms were which and then put big labels onto the doors in case they forgot.

Looking at the tin now in her bedroom, Lise was jolted out of her reverie when her phone rang. She took the call while Maisie went off to look at the rest of the house on her own.

'Hi, Mum. Yes, we're here safe and sound. Maisie arrived a little while ago.' She was still getting used to having these sorts of conversations with her mother, even though they'd worked on their relationship over the years and had reached this point some time ago. It had never been a case of forgetting but rather accepting and forgiving the way things were when she was growing up, with a lot of talking in between in order for them to get to a better place. 'Thank you for having her to stay with you in London.'

'It was my absolute pleasure. It was proper nanna and grand-daughter time.'

Shelly Baker had fallen in love with her granddaughter the first time they met when Maisie was only a few weeks old. Lise hadn't expected much in the way of affection from her mother but it was like this tiny bundle of joy had been an extra bridge for them to pull them closer. Shelly had visited Lise in Paris for three days and showed up with a basket of gifts – not the impractical designer items Lise might have expected but rather things she actually needed as a new mum, with everything from nappies and plain, no-fuss outfits for the baby to luxury chocolate and bath salts for Lise.

Shelly had been an unlikely ally for Lise after her falling-out with Emma too. They'd talked a lot. Dealing with it all on her own had been hard and rather than feeling lost and alone and not knowing what to do with the mess she'd got herself into, Lise had had someone on her side, someone who knew her and Emma, the history of their friendship. The time she and her mum spent together became easier and occasionally, when Lise watched Shelly with Maisie, she'd note a look on her mother's face that suggested she didn't need to be told how much she'd missed out on with her own daughter.

'How is it being back at number twelve?' Shelly asked as Lise went down a floor to open up a few windows and get some air circulating.

Lise still wasn't used to those sorts of questions either. It wasn't: *How is the house?* Or: *What state did they leave it in?* but rather asking how she was. It wasn't the way it had been in her younger years and some days, she had to remind herself to relegate those thoughts to a different compartment in her mind in order not to hold on to the resentment that would threaten to bubble up now and then.

Lise talked about the funeral, the wake and the neighbours she'd seen and when she reached the ground floor, she opened up the kitchen window. As she sat on one of the tall stools at the kitchen-island bench – it had been ahead of its time in design back when it was installed but times had changed – she turned up her nose. 'Ew, I just noticed the sides of the oven.'

'The food traps...' Her mum laughed. 'That was what I called them.'

'I don't remember.'

'That's because I did my best to keep anyone from noticing them. I'd have been mortified if anyone had picked up on how much dirt could accumulate there. I had a special, thin, cleaner thing that I slipped along the sides. I'd get down on my hands and knees and move it back and forth until I got any debris out.'

Shelly had always been so polished, Lise couldn't imagine it.

'Tell me, Lise, how's Emma?' When Lise and her mum had got back in touch with one another, she'd wanted to keep Lise as her name. She hadn't wanted to fall back to Annalise, be that young girl who was so unsure of the world and her place in it. And for the

most part, her mother remembered to say Lise, although sometimes she forgot.

'Not talking to me. Well, she is, but what she says isn't particularly nice, nor does it give me much hope that we'll ever resolve
things.' She recapped the way Emma had dismissed her attempts
to talk.

'Give her time. You two have something special; you'll work it
out.'

'I'm not so sure. We had something special once, and I'll try
with her again, but I can't work miracles.'

'You're there – that's the main thing. Don't close the doors to
the past, not unless you're really sure it's the right thing to do.'

Every time Lise thought she was coping with coming back,
with memories fired from all directions, something else reminded
her of everything that had happened and she felt her emotions
churn.

When she'd finished her call, Lise went back up the stairs to
find where Maisie had got to. *Don't close the doors to the past,* her
mum had said. Lise was trying not to, but it was hard.

Her mum was talking from experience. Over the years, Shelly
had opened up more and more about her relationship with Lise's
dad, Randall. It hadn't come out in a dramatic monologue but
rather it had been revealed over time. The first time she'd
mentioned their marriage in any detail was when Lise and Shelly
met at a brasserie in Paris. Maisie had been in her stroller at Lise's
side and content with a picture book now she was sitting upright
and taking more of an interest in the world. Their pastries had
gone with nothing left but crumbs, the passing waiter had delivered a bottle of iced water and talk had turned to Emma and the
Millers.

After Shelly finished tucking the blanket around Maisie's legs to make sure she wasn't chilly, Shelly admitted, 'When Randall and I got together, I dropped my friends.'

It was news to Lise but it made sense now why her mother had never had much of a life outside of the house or Randall's business dealings. 'Why would you do that?'

'It was never my intention but gradually, it happened. I spent all my time with your dad. We saw each other and not many other people. I gave up my job because he was working such long hours, so I wanted to look after the house and be able to go away with him on business trips.'

Lise remembered those and that her mother had gone sometimes when she was little. She didn't go every time but as Lise grew older, she soon started to. Shelly confided that he'd wanted her at his side. 'And I was insecure,' she told her daughter. 'I thought if I didn't go, he might meet someone else, have an affair, affairs. I was always waiting for the worst.'

'But why? He married you.'

'I can't explain why; it was the way I was.' Shelly moved from toying with the napkins to scratching a fingernail down the waxy residue on the outside of the candle bottle on their table. 'He liked me to wear nice clothes, jewellery, do my hair. And I felt like a princess. I felt spoiled and I'm afraid to say, I lost myself in his world. When you were born, I thought things might change but they didn't. We hired a nanny because he wanted the best for you – that's how he explained it to me anyway.'

'Nanny Mo.' Lise smiled. 'I loved her.'

'I know you did.' Shelly paused. 'She died when you were still a little girl and I couldn't comfort you.'

'I remember crying. A lot.' At the time, Lise had felt like she'd lost a mother. Nanny Mo always had time for her. Nanny Mo met her from primary school, took her to the playground, played board games, helped her with her school projects. She'd watch cartoons with her when her dad wasn't in the house. They'd build camps with old sheets and towels when it was just the two of them.

'After she died, I talked to Randall,' Shelly explained. 'I said I thought I should be at home more, for you. He convinced me you were older now, that it was good for you to not need us around all the time. And then he suggested boarding school.'

Shirtily, Lise told her mum to leave it when Maisie dropped her picture book. She picked it up and handed it back to her daughter, pointing at a couple of pictures of zoo animals, smiling, and saying the names of what Maisie was seeing. She was beginning to make attempts to say them back and Lise loved listening to her. She couldn't ever imagine sending her away, nor employing anyone else as her primary carer.

'I thought you'd enjoy boarding school and the way you were after Nanny Mo, when I couldn't console you, it felt like the right thing to do.' She looked sheepish. 'Did you really hate it?'

'At first I did. I hated being away from Emma, but I made friends, I had a lot of fun and I got the grades for university.' And what was done was done – no point raking over it now, not today at least.

'Your dad wasn't one to show emotion. Sometimes, I questioned whether something was wrong with him because he couldn't express the way he felt. His own father was the same. He encouraged Randall to do well at his studies, dedicate himself at work, and slowly without him realising, your dad became his father and he couldn't see it. I tried to point it out but he wouldn't be criticised. It had been too long; his behaviour was ingrained and I was too afraid to rock the boat. And so he did what he knew how. He bought you whatever you wanted, and our lives carried on with me at his side and the last few friends I'd had slipped away. Looking back, I could see he was overbearing – if friends ever came to the house, he'd appear out of his study and although he was pleasant enough, it was never relaxing, never like we could all be ourselves, and slowly they stopped coming. Then I couldn't accept their invites because there was usually something Randall had going on, a reason I couldn't make it.'

'Well he was right about one thing.' Lise glugged some of her water but slopped it down her black blouse. 'You guys gave me everything I could've wanted.'

'Apart from ourselves.' It was the first time Shelly had admitted it out loud and it stopped Lise wiping at her blouse with the cloth napkin. 'I didn't see it, not properly, not until he'd gone – how he had to have everything his way, how he wanted me to be, well, a bit of a puppet really.'

Lise grabbed the waiter's attention and asked for a bottle of wine. She'd declined earlier but she couldn't stop the conversation there. She had her mum talking openly for the first time ever and she wanted to keep it going.

'Puppet,' Lise repeated with a smile when the waiter left. 'I once said to Emma that you were Dad's puppet.' What she'd actually said was that she was his *fucking* puppet but there was no need to embellish now.

The waiter appeared swiftly and poured them each a glass of wine.

'I hate that you noticed.' Shelly rested the fingers of one hand on the stem of her glass, crestfallen. 'You and Emma were always close and you fell in with the Millers so easily.'

'They were always kind to me.'

'Seeing how you bonded with them made me feel worse. Part of me was glad you had people looking out for you, but every time you came back home, I could tell where you'd rather be.'

Lise couldn't deny it.

'Your father never should've let his own childhood shape his parenting, but it did.'

Lise admitted, 'I bet it's common, not that that makes it any easier.'

When Maisie began to get fractious, Shelly insisted Lise relax, and she picked the little girl up for a cuddle. 'I would hate to see you and Emma not work this out. I know I've got no right to try to give you advice...'

'Mum, I appreciate it.'

'Then all I'll say is that you need to do as much as you can to salvage your friendship. It's important. Don't let people fall away like I did.'

Lise had taken the advice and hadn't given up with emails and letters, not at first, but after a while, it felt like banging her head against a very solid wall. Emma wasn't budging. Emma wasn't interested.

But now here she was, back in Bath, ready to keep on trying.

'Who were you talking to?' Maisie asked the minute Lise found her in her bedroom looking through the box of photographs Lise had opened up and rifled through herself.

'Nanna. She sends her love.'

Maisie had the framed picture of her and Emma on the night before the new millennium in her hands, their smiling faces looking back at her and over to Lise if that was possible. 'This is a great picture.'

'It was a special night.'

'I wonder what happened to her... Emma.'

Maisie knew there was an Emma, that they'd been friends, but Lise had never told her daughter that the pair of them had had a major falling-out and not spoken since. As far as Maisie knew, they'd simply drifted apart and lost touch.

Maisie lifted out another pile of photographs. 'Mum, what's this?'

Lise looked at the print on top. It was of her holding the item Maisie was confused by. 'That's an ear-piercing gun.'

'No way.'

'I kid you not. Back in the olden days, that's what they were like.'

'But you're holding it.'

'Yup.'

'Don't tell me you pierced your own ears.'

Eyes innocently wide, she answered, 'Of course not.' And with a grin added, 'We pierced each other's.'

'You'd *murder* me if I did that with one of my friends.'

'Too right I would. So no getting any ideas. Now come on, I'm hungry. Let's head out and find somewhere for dinner. The kitchen here needs more attention before I attempt anything other than a bowl of cereal in there.'

They made their way downstairs, leaving the memories in her bedroom in the box of photographs. She wasn't yet sure how she was going to explain Emma's presence in the local café to Maisie and that was only the start of it; she had a lot more explaining to do than that, but all of it could wait for now.

6

NOW: 2023

Emma

'She's a credit to you.' William, regular customer in the café, watched Emma's daughter Naomi head out of the front door and wave as she made her way past the windows again, sports bag over her shoulder, her badminton racquet poking out of the top. Ever since she'd found Toby's old racket in the shed a couple of years ago, she'd been hooked on the sport that had been Toby's activity of choice after rugby.

'Thank you, William.' Emma set down his bacon sandwich on wholemeal bread and the requested bottle of brown sauce.

'She's got her head screwed on right.'

'Because she's playing badminton?'

'Because she's doing her own thing. I see girls her age hanging around in groups smoking or with those silly pen-type things in their mouths.'

Part-time helper in the café, Tara, walked past with a pile of empty plates to take out to the kitchen and leaned in. 'They're called vapes.'

'That's it.' William gave Tara a grateful smile.

William had been coming into the café for years, since Keely and Brendan Miller were at the helm, so he'd known Naomi since she was little. He was still a good friend to Brendan too and visited him a few times a week, which made Emma more grateful than he'd ever know. She might live in the same townhouse as her dad, albeit on different floors so there was some independence on his part and on hers and Naomi's, but company his own age was a unique kind of wonderful.

'Your Naomi keeps trying to get me to give badminton a go.' His smile made his entire face crinkle and his eyes light up.

'She never gives up on people so consider yourself warned.'

'Oh I'm far too past it for racket sports, but I appreciate her being interested in an old man like me.'

'I think I got lucky with her.' Emma smiled. 'She's thoughtful, tolerant and seems to know herself better than I ever did at her age.' When Emma was sixteen, she'd felt like she wasn't quite in the right skin. She wasn't cool; she wasn't confident. Lise had helped a lot by encouraging Emma and insisting she absolutely *was* good enough. Lise had assured her that she'd find her groove and she'd been right because at university, the shyness and the unease had gradually fallen away. Lise's voice of encouragement had been in Emma's head for many years. Until it wasn't.

'She was raised right.' William set the top layer back on his sandwich now the bacon was covered with a generous serving of brown sauce. The thought of her daughter rid Emma momentarily of the stress of thinking of Lise, of wondering why she'd turned up here now and whether she was hanging around for long, or if she was going to bump into her again.

'Talking of raised right...' She nodded to the door as William's son Max arrived. 'I'll be back to take his order.'

Max and Toby had played rugby together and Max had spent

almost as much time at the Millers' as Annalise had. After Toby died, Max hadn't faded away either. He'd never left Bath and had stayed in the Millers' lives, comfortable regaling them with tales of Toby when plenty avoided bringing up his name because they felt awkward or didn't know what to say. And these days, now Brendan wasn't in the café any more, Max often headed over to see him at number four, with or without William.

The café was busy today – late morning usually was, even on a weekday. Some customers were brunch people; others wanted an early lunch. Emma gave Max a wave and headed back to the kitchen. As she poached a couple of eggs on the stovetop, Emma smiled. Her daughter, who'd turned sixteen in the summer, was a credit to the family for sure and she couldn't be more proud of the young woman Naomi was growing into. She was sweet and kind to friends and strangers. She had the same red hair Emma had had at that age and the pale-blue eyes, but whereas Emma had been one to stand back from the crowd, Naomi took after her father, with his bubbly personality and enthusiasm for whatever he threw himself into.

The next hour was so busy, Emma barely had time to stop and when Max came to pay his bill, he asked about Lise.

'I thought I was seeing things,' he said.

'You weren't.'

'So she's back?'

He handed over his card after she'd punched in the correct amount on the payment machine for him.

'Something like that.' She said it as though he was talking about a neighbour nobody really knew except to say hello to in passing. She handed him his receipt.

He pushed the slip of paper into his wallet. 'I know you and she had some kind of falling-out...'

She softened. 'Sometimes I hate it that you know so much

about me.' But of course she didn't really. Max had been a connection to Toby when he died and all of the family had grabbed hold of it with both hands, including her.

'Have you spoken with her?'

'Briefly.' She recapped that Lise had shown up at the funeral, then at the end of the wake. She'd kept herself off most people's radars at the service itself, and by the time she showed her face in the café, Max and William had already gone.

Max didn't push her on it, and she saw to a few more orders when he and William said their goodbyes.

When things in the café quietened down enough, Emma checked with Tara before she ducked across the street to see her dad. She didn't like to leave him alone for too long and, as the house was only thirty-odd metres to the Café on the Corner, nipping home was easy enough. William had seen him first thing for a coffee and dissection of the newspapers, one of their favourite pastimes, but with his mobility not what it was, she usually went in once or twice throughout the day.

When Emma had come back to Bath after the falling-out with Annalise in her late twenties, she'd moved in with her parents, who had inherited the grand townhouse in Honeybee Place soon after they married from Keely's late parents. The Millers often said they wouldn't be able to afford such grandeur if the home hadn't been passed down and in some ways, it was too big for them, but its position was perfect for the city and for the café they'd really only known about because they were so familiar with the area.

Emma had landed a job at a local school teaching English very quickly after she returned to Bath. The return home to Honeybee Place was supposed to be a stopgap but it wasn't long before she fell pregnant. She'd done everything in the wrong order – had the baby, then got married, then moved out. And when her husband died suddenly seven years ago, after the loss of her brother Toby already, she'd almost fallen apart. The best thing all round had been to move back in with her parents yet again, until she found another place with a smaller mortgage and not so much garden. If she'd stayed in her former home, she wouldn't have been able to cope without employing a gardener. Her husband had been the nature-loving one, the person who spent all his time outdoors, the one who transformed an overgrown, neglected garden into one with flower beds, a swing set for Maisie, a wooden swing for Emma to laze on and read in the warmer months.

The Millers' Georgian townhouse was, like the other houses in Honeybee Place, spread over five floors and when she'd been there a couple of months with nothing turning up on real estate listings in her price bracket, her parents had suggested they make the top two floors hers and Naomi's. They shared the first floor with its lounge room and study, they shared the ground floor with the kitchen and access to the courtyard, and Brendan and Keely had the lower ground floor with its cosy snug and little library and a large bedroom with adjoining bathroom. They'd never talked about it being permanent but that was what it had turned out to be.

'Dad, only me,' she called out as she dropped her keys on the wooden shelf in the hallway and waited for a response to know whether he was on this level or down one. The stairs were getting harder for him but he said he wasn't about to stop going up and down them, because if he did, he'd never start again. He didn't go outside the house much at all apart from the courtyard garden now, not unless he had an appointment, but he was mostly content in the home he'd lived in ever since he married his sweetheart.

'In here,' came a voice, indicating she needed to go down to the lower ground floor, which had access at the end of the thin hallway to a small, enclosed, outdoor area. The main courtyard garden was accessed from the ground floor beyond the kitchen.

Emma found her dad in the little library in his vintage, leather, button-back chair, one of a pair surrounded by floor-to-ceiling bookcases. He'd always favoured the one chair because the window was behind him and gave him plenty of light for reading. Emma's mum hadn't read half as much as her dad but she'd come in here sometimes too, taken the chair opposite – the chair Emma sat in now, which was significantly different to the other with its level of wear and tear. Emma's chair was reasonably robust with little in the way of everyday marks and scuffs. Her dad's chair looked well loved, worn, and his small frame sunk into it as though it was designed purely for him.

'You shouldn't come back every five minutes, Emma. I've got my phone; I can call if I need you.'

'Gives me a chance to get off my feet for five minutes.'

He closed his book now he had company – a biography of a cricketer Emma had bought him last Christmas. 'I remember the desperate need to do that when we first started the café. I'd make your mother take five minutes and sit with her feet up, quite literally.'

'You two worked hard and made the café what it is today.' And now it was hers. It wasn't what she'd wanted at first but it was their legacy and when she took it on, she'd slowly slipped into the role of café owner and found herself falling in love with it as much as her parents had. Some days, it felt like an extension of home: she had plenty of visits from friends and neighbours, a variety of company.

She picked up the cup on the table next to him. 'Right, what can I get you? Save you going up those stairs again? Another cuppa?'

'Not just yet, pet.' When he smiled, he looked so much like Toby. It had almost physically hurt when they first lost her brother but over time, Emma had got used to seeing it and embraced the warmth it gave her, the feeling that a part of Toby was still with them.

She stayed and chatted to her dad for a while and when she got back to the café, it was straight into the kitchen to help Tara, who'd just taken an order for a party of six. And her day carried on much the same way, never finding another opportunity to sit down and only just managing to lift her head and smile when Naomi came in after the late lunchtime rush died down enough that she could bag a table.

Emma eventually got to her daughter and felt bad for planting a kiss on her head when she registered that she was sitting with another girl about her age. 'Sorry.' She grimaced to the other girl. 'Naomi will tell me off for that later.'

'My mum would do exactly the same,' the other girl groaned, sharing a conspiratorial eye-roll with Naomi. 'No PDAs, I tell her.'

'Public displays of affection,' Naomi clarified in case Emma didn't know. 'This is Maisie. We met at badminton.'

'Lovely to meet you, Maisie.' Emma flipped over the page in her notepad and clicked the end of her pen. 'Now what can I get you both?'

'The milkshakes – chocolate – are the best. You have to try one.' Naomi made the decision for them.

'Two milkshakes it is.' Emma scribbled on her pad. 'How was badminton club?'

'Great,' they said together and then laughed.

Tara floated past and took the order from Emma. 'Thank you, Tara.' She turned to the girls. 'She is the most amazing assistant. You don't even have to ask and she's already done what you needed her to.' She looked at her daughter's friend. 'Do you live close by?'

Naomi told her, 'Maisie just moved in to Honeybee Place.'

'Oh, number seventeen. I wondered who was going to be living there. You'll love it here – you'll soon feel at home.'

But the girl shook her head. 'No, we're number—'

'Twelve,' came a voice from behind them. A voice Emma knew only too well.

Maisie made the unnecessary introduction. 'This is my mum – Lise.'

And in the silence that ensued between the two women, it didn't take much of a genius to work out that these two not only knew one another but also that there was a lot the teenage girls still didn't know about their mothers and what had gone on between them.

Only in time would they begin to find out.

7

THEN: 1996

Annalise

'Sorry, Mr Miller!' Annalise apologised desperately as the poor gearbox crunched again when she attempted to put the little Vauxhall Nova into reverse and manoeuvre the car closer to the kerb. She was mortified. Emma's brother Toby and his mate Max were standing right outside the Millers' townhouse and lucky for Annalise – or unlucky in this case – that was where there was an available parking spot. Right now, she wished they'd had to park way over the other side of Honeybee Place, beyond the grass square in the centre, because the boys were pointing and laughing.

'Take no notice of them.' Mr Miller waved them away and then wagged a finger that had Toby doing as he was told and scuttling away. Mr Miller was a lovely man, calm and collected, but he knew how to discipline. 'Nerves are understandable. You're doing well, Annalise.'

Emma had lucked out with her family and that included her dad. He was a gem. And having already started driving lessons for seventeen-year-old Emma a couple of months ago, he'd volunteered his time to teach Annalise when she was home for the summer too. Annalise's parents had paid for her to have lessons with a proper instructor – her dad didn't have the time and her mum didn't even drive – which had been all well and good until the instructor had destroyed her confidence after only three lessons. She'd ended up in the Café on the Corner sobbing, telling the Millers that the driving instructor, Dave, had fired her as a pupil for being too anxious and not keen to get out of third gear.

'He just wants the easy cases,' Mr Miller had chided, sipping from his mug of tea in the café on the slow evening before he lifted it up to make his point. 'He wants eager, overconfident boys who want to put their foot down before they even know the rules of the road.'

'He's an arse.' Emma had announced as she brought her best friend a big mug of hot chocolate with a ridiculous number of marshmallows bobbing on the top.

'Language,' Mrs Miller had warned her daughter before looking at Annalise, who was devastated and wiping at her eyes. 'But it sounds as though, in this case, he *is* an arse.'

Mrs Miller's use of the word *arse* had both girls laughing and Mr Miller had volunteered his services to get her started before she braved lessons with a different instructor.

Annalise had had about twelve hours' practice with Mr Miller by now and her first official lesson with a new instructor was on Saturday. Today was her final practice before then and driving in Bath was a challenge at the best of times, with its hills and insane road layout, but with Mr Miller's calm approach, they both survived. She only stalled three times, and the hour was relatively drama-free.

Mr Miller headed for the café after he let Annalise into the house and she ran up the stairs two at a time, ignoring jibes from Toby about her parking skills, or rather lack of, and how they might need to catch a taxi to the kerb when they wanted to get in the car again. Annalise hadn't wanted him and Max watching earlier on but the teasing? Well, she didn't mind that at all. Her house was so quiet and so dull; she much preferred the boisterous behaviour of two rather annoying boys and the noise she found within these walls.

'How was it?' Emma looked up when Annalise went into her bedroom. She was lying on her stomach on her bed, doing homework.

'Ugh, is that French?'

'*Oui, bien sûr*. And I thought you liked France – you want to go someday.'

'I do and I'd happily learn French in France, but in the class-room it's so boring.' She flung herself down next to Emma.

'But you're doing the work, aren't you?'

'Yes, Mum.' Annalise grinned.

'I remember the few French lessons we had at primary school.'

'So do I. The teacher hated me!'

'She did not hate you. She was just unimpressed that you knew more French swear words than she did at the tender age of nine.'

Annalise shrugged. 'We had a few holidays in France – I picked it up from the locals.'

'France fascinates me,' Emma admitted although she seemed to have lost interest in her homework now her friend was here.

'We should go together,' said Annalise.

'Yeah?'

'Sure... we'll share an apartment and fall in love with Frenchmen who spoil us rotten.'

A smile spread across Emma's face. 'You forgot to mention the freshest croissants for breakfast every day, baguettes with gooey cheese for lunch, wine because we'll be old enough to drink whenever we like, the finest chocolates at our disposal twenty-four seven.'

'Trust you to think of the food.' Annalise laughed.

'We should do it. Not just dream about it.'

'Okay... when?'

Emma bit down on her bottom lip. 'After university.'

It felt a long time away but it would be even better when they were older. Both of them had plans for university – Annalise wanted to study public relations and all of her university preferences involved moving out of home, which was as attractive as getting a degree. The sooner she escaped the suffocating confines of number twelve, the better.

Annalise flipped onto her back on the bed, hands clasped behind her head. 'Your dad is a saint by the way.'

'He's patient.'

'Want to swap parents?'

She smiled in a way that said she'd rather not answer the question with brutal honesty. A couple of weeks ago, Annalise had been thrilled to be asked to help out in the café with Emma. She was on holidays from boarding school and she was bored beyond belief. She'd managed a total of four shifts before her dad let it be known, in front of Emma, that it wouldn't be happening any more. He said she had far too much work to do for school and should be putting her energies into that, not a café. Anyone who didn't know him might have been thinking that he cared about his daughter's education, that he was happy to fork out for extra pocket money so she could focus on her studies. But Annalise knew that wasn't it. He thought the Bakers were too good for a street café.

And she hadn't even had to convey that to Emma. Emma knew enough about Annalise's dad to know when there was an unspoken judgement. She hadn't told Emma what her dad had said that evening to her, though – *No child of mine is going to fail because they were too busy working in a greasy spoon* – it was too hurt-ful. She would've liked to tell Emma that she'd answered back, told him it was far from a greasy spoon, but all she'd got out of that was being sent to her bedroom and told to show a bit of respect.

She and Emma had spent the next evening thinking of ways he could be worse – they'd come up with violence and yelling and having Annalise living in squalor but Annalise, although laughing about it on the surface, had sometimes wished that was the way he treated her. It might be easier to explain to outsiders, easier to find a way out of there. As it was, he wasn't terrible – he gave her every-thing she ever wanted except for his unconditional love. Emma thought perhaps it was buried beneath the surface and Annalise had made a joke that they'd need some industrial digging equip-ment to find it.

'I need to finish this homework,' Emma said now, picking up her pen.

'It's the school holidays. You've got ages.'

'Said every single person who leaves it to the last minute and then finds they've got too much to do.'

'You're such a goody two-shoes.' But she got up. 'Come find me when you're done. I'll be at my house or at Mrs Griffin's.'

'Promise I will.' Head down, she was already getting back into her French homework.

Annalise headed back home to change into some shorts – it was warm enough today for summer clothes and no sign of the rain that had been on the weather forecast.

Mrs Griffin was heading up the street and waved at her.

'I was about to come and see you.' Annalise smiled. 'Come have a cup of tea with me.' Her parents were out and it felt like a luxury to have the freedom to invite a guest inside.

Annalise had always thought Mrs Griffin was very serious when she was little but had soon warmed to her, ever since the day

Mrs Griffin had seen her picking the petals from the roses grown at one corner of the grassy square in the centre of Honeybee Place. She'd expected to be yelled at but Mrs Griffin had asked her why she was doing it. She'd told her she was making perfume and Mrs Griffin had told her to leave the roses in the square because they were for everyone, but to go to her place and pick as many as she liked. She'd done exactly that – pink ones, reds, whites, an orange colour – Mrs Griffin had so many and had let her stay all afternoon when Annalise told her that her parents were too busy to play games.

Annalise, even as a young girl, never missed the looks people gave her or each other whenever her parents were brought into the conversation. She'd got so used to it. But the day she'd heard Mrs Griffin talking with the Millers in their house had made her cry. She and Emma had been at the top of the stairs at the Millers' and were heading down for some drinks. They'd stopped when they heard Annalise's name. They'd sat down on the top step and listened to Mrs Griffin say, *It's not right; they neglect that girl.*

And Mrs Miller had replied, *Then it's our job love to make sure she comes to no harm.* Emma had put her arm around Annalise's shoulders and Annalise had cried properly for the first time in front of her friend.

Annalise let herself in to the townhouse now and punched in the code for the alarm. Walking through the door usually deflated her but with the promise of the company of one of her favourite people, she could put those feelings aside.

She opened up the window in the kitchen because the whole place felt more stuffy than usual – it was never stuffy at the Millers'. There, the air circulated, hot or cold, the noise filled every corner, the love bounced off the walls. In the lounge, she flung open that window too and went over to select a CD, a classical collection Mrs Griffin would be happy with in the background, just to get some noise going in the walls of number twelve, which were woefully devoid of much apart from plush furnishings and the sound of the carriage clock her dad had got from work to celebrate twenty-five years of good service. Every time she heard it tick, it felt like it was taunting her, reminding her that work always came first for Randall Baker.

She wondered what she could give her dad as a gift rather than a clock. What did you give someone for eighteen years of providing food and shelter, not being nasty and mean, giving her everything she could've asked for apart from the one thing she really wanted? Love and acceptance.

She put the music on in the kitchen and made the tea as they chatted. But when Annalise became twitchy because she noticed the time and knew her parents would be back soon, Mrs Griffin picked up on it. She was expecting visitors later so she invited Annalise to her place to help her bake a cake – or rather three separate cakes – one of which she wanted Annalise to deliver to the men temporarily occupying number twenty-nine.

Emma found her on her way to make the delivery.

'Mrs Griffin has made me her cake mule.' She indicated the tin.

'Sounds mysterious,' said Emma.

'Apparently, there's a guy and his dad staying there while Mr Harp is away and they're renovating. Mrs Griffin wants to make them welcome but she's waiting for visitors so didn't want to leave the house.'

They knocked on the door to number twenty-nine and it took four tries to get anyone to come to the door.

Annalise didn't miss Emma's mouth almost fall open at the guy standing there on the other side, slightly out of breath, a grey T-shirt covered in dust that had been brushed onto his face. He had kind blue eyes that, now he'd seen who had disturbed him, didn't seem the least bit bothered.

Annalise garbled out a hello and an explanation about what was in the tin and handed it to him.

'Thank you. Appreciate it. But we don't live here; we're just the workers.'

'We know,' said Annalise, 'so does Mrs Griffin.'

'Well, thank you again.' His eyes kept falling to Emma but Emma was too shy to really look at him.

'I'm Annalise,' she said, 'and this is Emma.'

It did the trick. Rather than a stilted conversation, he stood back and opened the door and asked them in to have a slice of cake and a cup of tea. 'I was due to have a break.' He smiled.

The girls ended up staying almost two hours. They found a lot to talk about – the guy's name was Sam and he worked for his dad as a labourer every school holiday. They had a job and lodgings here for a few weeks and he had absolutely no intention of taking on the family business when his dad retired.

'So where do your passions lie?' Annalise asked him. Honestly, Emma was going to have to up her game. This guy clearly liked her and she was oblivious.

'I want to go to university. I'll be the first in my family.'

'What will you study?' Emma asked.

'Meteorology. I'm fascinated by it.'

Annalise looked out of the window. 'All I need to know about the weather is that it's turned. What happened to the sunshine?' What had been a sunny, dry day was now overcast and threatening rain if the grey skies were anything to go by.

Their talk of university and career choices ended when Sam realised the time and that his dad would be here soon – having gone to collect materials – but Annalise wasn't going to let this guy go, not when he was clearly so interested in Emma, and so she invited him to the movies with them that evening.

He came and he was great company. And after the movie,

they'd all agreed to meet for lunch at the weekend, and then again a few days after that.

But rather than the romance Annalise had seen potentially blooming between Emma and Sam – Emma denied she had an attraction to Sam; Sam showed no signs of making a move – what evolved was a lasting friendship between the three of them, a friendship that carried into the Christmas break, Easter and the following summer too.

8

THEN: 1997

Emma

The summer of 1997 – when both girls had turned eighteen – seemed to go on forever but in a good way. They had only a month until they started university. Emma was going north to study English literature at Durham; Annalise was heading to Exeter to study public relations. And their friend Sam had stayed true to his word. He hadn't gone into the family building business but instead was heading off to university in Scotland.

'Who fancies giving me a lift up to uni to drop me off?' Sam leaned forwards from the back seat as Annalise drove them all to the campsite down in Devon. She'd passed her test a couple of months ago and her parents had promptly bought her a Toyota MR2, bright, shiny red and purring like a kitten as they drove around the English countryside. She'd told Emma that she would've rather had the celebratory tea that Emma got when she passed her test, with homemade Bolognese and a big wedge of chocolate cake. But she'd seen the benefits of her gift when they talked about going on a getaway while none of them had any other commitments.

'I'm not ferrying you all the way up to Scotland,' Annalise said with a laugh.

'It's a long way,' Emma agreed, 'and I don't have a car. I share my parents' car with them and my brother. And batting those crazy-long eyelashes at me won't work.'

It wasn't fair that Sam, a male, had eyelashes girls would kill for, the sort that would take a decent set of extensions and maintenance. He really was quite adorable – blond hair, a kind heart and a big smile. When they first met, Emma had wondered whether he liked her as more than a friend but he'd never made a move and it worked between the three of them. They had a ball whenever they got together. Sam was funny, a gentleman, and rather than coming between the girls, he made things more interesting with his quirkiness and intellect. Every time he talked about the weather, there was a lot of teasing from the girls but only because they were so comfortable with him, they knew he could take it. Emma loved how clever he was. He was going to do well at university and in life.

The campsite had basic amenities and after they'd pitched the tents, they headed to the nearest pub – a good mile's walk away – for dinner.

'What happened to cooking over our little stove?' Emma asked as they took off their waterproofs and sat down at a corner table. True to form for England's weather, it had begun to rain the moment they'd arrived at the campsite and the drizzle that had made them put up the tents quickly had soon turned to a downpour.

'In this?' Lise asked.

'Yeah, fair point,' Emma agreed, picking up a menu.

'Maybe tomorrow night,' Sam said softly while Annalise looked around for a sign to the bathroom.

Emma wasn't sure but she thought she felt him shuffle a bit closer and she didn't mind one bit.

The rain had stopped by the time they got back to the campsite and so they sat outside on the low camping chairs they'd brought along and gazed up at the stars. Sam knew a lot about those too. Emma guessed it fitted in with his love of meteorology although did stars even have anything to do with the weather? She didn't think so but she wasn't going to ask. She didn't want to appear dumb.

Sam went into his tent to get a book to look something up when Annalise asked a question about the clouds and pondered how rain fell. Emma ignored her friend's rushed whisper and claims that he was definitely into her.

'Be quiet,' she told Annalise. 'He's a friend – that's it. We are all friends.' She wasn't sure why she was denying it so much to her best friend – probably because they were all so close and she loved the times when they joked around together. She didn't want to ruin anything.

The massive book was more interesting than either of the girls thought it might be. Emma was fascinated by all the information about the forces that govern the weather; Annalise wanted to know all about typhoons, dust storms and tornadoes. They only called it a night and went inside their tents when the rain started up again.

They managed the fire the next evening and the one after that. They cooked sausages on the open grill; they drank beer and wine and toasted each other, assuring themselves that this wouldn't be the end of the friendship and that they'd all stay in touch.

When they arrived back at Honeybee Place and Annalise began the slow cruise to find a parking space, Sam asked again whether they'd both visit him in Scotland.

Annalise's focus was on the road so Emma answered, 'It would be nice but it's a long way to go.'

'You know that someone very clever and kind invented trains, don't you?' Sam had locked eyes with her and it made her feel things she hadn't felt before: a fizzing in her tummy as though she were a young teenager rather than eighteen and an adult.

Annalise spotted a parking space and pulled up alongside it. 'Do you think I can get in there?'

'No,' Emma said matter-of-factly. Annalise was terrible at parking and worse if she had someone behind her. 'And neither could I if that makes you feel any better.'

'Want me to hop out and guide you a bit?' Sam offered.

'Or you could park it for me,' Annalise suggested.

'You try it first.'

Emma loved how he was kind but part of the kindness was to help others be their best. He wasn't letting Annalise give up.

Annalise grunted. But with no pressure of any cars trying to drive around the street, it wasn't long before she was tucked into the space. It might have taken four or five goes but she got there in the end. 'Damn, he's patient,' she said to Emma, unclicking her seatbelt.

'I'll miss him.'

Annalise leapt straight on the comment. 'He'll miss *you*.'

Emma did up her window. 'Would you stop saying that? He doesn't like me as any more than a friend. He doesn't,' she insisted again when Annalise failed to keep the expression of doubt from her face.

'Whatever you say.' Annalise climbed out and locked the car.

Sam said his goodbyes but not before he checked that both girls were going to the pub tonight. There was a great bar not far from Bath Abbey and to celebrate their A-level results, which had come out a few days ago, a whole load of them were congregating there this evening.

Tonight was going to be another reminder that everything was about to change. Emma wanted to go to university. She wanted it so much, but she never wanted to lose what she had here. And that included Annalise and Sam.

* * *

'It was sad saying goodbye to Sam tonight,' Emma admitted. She linked arms with Annalise as they stumbled back to Honeybee Place from the city.

'So sad,' Annalise agreed. 'You should've kissed him goodbye. Or did you? When I wasn't looking?'

Emma rolled her eyes. She'd had a few drinks herself – more than a few – but not quite as many as Annalise, who'd kicked off her heels to walk the streets of Bath barefoot.

When Annalise dropped her arm, Emma readjusted her messy bun and the highlighted strands that had fallen down after some energetic dancing this evening.

'You have no idea how sexy you are.' Annalise said it none too quietly and Emma laughed, hurrying her on by hooking her arm into her friend's again. 'Sam has an idea... Sam knows,' she said with glee. Annalise looked about to say something else but stubbed her toe on a paving slab that wasn't quite level. 'Bollocks!'

'Get all the swearing out now before we're back to your place.' Emma giggled. 'You got hot chocolate?'

'Sure have. And plain chocolate Hobnobs.'

'Come on, Hopalong; the sooner we get there, the sooner we can gossip.'

They didn't have sleepovers at Annalise's – neither of them wanted to endure the rules and the torturous formal breakfast the next day – but a visit was fine. Annalise's parents were three floors up and, as it was past midnight, would be asleep, giving the girls the kitchen to talk well into the night. You couldn't do that so much at Emma's. Toby had an intrinsic ability to pop up exactly when he wasn't wanted, usually with Max or one of his other mates in tow, given the Millers were pretty flexible about friends coming over, and they'd all park themselves up as though the girls wanted nothing more than their company. At least at Annalise's, her parents let her be at this hour and the girls would be quiet enough that they wouldn't be any trouble.

That had been the theory anyway, until Annalise announced their arrival home by tripping up the front doorstep and falling into the hallway. Emma found herself laughing hard and the more she tried to help Annalise up, the weaker she was and the more her tummy muscles ached from the laugher. They were still giggling and shushing one another in the hallway when a light came on and Emma saw Mr Baker coming their way, glass of something in hand, and a look on his face that wasn't the most welcoming.

She cleared her throat, going for politeness. 'Hello, Mr Baker.'

'Emma. Isn't it time you got home?'

'She's my friend,' Annalise butted in. 'Emma, you're staying.'

Emma only looked at Annalise. 'We'll have our hot chocolate tomorrow.'

If only Annalise hadn't tripped, they might have got away with their homecoming, although it seemed Mr Baker hadn't been three flights up at all but had come from the direction of the study. And he still hadn't retreated like he usually did. Instead, he was watching his daughter.

'Annalise, you're drunk. You need to get yourself to bed right now. We'll talk about this in the morning.' There was a lack of warmth in his demeanour and his words, he was abrupt and detached despite making an attempt to sound like a concerned parent. Emma wondered why he bothered sometimes. She and Annalise thought perhaps it was because he thought he should rather than because he was actually invested in the relationship. They engaged in regular assassinations of his character but now, facing him in the flesh, Emma was less confident with criticism and just wanted to magic herself out of there and back home, especially when it appeared Annalise was ready to do battle.

Annalise slurred, 'Not tired.'

Emma cringed, wishing Annalise wouldn't answer him back. From what her friend had told her, he'd never raised a hand to her, but Emma was scared enough of the voice, of the looks. She tried to imagine the same expression on her own dad's face and couldn't quite do it. Even at his angriest, she could still imagine the cuddly bear beneath.

'I have a phone meeting in ten minutes, Annalise. I'd appreciate some quiet.'

Emma knew Annalise's dad did a lot of international business. It was what kept him in the office at peculiar hours or working at home late into the night. At least with the Miller family café, Emma and Toby could drop in whenever they liked and there was an opening and closing time. For the Bakers, it seemed every hour of every day was a business hour.

Annalise shushed them all with a finger to her lips. Unfortunately, it made her look even less sober. 'We'll be as quiet as a mouse... as mouses... as mice...'

She was making this worse.

'Don't question me, Annalise.' He must have been clenching his teeth because his jaw took on a whole different shape. 'Now it's time your friend went home and you went up to bed.'

Emma saw a solution. 'You can come to my place. Sleep over.'

'I don't think so,' Mr Baker was quick to say. 'Annalise should sleep off whatever she's been drinking. And she should do it here. We'll talk about this in the morning.'

He didn't say another word before he headed back to his study.

He knew his word was always the last, although Annalise had other ideas and as soon as he was gone, she muttered, 'Fucker.'

Emma prayed he hadn't heard that one.

And Annalise hadn't finished. 'He won't be talking about it in the morning either. It'll be Mum who lectures me about drinking even though she has her gin every night and he has whatever revolting brown stuff was in that glass.'

Emma knew she had no choice but to leave now before Annalise went on so much, it drew her dad out into the hallway again. This way, at least Annalise would stumble up to bed with nobody left to talk to.

'I'll see you tomorrow, Annalise. It was a great night.'

'It was, wasn't it?' Annalise leaned against her friend as Emma walked her up the stairs to her bedroom, lifted her legs onto the bed and covered her with the duvet before creeping down the stairs again.

She closed the front door quietly behind her before she headed back to number four, the streetlamps giving enough light to guide her way. She closed the front door behind her and bolted it before taking off her shoes.

She looked up when her dad emerged from the kitchen. He was in his checked pyjamas, his dressing gown over the top, maroon slippers on his feet.

'Did you have a good time?' He was obviously tired but clutching his book – he must've been reading and waiting for her to come home. He denied that he did it now she was eighteen but she knew full well either he or her mum always stayed awake until both of their children were safely home.

'The best.' At least until they'd got to Annalise's house.

He held out his arms. 'Good. Now, I'm too old to be up at this hour so it's bedtime for me.'

She held on to him tighter rather than the cursory hug they

would usually have when they did it every so often. 'I love you, Dad.'

He pulled back. 'What's wrong? You need money? Are you in trouble with the law?'

She began to laugh, as was his intention. 'Neither, Dad. I just wanted you to know that.'

'And I do, love. I love you too. Goodnight, sweetheart.'

'Goodnight, Dad.'

9

NOW: 2023

Lise

Lise almost jumped out of her car seat at the beeping going on behind her.

'All right, all right, keep your knickers on!' she yelled to the driver behind, except it was only her who could hear in the confines of her car. She wondered how long the traffic light had been green.

Lise's mind hadn't been on driving but rather had drifted back to the events of yesterday. That awkward moment where she'd passed the Café on the Corner walking into the city and spotted Maisie in the window with another girl with the most beautiful red hair and smile she'd know anywhere. Emma had once smiled like that when they'd been sitting at the very same table in that very window. A woman had bumped into Lise when she stopped dead in the street because it was like being sent back in time. Lise had known Emma had a child – she'd found that out a while ago – but she'd never known anything other than the bare fact. And she never would've expected her daughter and Emma's to be together. Not in a million years.

'Twelve...' Lise had corrected Emma when she overheard her conclude that Maisie must be moving in to a different house with a *sold* sign out front.

After the girl who worked in the café delivered two oversized chocolate milkshakes to the girls, Lise had rallied, smiling at her daughter. She'd loosened the top few buttons on her coat. 'Who's your friend?'

'This is Naomi.' Maisie had beamed. 'I met her at badminton and this is her mum's café.'

Emma had tapped her pen against the little white notepad in her hand and almost leapt on the next customer through the door, showing them to a table she wiped down right there and then before indicating the menu.

'I was just passing and saw you.' Lise had tried to act normal in front of her daughter but Maisie wasn't stupid. Neither girl was – given the looks that had been exchanged. 'I thought I'd say hi, but I'd better get going to the shops.' It was a tiny lie. Really, she'd left the townhouse for a break in search of a decent coffee from somewhere in the city but she couldn't tell Maisie that, as Maisie would likely point out the obvious – that they were in a café already.

Lucky for Lise, Maisie had been more interested in her new friend than what her mother needed at the shops and Lise had made a sharp exit. She wasn't sure how long she'd walked for – way further than she needed to for a coffee – but she'd ended up in a quiet café at the opposite end of the city and stayed there for more than an hour to read her book although she barely read half a page, her head all over the place. She'd spent most of her time gazing out of the window. Her daughter making friends was something Lise was concerned about especially when she wasn't sure quite how long they'd be staying in Honeybee Place. She'd told

Maisie that there was a strong possibility she'd sell the townhouse but she'd never been able to fully explain why.

Her mother's advice about not giving up on her friendship with Emma was still ringing in her ears now when the car behind her at the traffic lights gave a long, angry beep that meant get a move on.

Back in Honeybee Place, Lise had to do a lap around the road that bordered the small, shared garden for residents in the centre but there were no spaces, at least not until she spotted a bright-yellow car pulling out of a space up ahead. Since she'd come back, she'd tried to park as near to number twelve as she could every time she returned to the townhouse, praying she wouldn't have to be too close to the Millers'. But today, the gods of parking were having a total laugh because this space was slap bang outside Emma's house. Still, at least Emma didn't know the car and Lise could discreetly move it later as soon as a better space became available, preferably under the cover of darkness.

She pulled up parallel to the car in front of the vacant space and in one swift manoeuvre, she was tucked in and nicely close to the kerb.

She almost jumped out of her skin when a set of knuckles rapped on her window as she was putting her phone into her handbag on the passenger seat. She was about to wind the window down a fraction and ask whether she could help the man when she recognised exactly who it was.

'Max!' She beamed from the other side of the glass and it must have been her smile that let him know it was all right to open the door for her.

As she stepped out onto the pavement, he whistled. 'Great parking, saw the whole thing and assumed it was a local, not a visitor.'

'I suppose I'm kind of local,' she said. 'And believe me, parking wasn't always easy for me.'

'Oh I know; I watched you enough times.'

'That's right, you and Toby used to have a good laugh at my expense.' But she was laughing now too. 'I got much better after I spent a lot of time in Paris. The drivers over there are absolute nutters. The parking is atrocious, and I guess I got used to it.' She couldn't stop smiling. 'How are you? You've barely changed.'

'Thank you... I think.' He grinned. 'And I'm well... wow, what's it been? Well over twenty years?'

His dark, dark eyes were trained on her. They had a softness she remembered from millennium eve as she'd looked into them after a spine-tingling kiss. He still had the same smooth, naturally dark skin, the same solid build. Smooth facial features had given way to a rougher complexion and creases at the sides of his eyes when he smiled but it took nothing away from him. If anything, it added something.

'Stop. I feel really old now.'

'Better to be old than the alternative...' He said it with a smile but both of them realised the significance. 'Sometimes, I can't believe Toby isn't here any more.'

'Me neither.'

'You didn't come back for the funeral.'

Momentarily, she wasn't sure how to respond. She hadn't expected him to bring it up – Emma, sure, but not Max. 'I couldn't—'

'Couldn't or wouldn't?' he interrupted.

She smiled gently. 'Definitely *couldn't*. I was very pregnant with my daughter Maisie and so travelling from another country wasn't an option. I would've given anything to have been here.' He had no idea how much.

Max smiled either in relief she'd had a genuine reason or because she was a mum – Lise wasn't sure. 'I didn't realise you had a daughter. I'll bet she looks like you.'

Lise smiled. 'Actually, she does.'

'And are you here with her dad?' He cleared his throat.

'No, her dad isn't here. And I'm divorced. Happily so.'

She thought she detected a bit of a sag of relief in his shoulders.

'Same here. All amicable, kind of.' He raised his eyebrows to suggest perhaps it hadn't been as pleasant as he was making out, but if he was anything like Lise, he wouldn't want to dwell on it. 'Your daughter must be around sixteen now then.'

'You've calculated correctly. You're good at maths – never knew that about you.' She shifted to his side to let a man walking three dogs past.

'As I remember we didn't know much at all about each other. I was Toby's annoying mate who laughed at your driving.' He shook his head. 'That and the guy you kissed on New Year's Eve.' So he was going to mention it then. 'Oh what it is to be young.'

'You mean you don't do that every year?'

A gentle chuckle erupted and made those creases beside his eyes crinkle all the more. 'I'm forty-seven. I think that classes me as a dirty old man in the pubs now, doesn't it?'

Lise hadn't laughed so hard in days and it felt like a good release. 'You've kind of got a point. Maybe don't do that.'

'So how long are you here for?' He checked his watch and Lise was distracted by the dark hairs on arms, which she remembered as strong, wrapped around her as they kissed that night so long ago. 'I'd love to have a proper catch-up but work beckons.'

'I'd like that. And I'll be in Bath for a couple of years at least – school for Maisie.'

He nodded. 'And you're staying at your old house?'

'It needs work, so yes, for now.'

His expression suggested uncertainty as he added, 'And what about doing some work to resolve things with Emma?' She knew her face gave away something because he said, 'Come on, one of us has to mention it. I know something went down with you both. Toby told me you fell out but he didn't give me any of the important details.'

'Men,' she sighed. 'And I do intend to try with Emma, but remember, it's a two-way street.'

'Sounds difficult.'

'Yeah, that about sums it up.'

He reached into the back pocket of his jeans and took out his phone. 'I really do need to go but give me your number and I'll give you a call?'

'You weren't this persistent on millennium eve.'

'I think I was very drunk on millennium eve. Not too drunk to enjoy the kiss but far too drunk to appreciate the good thing right in front of me.'

'Flattery will get you nowhere.' She was enjoying this, because as confident as he came across when he'd first said hello today, right now, he reminded her of that man in his mid-twenties who'd kissed her as the fireworks exploded into the night sky and then pulled back as though it was all make-believe and he had no idea what to do next. From memory, she'd found Emma and that had been it. She'd bumped into Max again at the Millers' on the odd occasion after that but neither of them had spoken about their moment of passion. Max had been a midnight kiss and a memory that had faded away, although now it seemed to be coming back to her in glorious technicolour.

'Stop torturing me and give me your number.'

She took his phone, tapped in her number and handed it back. 'I promise you it's even the real one.'

With a laugh, he set off down the street and as she was opening up the boot of the car to get the shopping bags, she saw him turn at the corner to give her another wave.

Max. After all these years. Perhaps a catch-up would be fun. She hadn't bumped into many other people she knew from back then apart from neighbours and she'd never been close to that many of them apart from Mrs Griffin. Emma probably knew all of them and it was another reminder that the girl she'd once called her best friend had a whole new life of her own in their home town. And here was Lise barrelling into it like a meteorite. Perhaps too much had gone before, too many years had passed to ever be those girls again; maybe her efforts were futile.

Lise hauled the first overly loaded shopping bags to number twelve and dumped them in the hallway. Maisie had gone out again – that or she was ignoring her mum when she called out a greeting, which was always a possibility. Lise trudged back for the rest of the bags.

She was about to walk away from the car, bags looped over her wrists, when she turned her head at the same time as the front door to number four opened.

Her heart almost melted at the sight of Brendan Miller, standing there looking at her. He was smaller than she remembered – she'd only got a glimpse of him at the funeral – and he had a walking stick at his side. But his smile was the same as it had always been and she didn't know how she'd convinced herself that avoiding him for as long as possible was the best thing all round.

She walked straight up the path, let her bags drop onto his front step, and wrapped him in a hug that unexpectedly caused her emotions to run haywire and a lump to come to her throat.

A tear spilled over and down her cheek when they pulled apart. Her bottom lip wobbled.

'I don't look that bad, do I?' he joked.

'Of course not.' She managed a smile and a gentle laugh. *Thank you, Max. Thank you, Mr Miller.* It felt good to feel some sort of welcome, a happiness of sorts at being back here. She briefly looked up to stem the threat of any more tears. 'It's good to see you.'

'Go and put your shopping away and come back,' he said. She opened her mouth to argue but he interrupted her. 'Emma is at the café, only just checked on me. The coast is clear.'

This man was impossible to say no to. She barely nodded.

Back in the townhouse, Lise unpacked what needed to go in the freezer and the fridge and then she returned to number four. Mr Miller had waited inside the doorway on the hallway bench that had always been there with its sections holding shoes beneath. He led her into the kitchen that had been updated. Gone were the dark, wood cabinets and cream benchtops that had been almost falling apart when she was last here and in their place was periwinkle blue cabinetry with off-white tops with a thin grey vein running through them. The table was still the same oak eight-seater though, positioned at the end of the kitchen, bathed in plenty of daylight.

'Let me do that, Mr Miller.' She immediately took the tea caddy when she noticed he was trying to host her by making the tea. 'You sit down.'

'On one condition… you stop calling me Mr Miller and call me Brendan.'

'You'll always be Mr Miller to me.' She lifted teabags out of the caddy for the two awaiting mugs he'd already plucked from the mug tree.

'Very well.' But his smile showed that perhaps he liked it. Maybe it reminded him of their younger years, both his and his wife's.

While they waited for the kettle to boil, Lise looked out of the back doors and onto the courtyard garden. 'It's so neat.'

'Emma keeps it shipshape even though she's not a keen

gardener. She lives upstairs,' he added by way of explanation, 'her and Naomi.'

'I met her. Naomi, I mean.' Arms folded, she leaned against the door frame and explained their encounter at the café. 'She's the spitting image of Emma at that age.'

With fondness, he talked about his granddaughter. 'She's the light of our lives. She would've loved her uncle Toby.'

Lise caught sight of the photograph of Emma and Toby on the cabinet beyond the table. They were kids in the picture, not quite teenagers, both pulling faces for the camera as they posed near Bath Abbey, bundled up in their coats and scarves and woolly hats. 'I bet she would've done too.'

Lise made the tea and took both cups over to the table. Talk dissolved into memories of Toby, the way she'd known it would – some of the laughs, some of the perils of growing up – all bringing a softness to Brendan's face along with the inevitable sadness.

'I'm sorry I didn't make it back for his funeral.'

'You had your own life to lead, Lise.'

'It wasn't that...' She could be honest, at least partially. 'I was heavily pregnant. I couldn't travel.'

His face spread into a smile. 'You have a child.'

'Maisie – she was born on the day of the funeral; that's how pregnant I was.'

'Well now, you wouldn't have wanted to give birth at the church in front of all of us, would you. Although Toby might have seen the funny side.'

'Yes, I bet he would.' It felt good to be able to talk about Toby.

'I hope I get to meet Maisie some day,' said Brendan, leaving no doubt to Lise as to the kind of grandparent he was – present, interested, invested. 'Is she in Bath with you?'

'She certainly is and I'm sure you'll get to meet.' How could she keep her away from this family who had meant so much to her growing up and still did? 'I ran into Max right before I saw you today.'

'Max...' Brendan smiled. 'He still comes to see us. He keeps Toby's memory alive. Well, you all do.'

Lise gulped back emotion at being included. Such a simple remark but it held a lot of power. 'I'm sorry.' She ran her fingers beneath her eyes. 'It's just being back here, in this house, talking to you... it's quite emotional.' She spotted another photograph of Toby and Emma taken on millennium eve before they went out, balloons with 2000 written on them in the background, coloured party streamers on Toby's shoulder.

Brendan followed the direction of her gaze. 'You were all so young at the turn of the century.'

'And hearing that makes me feel so old.'

'Do you remember how excited you were that night? You and Emma were noisier than ever with your constant giggling and chatter. Toby and Max kept setting off those blessed party popper things. And you were all joking about the world imploding if I remember rightly.'

'That does sound like us. I think we'd be more worried now we're proper grown-ups. Back then, I don't think we took it seriously.'

'Is your husband here with you and Maisie?'

'No, it's just the two of us. I'm divorced.'

'I'm sorry.'

'I'm not. I chose a man like my dad.' She didn't need to elaborate for Mr Miller.

'Oh dear.'

'It's fine. I got out. And my mother and I have reconnected too. We chat and see each other quite a bit.'

'Now that is simply wonderful. I'm really pleased.'

Talk turned to the work Lise needed to do on the townhouse,

her intentions and the choices facing her. She had no idea how to answer most of his questions – everything was so open-ended right now.

'I'm glad you'll at least be in Bath for a while,' said Brendan. 'Now, if you go over to that tin in the corner next to the tea caddy, you'll open it to find some carrot cake. I think you being here today deserves a bit of a celebratory slice.'

'I couldn't agree more.'

By the time Lise left number four and made her way back to her own townhouse to finish unpacking the shopping, she felt as though perhaps she'd taken a huge step in the right direction by talking to Mr Miller. She wondered how he'd react when he knew the whole truth but it wasn't time. Not yet. She didn't want to win him over by telling her side of the story; she wanted to be a part of life in Honeybee Place again as the woman she was now.

But one day, he'd know everything.

10

NOW: 2023

Emma

Emma loved living in Bath. This beautiful city had always been her home and she wouldn't change it for the world. She'd been to other places, she'd seen plenty, but her roots were here. And she didn't think she'd ever tire of an evening spent at the Thermae Spa. The historic city delivered in many ways and the natural thermal spa was one of them. Emma had come along with four other former work colleagues who all still taught at the school she'd left behind when she became full-time café owner.

She floated on her back in the water of the rooftop pool. She'd already been in the steam room and with so much going on in her head, she'd left the others to it and come out here.

It was twilight, the best time to come in Emma's opinion. It was raining and the cold raindrops mixed with the hot waters pumped from natural springs created steam rising from the water's surface and a magical atmosphere.

When she finally scooped her arms down into the water to

come from the floating position to upright, she spotted Laine, who had been at the school the longest out of the group.

'What I want to know,' Laine began, smiling at the sight of the mystical atmosphere created by the rain, 'is whether you're ever coming back. You know they'd have you in a heartbeat.' Laine was a no-nonsense maths teacher and Emma expected she ran her classes in much the same way, said exactly what was on her mind, asked questions of her students but listened to them as well.

'Some days I think I would. But the café...'

'You've found your true love. I mean, your carrot cakes say it all. I'd kill for one of those. I took one into the staffroom on my last birthday and almost got trampled with the stampede to get a slice.'

Emma swished her hands through the water. Going back to teaching was something she'd put to one side for a while. After having Naomi, she'd gone back on and off in a supply capacity but had never wanted to commit to a permanent position. Then her mum got sick and her parents struggled with the café and so when Naomi started school, Emma had been there to help out and get them to a stage where they could manage. That was back when they'd expected her mum to recover from her operation and be back to work full-time. Except that had never happened. At least not in the same way as before. She slowed down, she got sick again and slowly, Emma had fallen into working at the café in a full-time capacity. She knew it was her place now and she enjoyed it, but she sometimes missed the classroom and her colleagues.

'All right, I've mentioned teaching,' said Laine as they turned and leaned their arms on the very edges of the pool, looking out to the breathtaking views of the city that surrounded them. 'So how about dating? Anything to report there?'

'I didn't realise I was getting an interrogation tonight,' Emma said and sighed.

'I'm a bored, dissatisfied fifty-something.'

'How can you be dissatisfied? Your husband is gorgeous – you're as in love as you were the day you met – and you have two grown-up kids who seem to have their lives sorted.'

'Okay, so maybe I'm just in need of some excitement. Don't you have *any* gossip?'

Of course she did. 'Annalise is back.'

'And you're telling me this only now?' Laine gasped. 'Tell me everything.'

While she'd kept the details of what happened quiet from most people, she'd had to tell someone over the years and that person had ended up being Laine. She'd once joked that it was like going to confession, telling Laine every single detail in the staffroom one night when it had been just the two of them working on a project together. Laine was impartial and Emma had really needed that, and tonight, out of all the girls here it was only Laine who would know why an old friend's return had left Emma so discombobulated.

By the time she made her way back to Honeybee Place, Emma felt a bit less on edge about the possibility of bumping into Annalise. Laine was right that she and Annalise needed to put the past to bed, which would mean talking to her at some point. Laine said Emma had a classic case of lack of closure and her description had been apt. That was exactly the way she felt. And then Laine had lightened the mood and focused on her other favourite topic – trying to persuade Emma to wade into the dating pool again. She wasn't sure what was more terrifying – having it out with Annalise once and for all or the possibility of ever getting naked with a new man.

Emma found Naomi in the kitchen spooning out a generous helping of ice-cream into a ceramic bowl. 'Hello, darling. Is your grandad downstairs?'

'In the library, reading.'

'How was school?' Term was underway with Naomi starting sixth form.

'I've already got a stack of homework,' Naomi grumbled.

'How rude of those teachers.' She planted a kiss on Naomi's head. Inside their own home, she could still be Mum in full glory with displays of affection. She wondered what Annalise was like with her daughter as she made her way downstairs to see her dad. Their girls were around the same age. Which meant she and Annalise had been going through pregnancy at the same time. All those times when Emma had felt lost with a newborn who shook her world into something different. Had Annalise felt that way too? Would pregnancy and motherhood have felt less lonely and daunting with Annalise around?

Of course it would. And thinking this way just reminded Emma of how long they'd let the past come between them. But she wasn't sure she was strong enough to forgive, and she'd never forget.

Her dad looked up from his book when she went into the library and asked whether he wanted some tea or anything to eat. 'Not for me, thanks. How was the spa?'

'Wonderful, amazing, relaxing,' she said, eyes half closed remembering the bliss. 'And you look happy, which means you've had a good evening with William.'

'We had a couple of games of cards, put the world to rights as I'm sure you and the teaching crew did tonight.'

'Something like that.' But she'd hardly talked when it was the group of them. As long as you put in the odd few sentences, laughed, the group setting had the ability to carry you through even if you had a lot on your mind and weren't up for talking. Laine had obviously picked up on her state of mind and that's why she'd headed outside after her. They'd been joined by the others eventually and conversation had evolved, but by then, Emma had felt a bit better getting everything off her chest.

'I had another visitor,' said Brendan.

'Max came over too?'

He shook his head. She'd have to get the hairdresser to visit the house soon. His hair at the sides fanned out above his ears when he took off his reading glasses. 'Lise came to see me. Well, I caught her in the street – she wasn't going to stop by. I think she's too scared to bump into you.'

Emma wasn't sure how to feel. 'You always liked her.'

'She's a great kid.'

'Kid?'

'You two will always be young girls in part of my mind. And she's got a lot better at parking.'

That made Emma laugh and she sat in the stiffer of the two leather chairs. 'I should think so. It's been a while since she was a learner driver.'

'She's also got older.'

'We all have.'

'She has a daughter.'

'I know she does, Dad.'

'She's divorced.'

That jolted Emma a little – that fact she hadn't known. Xavier had never been right for her friend, in Emma's opinion, but she had assumed he was still on the scene.

He put his book down. 'I know whatever happened between you two isn't going to be swept aside just like that. Your mother and I never really knew what went on. I don't need to know now, but it always made us sad that whatever it was, neither of you found the strength to work it out. Is there really nothing more that can be done?'

Emma thought about her talk with Laine tonight. After Emma's dramatic announcement of Annalise's return, Laine had settled in to be an agony aunt. She was good at that. Emma didn't know whether it was because she had grown-up children who hadn't always been so level-headed, whether it was because her sister had been in a lot of trouble over the years and it was she who'd had to help her out rather than their parents, but she had a way of listening, a way of advising without lecturing or being bossy.

'I'm sad about us too, Dad.'

'You don't need to tell me. You're my daughter. I can read your mind more than you know.'

'Now that sounds frightening.'

'Don't worry, I'm not so clever I can always work out what you're thinking.' The laughter lines were replaced by deep creases on his forehead. 'I know when you're hurting, though. It's not a grazed knee or a headache or anything that can be fixed by something in the medicine cabinet, but it's a hurt that runs deep and I'd hate to see you carry it around with you for the rest of your life.'

With a sigh, she admitted, 'I've no idea where to start, Dad.'

'Your mother would have had some ideas. Once, she said she wished we could get Lise back in the country, get the two of you in a room together. She said she'd lock the door and refuse to let you out until you'd screamed, yelled, whatever it took.'

'That sounds like Mum. Remember when our cousin Felix fell out with Toby?'

'Do I ever.' His laughter made his whole face come alive.

Felix was Brendan's sister's son and when they were little the boys had played together a lot in the summer holidays. But they also got fed up with one another. One day, the boys started fighting for the third time in the courtyard garden and before Brendan could go and pull them apart, Keely had stood in front of the back door and said, 'Leave it. If they're still scrapping in another two minutes, I'll go out.'

They'd been scuffling around in the dirt, the rest of the family watching, and finally each of them ran out of energy. Both of them had lain there looking at the sky, dry mud caking their legs where the sunscreen had clung onto every piece of it. Emma remembered Felix getting another shove in, Toby retaliated just the once, and then that was it. They both stomped off their separate ways but by the time their parents took them all to the big park to play, they were back to being friends.

'I don't think Lise and I would get very far being shut in a room.'

He was smiling.

'What's that look for? You think differently?'

'Oh it's not that... it's that you called her Lise. You haven't done that since she got back here.'

'I miss her, Dad.' Her voice caught.

With a bit of effort, he got out of the chair and she stood up to meet him halfway and let herself be wrapped in a hug that reminded her of when she was much younger. The hug he'd given her when she passed her exams, then her driving test, the hug before she left for university, the hugs in between all those times.

'I'm going to go to bed.' He kissed her on the forehead gently. 'Have a think about it, Emma. I can tell you miss her and I know she misses you too.'

When he got to the doorway, he asked, 'Do you mind her daughter being friends with Naomi?'

'I don't. Somehow, they met by chance and they seem to get on. I won't be stopping them. I can imagine what Naomi would do if I tried.'

'She'd want to be friends with her all the more.'

'You understand how teenage girls work.'

'Should do – I raised one. A good one might I add.'

She took a curtsey, making them both chuckle, before he

headed off for bed and Emma went back up to the kitchen to make herself a mug of tea. She could hear the distant sound of the television from the lounge on the floor above while Naomi watched one of her shows, no doubt double-screening with her phone on her lap lest she miss any messages or gossip.

Lise. She'd called her Lise.

Because as much as she was upset, angry, resentful, that was who she was. And they had a history.

But was that all it was ever going to be?

11

THEN: 1999

Lise

Annalise and Emma were both in their final year at university and home in Bath for the holidays. Christmas came and went with the usual festivities, including a traditional midnight mass with Mrs Griffin, the day itself with her parents at number twelve, an escape to the Millers' on Christmas night for board games and lots of fun and laughter. And now, the millennium was fast approaching.

Annalise carried a heavy box in her arms and watched her footing on the front path – there was enough frost on the rooftops to indicate there may well be slippery pavements today. The last thing she wanted was to ruin what was to be the biggest New Year celebrations of all, with 1999 turning into 2000. Everyone was talking about the Millennium Bug, the term coined for the panic that computer systems worldwide would crash, planes would fall out of the sky, and medical devices would fail, risking lives. There had even been a story in the newspaper this morning about shelves of non-perishable items like bottled water and toilet rolls being cleared from supermarkets with people preparing for a major disaster.

Annalise heaved the box up again as she managed to open the front gate by balancing the box on one uplifted leg. She was going to dump it in the boot of her car for safekeeping.

Emma was walking her way, a dark-blue woolly hat covering her hair cascading down her back. 'What's have you got in there?'

Annalise turned to the side. 'Do me a favour? My car keys are in my coat pocket; the car's just down there past your place. Help me out so I can dump this in the boot.'

Emma plucked the keys out from Annalise's pocket and they started to walk again.

'My parents thought now was a good time to decorate, which means I have to move all my things into Mum's sewing room. Which means she'll have full access to my diaries and I don't intend to let that happen.'

'She won't look at them.'

Annalise just laughed. 'You say that because your mum respects boundaries. My mother thinks boundaries are for other people. She won't think twice about looking through and… well I can't have that.' Especially given a lot of what was in there was about her parents.

'Why don't I keep them for you, in my room. Nobody will snoop. That way you don't have to stick them in your car.'

'You sure?' She would rather they weren't in the car. She'd already had visions of it being stolen given it was a nice car. She'd imagined the thieves having a great time reading her innermost thoughts, which would circulate around the city of Bath and taunt her. 'It will only be for a couple of weeks. At most.'

Emma led the way down her own front path and opened the door. 'As long as you need – you know that.'

'Thanks, Emma.' She looked at her friend more closely. 'Are you okay?'

'Yeah, just a bit tired that's all. Go put the box upstairs in my room. I have to get to work.'

'Well don't work too hard. And I'll see you for movie night tonight? And we have to call Sam, remember?' Sam hadn't come back for the holidays; he'd stayed in Scotland and his family had travelled up for a millennium party at a castle. He was hoping for some brutal winter weather apparently, and that they'd all be snowed in and he could use it for research.

'I won't forget.'

'It's a shame he isn't back in Bath for the new year.'

Emma shrugged. 'We've all made new friends. Life moves on, I suppose.'

Annalise still thought he might have come home, perhaps finally asked Emma out, but maybe she was right. Life moved on.

Emma reminded her to give the front door a good tug shut when she left and went on her way.

Annalise went back to her own place after the diaries were safely ensconced at the Millers' and continued moving more of her stuff into her mother's sewing room, grumbling the whole time that they could've done this when she was back at university. Why did it have to start now? But when she'd asked the question, her mother had simply said they had to fit in with other people's schedules and the decorators were happy to work right up until New Year. She'd told Annalise to think about the lovely bright room she'd have to come home to next time. Annalise could barely keep her mouth closed that if she could afford to, if she got a job quickly, she'd be moving out permanently as soon as she could.

Annalise spent the remainder of the day shopping in the city to get out of the way of the decorators and briefly went home to get changed before heading back to Emma's armed with the snacks she'd bought for their movie night.

'I got popcorn!' She beamed when Emma opened the front door but her friend looked worse than she had earlier. 'You all right?'

'I feel like I'm getting the flu. Or a nasty cold. I kept sitting down today whenever I could. I'm exhausted.' She warned, 'Don't be sitting next to me. I don't want to pass it on.'

Annalise closed the front door. 'Thanks for the warning. You go put your feet up; I'll make the popcorn and bring it to you and then we'll call Sam before we do anything else.'

But Emma didn't chat much to Sam and the call wrapped up quickly before Annalise put the movie on. Emma ate barely any popcorn and before the credits to the first film even rolled, she'd lain down on the sofa, covered herself in a blanket and was almost out for the count.

'You're shivering. Let me get you a hot-water bottle,' Annalise suggested. 'You need to get better in time for the biggest New Year's Eve of all time. It's only a few days away.'

'I'll try. The hot-water bottle is upstairs, in my bed.'

Annalise went up the stairs towards Emma's bedroom but when she pushed open the door and saw Toby with one of her diaries in his hands, her legs almost gave way.

That was until her voice kicked into gear. 'What the hell are you doing?' She snatched it back.

'I'm sorry, I—'

'You're snooping. These are mine!'

'All right, stop yelling. I didn't realise until I opened it – my sister said I could grab some paper from her room earlier and so I came in to get it, saw notebooks and figured...'

'That you'd help yourself and read private diaries?'

'Lise, I didn't mean to snoop. I apologise, honestly, I'm so sorry.'

He called her Lise – nobody had ever done that before.

She yanked back the diary he was holding. 'What did you see?'

He held up his hands. He was a well-built rugby player at twenty-four, but he still looked terrified and it gave Annalise a little satisfaction despite the fact he'd intruded on her privacy. 'Not much.'

'Not much?' But not *nothing*.

'You lost your virginity to Davey Price?'

'Oh my God!' she yelled. He knew Davey Price because they played rugby together.

'I'm sorry, it was right there on the page when I opened it.'

'Well, as soon as you saw it wasn't the blank paper you were supposedly looking for, you should've put it down!' She shoved the diary he'd been holding back in the box before lifting the entire thing up. 'I should have put them in my car, not here.'

'I'm sorry, Lise.' He put a hand on her arm and the warmth of his touch had a tear snaking down her cheek, betraying her.

'Leave me alone.' But she didn't tug away.

'Lise—'

She didn't look at him, box still in her arms. 'Pass me the hot-water bottle.'

'What?'

'Just pass it!'

He did as asked and slotted the hot-water bottle on top of the box. She wished she could stop her tears but they were falling as if they were too scared to stop.

Downstairs, she put the box by the front door, filled the hot-water bottle for her friend who was asleep, and left.

And on the way home, she shoved the boxes in the boot of her car.

* * *

The next day, Annalise came down the stairs rubbing the tops of her arms despite the jumper she was wearing. She was about to close the front door at least partially so they didn't lose all the heat, given the inconsiderate painter and decorator had left it like that, when Toby appeared at the end of the path.

'What do you want?'

'Boyfriend trouble?' asked one of the painters who had squeezed past Toby at the gate and headed past Annalise and back inside.

'He's not my boyfriend.' *So fuck off and mind your own business,* she wanted to add.

Toby came closer. There was no sign of his cheeky smile, just regret. 'Lise, I'm so sorry I looked at your diary.' Lise, it sounded good, new, different. She liked it already. 'It was a mistake, and I've felt guilty all night. I barely slept.'

'Yeah right.'

'It's the honest truth. Please, whatever I can do to make it up to you, I will.'

She harrumphed.

'I mean it. I want to make it right. And not only because Emma doesn't know and when you tell her, she'll kill me.'

'How is she?'

'She's been up for breakfast but went back to bed. I told her you were tired last night so went home after you gave her the hot-water bottle. I didn't tell her what I'd done.'

She stood a little taller. To most people, those diary entries wouldn't mean much. They weren't terrible; there were no enormous secrets that would change the course of a life. But as well as the details of what she and Emma got up to, things they might not want others to know like kissing boys, losing their virginity and all the other cringe-worthy admissions of teenagers over the years, there were private thoughts: what it was like to live the life she was living, what it was like to be her. And that made her feel raw, exposed, like she was suddenly naked in front of a crowd with nothing to cover her modesty.

'I'm humiliated that you read any of it, Toby.' She couldn't look at him at first but she did when she asked, 'Was it just that bit? About Davey?'

'I'm not proud of it. My curiosity got the better of me and I may have flicked to another few pages. But that's it – it was barely anything.'

She didn't even want to ask what else he'd seen.

'None of it will go any further.'

He sounded like he meant it.

'I promise, Lise.'

'You keep calling me Lise.'

He shrugged. 'It suits you.'

She was trying to be nonchalant but after twenty-one years of being Annalise Baker and playing to her parents' rules and hearing her dad use her name and lecture her, perhaps Toby had unwittingly given her a bit of an out. She was growing up, moving in to her own place as soon as she could manage it. Perhaps it was high time she stopped being that girl – Annalise Baker, the girl from the diaries – and became Lise Baker instead.

Toby shifted from foot to foot, blew into his hands for warmth. She jerked her head for him to come into the hallway so he didn't freeze.

Annalise closed the door and claimed, 'I'm not doing it for you, you know. I'm doing it to keep the heat in. It's already bad enough with windows open to rid the place of paint fumes. And I hate being cold.'

'You know Davey is a total bellend, don't you?' he said.

She began to laugh. 'Yeah, we had a couple of dates if you can even call them that and then I realised for myself. You know he wanted to take photographs of me naked?'

He leaned against the wall near the bottom of the stairs and tilted his head back. 'No surprise there. And how long do you think before he showed them to other people?'

She shuddered. 'I'm glad I stopped seeing him.'

But then a thought came to her. An idea.

'You're smiling,' said Toby. 'Should I be worried?'

'You said you'd do anything to make it up to me.'

'Anything.'

'Right, then I want you. Naked.' She appreciated the sight of him gulping in panic. His usually gorgeous smile and alluring eyes held a sense of trepidation. 'Not for me. But you have to be naked and run around Honeybee Place, a whole lap around the railings.' The homes of Honeybee Place shared the garden square and it was big enough that a lap around its perimeter would take him at least five minutes, if he ran fast.

'Tell me you're kidding.'

'You said anything.'

'It's bloody freezing out there, not to mention it's daylight.'

She tilted her head. 'Well I can't do anything about the cold, but we can change the time so it's dark. You come back here, seven o'clock, strip, go for it.'

'I think your parents might have something to say about that.' But he knew when he was cornered. 'I think 10 p.m. otherwise I could risk seeing kids and I wouldn't want anyone traumatised.'

She twisted her lips together. 'Done – 10 p.m. And don't worry about my parents; they'll be out at a dinner function, which doesn't finish until midnight. The only thing they'll have to complain about is the fact that you're leaning up against a freshly painted wall.'

He leapt off the wall and tried to turn his head to see.

'Yep, a nice, pale blue for your hair and your T-shirt.' She grinned. 'Good luck getting rid of it.'

He grimaced. 'Your parents will kill me.'

But the eldest of the painter duo was coming down the stairs and just rolled his eyes, muttering 'kids' beneath his breath, before calling up to his sidekick that they had to repaint the wall in the hall.

'Relax,' she told Toby. 'They get paid by the hour. They don't care if it's another bit of work.' She ushered him towards the front door. 'I'll see you tonight. Don't be late.'

* * *

When 10 p.m. came around, Lise was watching from the corner of her bedroom window upstairs, light off with no curtains while it was being decorated. She was kneeling down and watching a very nervous Toby hovering at the end of the path. She couldn't believe he'd actually turned up.

All of a sudden, she wasn't sure she should've asked him to do this. Whatever had possessed him to say yes?

She put her serious face on as she answered the door. 'You came.'

'Said I would, didn't I? And if you breathe a word of this to my sister...'

'I won't. Now get your kit off.' This was helping her utter devastation at him having looked at her diary; this was helping a lot. She turned her back. 'Don't worry, I don't need to see it. I'll take the bare butt cheeks when you run past me. That's enough.'

She'd thought she'd have to nag him into hurrying up but in less than a minute of shuffling behind her as he tugged his clothes off, he shot past her. 'Later, Lise!'

Watching his firm, bare buttocks as he made a run for it, she couldn't quite believe he was doing it. He moved into the darkness surrounding the iron railings of the square garden in the middle where at least he had a modicum of privacy from the lack of street-light and the extra protection of the trees. Did he even have shoes on? She didn't think so.

'Good evening, Mr Walker,' she called out when the next door but one neighbour went past with his dog. Luckily, he wasn't one to chat so smiled in her direction and carried on.

Mrs Griffin came past next and looked Annalise's way. 'Did I just see...?'

Annalise flashed her a smile.

'You know what? I don't need to know...' And with a goodnight, she went on her way.

After almost ten minutes, Annalise was looking at her watch. Where was he? He was a fast runner and it wasn't the warmest of nights being December. What was taking him so long?

And then there he was. She put her hands in front of her eyes as Toby charged down the front path towards her. As soon as she looked again, she spotted Mr Walker closing his curtains at his front window and doing a double take in her direction. She waved, hoping he'd think he'd just imagined seeing a naked man charge into her house.

'You decent yet?' she asked, still at the door as she heard the clink of a belt and the shuffling sound of jeans being pulled on behind her.

He soon told her she could turn around. Bare-chested, he could've passed for a male model but she'd never tell him that and she knew if she mentioned it to Emma, she'd put her fingers down her throat.

'Are we even now?' He picked up his top from the floor.

'I suppose so.' She watched his chest rise and fall as he tried to get his breath back. 'You took your time.'

'I had to duck when I saw Miss Nevis at number twenty-one.'

Lise burst out laughing. 'She'd have you in her bedroom in under a minute if she saw you.' Their neighbour was in her thirties, unmarried and was seen recently dating a man at least a decade younger than her.

'Don't even joke.'

'I can't believe you did it.'

'I wanted to make it right after I snooped.'

The reminder had her uncomfortable but when she looked down at the wooden floorboards in the hallway, she noticed his foot was bleeding. 'You've cut yourself. I guess that answered my question of whether you had shoes on or not.'

Barefoot in jeans, he picked up his foot and inspected the sole. 'That'll be whatever I trod on when I was trying to escape Miss Nevis.'

'Sit down and let me get something to clean it with.'

While Toby sat on the stairs, she went to the kitchen and found the first-aid kit and some antiseptic wash. She mixed the wash with some water, soaked a cotton wool ball and went back to Toby. She brushed the cotton wool ball gently against the cut, watching his face to make sure she wasn't hurting him. She would've wanted to when she'd caught him looking in her diary, but not so much any more.

He winced. 'Stings a bit.'

'Not as much as knowing you read my innermost thoughts.'

'I thought you said we were even.'

'Relax – I'm over it.'

'You are?'

'Well...'

'Can I ask you a question?' He winced one more time before she finished cleaning the cut and put a plaster on it for him.

'As long as it's not too personal.'

'Do you still keep a diary?'

'I stopped, in my first year at university. I suppose I discovered there was more to life than focusing on everything that bothers me.' She'd started writing them when she was in her early teens. It was an avenue of release, a way to let go of the turmoil inside of her. She hadn't needed it as much once she was at university on her own terms.

'Your dad, you mean?'

She tensed, slopped the antiseptic as she faltered putting on the plastic top.

'That was the other bit I read.' He pulled a face at his admission that he hadn't shared with her until now. 'I shouldn't have, but you've been in my life for a while, Lise. I care.'

He cared. She supposed she was at the Millers' a lot, almost a part of the family. And oddly, she wasn't angry about this part of the snooping. It meant she didn't have to attempt to explain that her home life wasn't quite like his and Emma's. 'Well, knowing that you read something about my dad doesn't help me, Toby, because there is so much in there about him. None of it terrible but none of it great either. He didn't do anything bad to me. He didn't hurt me, he—'

'Not physically.'

'How much did you read?' She looked up at him, felt her vulnerability again.

'Not much, I swear to you. But...'

She filled in the blanks. 'I didn't hold back. You could've opened it at any page really—'

'Lise...'

'Don't apologise again. Honestly, I'm fine.' She put the bottle of antiseptic down. 'And I mean it when I say I don't write them any more. I don't know why I keep them. I think about getting rid of them, but I'm not sure how to do that. Know anyone with a garden incinerator?'

He shook his head. 'Don't destroy those diaries.'

'I don't ever want to read them again.'

'You might want to, one day. There must be some good things in there.'

She was about to shake her head but sat down on the bottom stair next to him. 'There's a lot about me and Emma.'

'See.' He nudged her. 'You and my sis are the very best of friends. Friendships like that don't come along often and one day, you might want to read about it in your own words.'

'Emma said the same, you know. We wrote each other letters when I was away at school but we made each other promise that those letters were destroyed, the evidence got rid of. It felt like a part of the adventure at the time but she mentioned the other day that she wishes she could read some of them again for the memories.'

'So she wants you to hold on to the diaries instead.'

'She does. A few years ago, when she knew she wanted to study English, we talked about diaries and how important they are. I joked that if mine were ever made public, I'd never be able to show my face again. But we also talked about the two of us reading them some day, being reminded of all the little things, like the time we fell out over Jaimie Walker, the boy who asked us both out on a date.'

'Jaimie Walker who used to live with his great-uncle at number fourteen?'

'The very same. He asked us both to go with him to the disco at the sports centre one night over the summer – I think we were thirteen or thereabouts. He was apparently hedging his bets, asked us both, we both said yes and he thought he could decide on the night who he would have as his date. We both turned up and he honestly thought he could select one of us and the other would toddle off home. I thought Emma was going to deck him. But she smiled, told him of course we were going to the disco, hooked her arm through mine and in we went. We vowed on that day that we'd never let a boy come between us ever again.'

'You two have so much history. Treasure it.'

'I will. And I do.'

'I have plenty of memories with you both in it. Remember the crumble recipes you came up with. The one with… what was it…'

'Strawberry and lime crumble.'

His laughter sounded more manly than she ever remembered, mature, not the laughter of the young Toby from before she'd gone away to university. 'Absolutely revolting, Lise.'

She shoved him playfully on the arm. 'You ate it!'

'I was being polite! Thought you'd have to cart me to A&E.' He looked sideways at her and she was sure his gaze dropped to her lips before it went back up again. 'See, you don't want to lose some of those memories.'

'Me and Emma agreed that we could look at the diaries when we were forty, with wrinkles and saggy boobs.'

'No comment I make will sound right in this scenario.' But he made an attempt anyway. 'Whatever your body is like at forty – which, I'm sure will be smoking hot – you won't be able to look at the diaries if they're gone.'

Smoking hot? That was new, a compliment she'd never thought would come from her best friend's brother.

'Keep them, Lise,' he said, using the name she was fast getting used to. 'Maybe in a safety deposit box might be the best idea, though. Away from prying eyes like mine.'

'Wherever I hide them, I'm going to put a note on top of them to say that these must not be read until I'm with Emma and we're at least forty.'

'What about the saggy boobs?'

'You're such a child. Behave.' But she had another thought. 'I could bury them.'

'You've been reading too many of Emma's *Famous Five* books.'

'I have not and she doesn't have those any more,' she said.

'She does – they're in the storage. You know Emma; she's very attached to her books.' He was watching her. 'Where do you intend to bury them exactly?'

'We could use the veggie patch in my garden – it's never seen a vegetable. It was mine as a kid but my parents never really helped me do anything with it. Mum tried once. She gave me some seeds but she's not one to get her hands dirty so I think I shoved them in and left them and that was that. Nothing grew.'

'That's sad.' How did he manage to give sympathy that didn't feel like pity?

'It's the perfect place to bury something,' she went on. 'It's just a patch of dirt now with a few planter boxes at the edges.'

'You'd have to bury it in tin, so the diaries stand the test of time.'

Deflated, she knew she didn't have what she needed. She only had cardboard boxes.

'I might be able to find something suitable at home.'

'Then what are you waiting for?' She leapt up. 'Let's do it.'

While Annalise found a big spade from the shed, Toby ducked home to see what he could get his hands on and came back with what had once been a tea caddy storage tin that had been in their shed, holding bits and bobs he'd transferred to an old biscuit tin. While he'd been gone, Annalise had written her note as discussed and put it inside a plastic cover she'd nicked from her dad's study – it wasn't like he was going to find it in her room or anywhere else, was it? – and with that fixed to the top of the tin box with the help of a lot of Sellotape, and her diaries stashed inside, she and Toby ventured out to the Bakers' back garden.

Beneath the moonlight and the cold winter temperatures, the pair took turns to dig down deep in the veggie patch and before too long, she buried her memories and a part of her pain about her relationship with her parents along with it.

After they'd heaped the dirt over the top, she smoothed the surface with the back of the spade and looked up Toby, the boy from a few doors away, her best friend's brother, a pain in the arse a lot of the time, but now a man who had sensitivity and understanding. 'Thank you.'

'Least I could do.'

When Toby left, Annalise lay down on the spare bed and stared up at the ceiling, trying to banish any panic that her parents might suddenly landscape the small garden they hadn't paid much attention to in the whole time they'd lived in the house.

'Lise,' she said out loud to nobody at all.

And she smiled.

Lise Baker. It sounded grown up, sophisticated. Thanks to Toby, she had a new identity almost and it felt fitting with the turn to the millennium fast approaching.

She turned over and closed her eyes.

From now on, she was Lise, she'd written in enough diaries, and it was time to get her life on track. It was time to move forwards.

12

THEN: 1999

Emma

Emma teased the few strands of her hair around her face so they sat perfectly. She could see her emerald dangle earrings, the gift from Sam all the way from Scotland for her twenty-first birthday. Her boyfriend at university, Stuart, hadn't appreciated the gesture but he'd relaxed a bit when she pointed out that Sam had got Annalise – or Lise as she'd been calling herself for the last few days, although that was taking some getting used to – a pair too. Emma had told Stuart that they were all friends; there was nothing more to it than that. But she hadn't told him she and Annalise had clubbed together to buy Sam a watch for orienteering when they heard he'd joined a society up in Scotland. He'd have handled that nugget of information the same way as he had the earrings and she didn't want any unnecessary fuss, especially because she, Lise and Sam had agreed that gifts ended now because they were all skint students.

When Sam had called to say he couldn't make it home to Bath for the millennium celebrations, Emma hadn't admitted how disappointed she'd been. But that was what happened with friends, wasn't it? You missed them; you craved their company. And she wasn't happy she and Stuart couldn't be together either. He'd chosen to go home to Wales because, like her, he wanted to be with family and old friends. They were meeting up a few days after but it wasn't quite the same.

'Can you believe Sam got a better offer?' Lise was in Emma's bedroom as the girls got ready. She adjusted her velvet mini skirt that showed off her super-long legs before squeezing in to check her reflection and apply her fiery red lippy that somehow she never got on her teeth.

'I think I'd have said yes to a party at a castle.' Emma finished with her lipliner before applying a glossy pink colour she knew would be on her teeth later. She didn't have quite the same elegance as Lise; at least she didn't feel like she did.

'It does sound rather glamorous. Talking of glamorous...' Annalise stepped back to admire Emma's outfit, a sparkly green top with a black mini skirt. Emma had dialled it up with make-up too, opting for candy-pink eyeshadow, black eyeliner and a good lick of mascara.

'You think?'

Annalise shook her head. 'You need more confidence.'

'At least the horrid cold has gone so I'm not covered in snot for tonight.'

Annalise laughed loudly. 'That would've been a good look. Honestly, you're utterly gorgeous, Emma. I'd kill for your hair for a start.'

'You would not, Annalise.'

'It's Lise, remember.'

Emma adjusted the bottom of her top to sit more flatteringly over her hip bones. 'What made you change your name?'

'I haven't changed my name. Just dropped the first four letters. Don't you like it?'

'Of course I do. I'm just used to full-naming you that's all.'

'It makes me feel different, being Lise not Annalise. I can't hear my dad announcing that Annalise will do better at a boarding school or that Annalise shouldn't be working in a café when she has studying to do, telling Annalise that her friend should be going home now. It's refreshing – that's what it is. They won't ever know I go by Lise either. I'm Annalise at home but when I step outside that door, I'm Lise Baker. And I love it.' Shoulders back, standing tall, she clearly did.

Emma knew better than anyone the crap Lise put up with at home, the parents who to most weren't doing anything wrong at all. Their daughter was safe; she had everything money could buy. But what she didn't have was the type of unconditional love every kid craved. And growing up alongside Lise made Emma appreciate her own parents.

The day the girls got back from university, Lise had come over to the Millers for a roast dinner with Emma's mum's renowned Hasselback potatoes. They'd had apple crumble and ice cream for dessert. They'd regaled everyone with tales from their universities and shared more risqué stories with each other behind Emma's bedroom door. And when Lise left for home that evening, Emma realised that her friend hadn't said much about her parents at all. And when she went to see Lise the day after, she bumped into Mr Baker coming out of the front door. He'd seemed surprised to see her there and flummoxed when Lise came down the stairs.

'Did he even know you were home?' Emma had hovered in the doorway as he set off down the path.

'Doesn't seem like it.' Lise had brushed it off, the way she often did, and they'd quickly headed off to the shops to choose new outfits for New Year's Eve. But all the while they were talking, laughing, shopping, Emma hadn't been able to get it out of her mind that Mr Baker's daughter had been home twenty-four hours and he had no idea.

'Tonight is going to be a blast, Emma.' Lise was full of New-Year spirit now.

Emma put a smile on her face and did her best to stop thinking about Mr Baker and how detached he was from his family life. It had always been that way, would probably never change, but she wondered how Lise could even stand it sometimes. Her mum wasn't the best but at least she was more present than he was. 'I've been counting down the hours ever since I got up this morning,' she gushed, hoping she could match her best friend's enthusiasm.

'Tonight, Emma Miller, we are partying in the city in our favourites pubs and at least one bar and then we'll pile onto the streets to see the fireworks.'

'Do you think we'll actually see any?' Emma had suggested they buy tickets to a venue away from the city but as soon as she realised how many people they knew were going to be around in the usual haunts, she had the urge to be in amongst it and they'd bought tickets for the bar they knew everyone else was heading for.

'Of course we will. I'd put money on it. You don't have to buy a ticket to look into the sky. Have you put your camera in your bag?'

'I got a disposable one – don't want to lose mine.'

'Good thinking.' Lise admired her reflection again. 'Is my eyeshadow too much?'

'No, I love it! Really suits you.' Lise had gone for bright blue on her lids, said she wanted to stand out on such an important occasion. It was striking, just like she was.

Lise put her arm around Emma's shoulders. 'I think we're ready. And Stuart doesn't know what he's missing.' She gave her friend a squeeze. She knew Emma was wishing her boyfriend was here tonight.

'I won't get a New Year's kiss,' said Emma.

'Who says you won't?'

'I'm not a cheater!'

'One kiss isn't going to destroy a relationship.' They bundled out of Emma's bedroom.

'Depends what sort of kiss it is.'

When they got downstairs, Mrs Miller insisted on getting Emma and Toby to stand together for a photograph before he went out with his mates and Emma with hers. And then after getting a picture of the three of them, they left Mr and Mrs Miller to their cosy night for two before a walk into the city as the time approached midnight so they could bask in the atmosphere.

Everyone was buzzing when they got to the bar and squeezed in, more than a little relieved they'd bought tickets and hadn't assumed they'd do what they usually did and turn up to one bar, then move on to another and another until they were done for the night.

Emma and Lise circulated, catching up with old friends until they found a space for a breather. 'It's hot in here.' Emma flapped her top with one hand, clutched her bottle of Hooch tightly in the other, paranoid someone was going to knock into her and send it flying across the floor.

Lise began dancing on the spot when the music changed to Shania Twain's 'That Don't Impress Me Much', her own bottle of Hooch lifted high in one arm. 'It's amazing to be back!' she yelled above the din. 'I love this city!'

Emma didn't care that it was hot; she started dancing again too, all the way through that track and another.

Lise waved over at someone and when Emma turned, she saw

Toby with his friend Max and a couple of other guys. She grabbed Lise's hand before she could object. 'Let's go!'

They danced their way through the crowds. Five or six years ago, Toby would've been mortified at his little sister approaching him in a bar but these days, he didn't seem to mind. Her brother wasted no time introducing his mates and when Toby's ex, Vicky, swooped in and commandeered his attentions, Max and the others chatted with the girls.

Max looked across at Vicky with Toby. 'She's...'

'Hot?' Emma concluded, admiring the blonde's curls cascading all the way down to her bum.

'Not shy,' Lise put in.

Max concluded, 'I'd say scary... She's almost eating him up.'

'Ew.' Emma zoned in on what he meant and saw Vicky snogging the face off her brother.

A little before midnight, a group of them spilled out onto the street, eager to get ready to see fireworks the second they welcomed in the year 2000. The countdown began loudly, excitedly, and as soon as the clock struck midnight, a big whoop went up. Emma hugged Lise first, glad to be welcoming the new year in with her best friend. The fireworks from more than one direction sent a riot of colour into the air, bursts of brightly coloured stars launching into the darkness, and they turned so the fireworks were behind them, their cheeks pressed together as Emma used her camera to capture the moment. Neither of them cared how cold it was. That wasn't important, not tonight.

They took at least ten shots, hoping one of them would be good, until Toby came over to hug each of the girls and took charge of the camera to do the honours for them. As soon as he handed the camera back, he hugged someone else, then another person, Emma hugged a girl from primary school who recognised her and the friend she didn't. They hugged strangers, with everyone high on tonight. If Stuart had turned up, Emma knew there was no way she would've been in amongst it like this. Tonight was *one for the books*, so her parents kept telling her, and perhaps that was why when a good-looking guy wearing a midnight-blue shirt and snug-fitting jeans planted a smacker on her lips, she didn't pull away.

'Happy new year!' he cheered after the kiss and she yelled the same. She couldn't stop smiling, laughing. Everyone was dancing in the street, Emma included, and she turned around to find Lise again. She couldn't see her at first, squeezed past a couple of guys with their arms around each other singing 'Auld Lang Syne' out of tune, past her brother who was being eaten up by Vicky again and then she spotted Lise, in full-on kissing mode with Max.

She hung back, smiling.

Emma joined in with 'Auld Lang Syne' for round three, or was it four? And by the time they were about to go for it and sing it all over again, Lise came to her side and tugged at her arm.

'You finished kissing the face off Max?' Emma asked, her volume lower out here than it could be inside the bar.

Lise couldn't stop grinning. 'He's a great kisser.' Her lipstick had been kissed off well and truly.

Emma shivered. 'Want to head inside?'

Lise surprised her by saying, 'I'm ready to head home.'

Emma leaned around her friend to spot Max talking to Toby, now that Vicky had released her hold. She was still lolling on his shoulder though. 'Aren't you tempted to go home with Max?'

Lise turned and when he saw them looking, she beamed a smile his way. 'Tempted to carry on that kiss, but no...' She turned back to her friend. 'Tonight is for you and me. We can talk about him, though – you know, he's got that really sexy, rugby-guy vibe going on, like your brother.'

'My brother?'

'Your brother, who plays rugby.'

'I know who my brother is but please don't use the name Toby and the word *sexy* in the same sentence again.'

Lise sniggered. 'Promise. Now come on, home time. And by home, I mean your place.'

'Do your parents know you'll be at ours?'

'No, but they won't be back until the small hours and it's not like they peek in on me so I'm not worried.'

Emma felt oddly sober for a moment, wondering whether Lise's parents had even done that when Lise was a baby. Surely they had.

But she wasn't going to dwell on that thought. She didn't want to let them take anything away from Lise tonight, in this moment, high on life and amongst friends. 'Come on... home.'

As Lise linked her arm, the guy Emma had kissed darted over, complaining that they were leaving the party.

'Something you want to tell me?' Lise asked when he left them to it. 'Who was that?'

'I don't know his name. But he kissed me at midnight.'

'Emma! You hussy!'

Emma stopped in the middle of the pavement. 'I just realised something.'

'Well can you realise it while walking. It's kind of freezing.'

'It's the year 2000 and so far, the world hasn't imploded!'

Their giggles rang into the night, best friends forever, the moment captured for a lifetime in their memories and the photographs of them welcoming in the new year, together.

13

NOW: 2023

Lise

Who needed a gym or weights when you had tins of paint to lift?

Lise lifted one tin in each hand and waddled – that was the only way to describe it – with them to the front door. She'd already put her bag over her shoulder as well as the other bag containing brushes, sugar soap and all the extra pieces of kit you needed for a spot of painting.

Lise had graduated with a degree in public relations and she'd worked as a PR officer in London for a few years prior to Paris. She'd begun to move into a similar role over there and would put the feelers out here once she knew what she was doing. For now, it was the town-house that needed her attention. Maisie thought she was crazy setting her alarm when she had all day to do whatever she liked but Lise liked her routine; it kept her sane. Last week, she'd been at a real loose end and got some quotes for the work she wouldn't be able to do herself: the kitchen makeover to replace broken cabinetry and damaged floor tiles; and the spruce-up of the bathrooms, including putting in a better shower cubicle and new flooring in the en suite as well as a new floor in the main bathroom. She'd also elected to have a better extractor fan in both given the marks on the wall that were either because the fans weren't good enough or because the renters hadn't bothered to use them when they showered or took a bath.

With the paint she'd just bought, Lise was going to work on the bedroom that was hers at the moment. She'd already had Maisie help her drag the queen-size mattress down the stairs to a bedroom on the floor below. They'd done it in hysterics – mattresses were heavy and when you least expected, they bent and tried to take you with them. She'd covered the base of the bed rather than moving that as well as the chest of drawers, which she hadn't unpacked anything into and didn't know if she ever would, and she'd already dragged her suitcase and boxes out of the way too.

Lise set the paint tins down in the hallway and sat on the bottom stair to take off her shoes. Maisie had already texted her to say she was heading to Sally Lunn's, the historic eating house in the city, with some of the badminton crowd. Rather than wonder whether she was in for dinner, Lise messaged her back to have a nice time. She wondered whether Naomi was with her and if she was, were they getting closer?

After a glass of water gulped down in front of the kitchen sink, she ventured outside to get the stepladder from in amongst the cobwebs lining the shed, and with everything she needed upstairs, she wound her hair up into a clip, pinned it in place, and hooked the wisps that fell onto her face behind her ears, even though she knew they wouldn't stay there. She flung open the window and took in the view across Honeybee Place. She'd always loved the view from her bedroom one floor down, but it was even better up here. She looked across the rooftops beyond, houses as far as the eye could see, people just like her living beneath the roofs, small families and large, couples, children, all making their homes in whatever way they could.

Down below, everything looked so small – the green space with its graceful, old beech trees and grass dotted with leaves that had already begun to fall, the winding path in the centre bordered by flower beds, the surrounding road. The cars looked like those toy versions she'd seen on the carpet road maps she'd never played with unless she was at someone else's house. She'd asked Father Christmas for a toy garage for Christmas when she was five and had been devastated when she didn't get it beneath the tree in the morning. Instead, she'd got a doll and a pram.

The breeze that filtered into the room was welcome. It was early October and gone were the sweaty nights of summer, but it wouldn't be long before a gentle breeze like they had today turned into the biting winds of late autumn and early winter. Time passed too quickly as you got older.

With a bucket filled with hot water, a squirt of sugar soap and the brand-new, ginormous sponge, Lise got going. She hummed away. She was going to do a feature wall in here with a nice solid colour. The other walls she'd do in the shade she'd picked called Chantilly Lace, which was a shade of white.

As she cleaned, the water trickled down her forearms and seeped into her shirt sleeves, which were pushed up but not quite enough, and when she was done, she dried her hands on an old towel and went down to make a cup of camomile tea. She was back in the bedroom and about to enjoy her tea while soaking up the view of the world beyond her window when she caught sight of the old tin box again. It was just sitting there. Tempting her. She'd vowed not to look inside, at least not properly, not unless she was with Emma, but it wasn't easy.

Giving in to temptation, she opened it up and looked inside.

But she only picked up the first diary before she talked herself out of it and put it straight back. She couldn't. She'd promised.

But before she closed up the tin again, she spotted something else – a note on a piece of folded-over, lined paper in a second plastic cover that had slipped down next to the diaries.

She pulled it out. She didn't remember putting anything else inside and she'd never tucked notes into her diaries either. She reached into the plastic cover and pulled out the piece of paper and when she read the words, she slumped onto the floor and promptly burst into tears. It was a note from Toby. He must have sneaked it inside without her ever knowing. It made her smile, it made her cry, and she clutched it against her chest. A piece of Toby right here and the memory of the night he'd run around Honeybee Place naked. She laughed and cried all over again for the boy who'd become a man, a decent man, and who would be forever twenty-nine.

When her phone bleeped, she wiped her eyes and put the note back inside the tin before closing it up again.

She pulled her phone from the pocket of her jeans and smiled. Max. Making her feel better all over again.

His message read:

Dinner? Tonight?

What was it she always told Maisie if a boy texted? *Don't reply straight away; that's far too keen.* Not that there had been many boys, just a couple, and none of them had held her daughter's attention for long. Something Lise wasn't particularly devastated about.

Lise waited until she'd dried her eyes properly, blown her nose and made another cup of tea to take up to the top floor, and when she was back with the paint pots, she typed out her reply and pressed send.

Who is this?

That ought to keep him on his toes for a bit. She put her phone down on the mantel and started washing the skirting board on the wall with the window.

When another ping came, she waited as long as she could before texting back in response, although not too long because looking at the time, if she was going to go out for dinner, she'd have to get herself into the shower, wash her hair, so she needed to know details.

It's Max. You know, the boy you kissed at midnight.

That made her laugh like she was back in her twenties. How did male attention make you do that so easily? Revert to your younger self? At least the welcome sort of attention, anyway.

She replied to accept the invitation and when he suggested a few places, they settled on a time and she told him there was no need to come to the house to pick her up; she'd meet him at the entrance to Bath Abbey. There was something she had to do first.

The Café on the Corner was busy when Lise went inside. After a shower, she'd swapped her old jeans and shirt for a royal-blue dress that came to just below the knee, together with her black leather jacket.

It took Emma a while to register she was here. She was laughing and joking with a lively table of customers in the far corner and when she turned and saw who'd just come in, the smile fell away.

Lise went to the counter, intercepting Emma, who plucked a

few dessert menus and took them back over to the group she'd been talking to. This time, there wasn't much joviality with those customers, just the statement that she'd be at the counter and to give her a wave when they were ready to order.

'What can I do for you?' The formality of the greeting, although not unexpected, saddened Lise all the more.

'I can see this isn't a good time. I thought it might be quieter.'

'Early evenings tend to be busier than lunchtimes.'

'Yeah?' A moment passed between them, an almost-conversation until they each remembered who they both were now.

'You're dressed up.' Emma thanked a customer who left but passed by the till to drop a few coins into a tip jar.

'I'm going out. With a friend, or maybe it's more of a date.' Why had she said that? She sounded lame, desperate. But she was fighting for a bit of normality and as a result, had blurted out the first thing that came into her head.

'Didn't take long.'

Lise, aghast, didn't have time to retaliate before Emma apologised.

'I'm sorry, that was unnecessarily bitchy.' Emma took a breath. 'Have a nice time. Enjoy the city – it's beautiful out tonight.' She was rambling. She'd always done that when she got nervous.

Emma wasn't giving her much but she had apologised for being nasty and at least she wasn't walking away. Yet. 'It's easy to forget the beauty of the city when you've stayed away as long as I have.'

'It's home,' said Emma and Lise wasn't sure for whose benefit her comment was made.

'I came in to say thank you for not making things awkward with the girls.' Actually, she'd come in here to see whether Emma would talk to her, but the excuse seemed a better thing to say in the moment.

'Of course.'

'You're okay with them being friends?'

Emma shrugged. 'Naomi is old enough to choose her own friends.'

'I saw your dad,' she said when conversation stalled. 'He looks well.'

'He told me you'd visited.' Emma's face softened ever so slightly. 'He told me you're divorced.' It wasn't said with malice but rather a statement of fact.

'Right. Yes. All true.'

'He appreciated the visit.'

Lise was always going to go round to number four eventually, but she certainly would've put it off as long as she could. Mr Miller hadn't given her much choice in the matter but somehow, as he'd always managed to, he'd done the right thing.

Without looking at her, Emma said, 'You can see him again. It's fine by me. He likes the company these days. He doesn't get out much.'

'That would be nice. I enjoyed chatting to him. And I've got a bit of time on my hands apart from doing up the townhouse.' She thought her comment might ignite a spark of conversation, questions, if only to find out when Lise was leaving again, but it didn't.

And the group in the corner were waving Emma over now.

'I'll see you then,' said Lise.

'Have a nice time.'

Surprised at the well wishes, Lise left the café wondering where they could go from here. But Emma exchanging any pleasantries was at least a start.

* * *

If it was possible, Max looked even more gorgeous when he met her outside Bath Abbey. He leaned in and kissed her on the cheek, and she got a pleasant waft of a fresh aftershave with possible notes of mint or berries. Whatever it was, it screamed sophistication, like it should only be worn by people who were old enough to remember the millennium celebrations. Back then, she was pretty sure the only smell she'd noted on either of them had been beer or spirits.

'You look beautiful.' When it was offered to her, she slipped her hand through the crook of his arm. 'Shall we?'

'Very gentleman-like,' she approved. 'And you look pretty good yourself.' Although he'd asked her out as a friend, to catch up after all these years, the fact they barely knew one another apart from bumping lips one night made Lise feel like this was more of a date. And dating wasn't something she'd done in a while.

'My mother taught me good manners. And she'd kill me if I didn't treat you like a lady, which you deserve by the way, whether this is a date or just friends catching up.'

They turned onto the main street to walk past small shops and bigger stores closed for the night. 'You're talking about your mother on our first not-a-date?'

He burst out laughing as he gently pulled her to one side when a group of lads came barrelling onto the pavement from a side street. 'Right, no talk of parents.'

Lise had expected to wander aimlessly with Max to find somewhere to eat but he'd made reservations at a gorgeous, and somewhat romantic, Italian restaurant – which immediately had Lise realising this was most definitely a date.

They were shown to their table and Max ordered the wine after Lise insisted she'd be happy with anything red. She didn't want to have to think about it, to make a choice. She never had with Xavier. He'd always known what to go for and sometimes, it had bothered her that he never asked her opinion, but with Max tonight she was happy for him to take the lead because it was done without the accompanying arrogance or assumption she knew less than he did. She hadn't seen those sorts of faults with Xavier when they first got together; rather, she'd seen those qualities as attributes. Part of what had attracted her to him in the first place was his confidence and strength of personality.

As they enjoyed the wine, which was bold and smooth, they talked about work – both of their career journeys thus far. And Lise watched Max as they talked and laughed. He'd filled out from what she remembered – not that he'd been skinny back then, but he seemed stronger now. His olive complexion and neatly clipped beard suited him, as did hair that wasn't quite as dark as it had been almost two decades ago and had a few tell-tale greys here and there, which only distinguished him all the more.

When he smiled across at her, his cheeks didn't dimple, but creases on either side of his mouth like brackets deepened. 'See anything you like?'

'What?' She'd been staring; she knew it. Hard not to. He looked so handsome in the dark, ink shirt open at the neck, no tie.

Laughter accompanied, 'On the menu, I mean.'

'Right, yes, the menu.'

She wasn't usually like this in male company. It was like being a teenager all over again. She didn't even remember being this all over the place the night they'd kissed. And of course, thinking about that night and the fact she'd kissed those lips had her fluffing her words again. She gulped back the remains of her first glass of wine quickly and lost herself in the menu.

She relaxed as they ordered their food and conversation switched to talking about Bath as a city, the house she was sprucing up, the beautiful canal walks she hadn't done for years but that Max did with regularity. Max told her briefly about his divorce – he'd been married for almost a decade, no kids – and the evening rolled on easily. They enjoyed shared starters of bruschetta, portobello mushrooms topped with pine nuts and goat's cheese, baby calamari with garlic aioli.

'Are you going to try talking to Emma again?' Max asked after the waiter delivered their main courses. He knew she'd stopped by the café on her way here.

She cut into a piece of potato without hesitation and popped it into her mouth. 'You know we're going to stink of garlic...' She used her knife to indicate the roasted garlic bulb next to her beautifully golden, roasted potatoes with garlic and rosemary.

'Don't change the subject.'

'I'm not. And these are delicious. Want to try some?'

He relented with his questioning. 'Go on then.'

She speared some on a fork and passed it over to him. She wasn't ready to be feeding him across the table. 'Good?'

'Very good,' he said, hand across his mouth.

When he finished and turned his attention to his dinner, he looked up at her from beneath those dark eyelashes. 'So... Emma.'

She took a deep breath. 'I'm doing what I can. But maybe you could put in a good word for me, ask her to actually talk or maybe listen to me and give me a bit of a break.'

'Maybe, although I'd hate to interfere too much.'

'I can understand that.' She sliced into the most tender chicken she'd ever eaten, more so than anything Xavier had ever cooked, which gave her a little boost inside, a bit of amusement.

'You guys were such good friends. I remember Toby telling me about you two heading to Paris, how excited you both were. But then all of a sudden, she was back and you weren't.'

'A lot happened in Paris.'

'You learned how to park.'

She laughed. 'Yes, there is that. It served me well.'

He took a sip of his wine. 'You're not going to tell me much more, are you.'

'I will some day.' She caught herself, aware she was suggesting they'd keep seeing each other and she realised that was exactly what she wanted. 'Emma and I need to sort things out between us first, I think.'

'Fair enough.' He offered her a taste of his pasta with lamb ragout but she declined.

'I went to see Emma's dad.'

'I bet he liked that. I try to pop in with or without my dad – they're good friends. Brendan is always up for company; I don't think he's ever wanted to decline. If he has, he's far too polite to say.'

'He's always enjoyed being social, a lot of noise around him. Their household was never quiet – kind of the reason I loved going over there.'

'I take him dinner sometimes – gives Emma a break when she's so busy at the café.'

'You're a good man.' Her fork hovered mid-air as she made her point.

'I like to think so.' He set down his wine. 'Brendan loves a good chinwag about Toby, which is surprisingly nice. Most of the guys from the rugby club have moved away or else they're settled down and busy with their families. I don't see many of the old crowd so there aren't many people who knew Toby as well as I did.'

'Do you still play rugby?'

'Not for years. I'm done with the rigours of winter training. Still like to watch a game, though. Toby and I went to plenty of local matches, always a good way to spend an afternoon or an evening.'

'He loved it, didn't he?'

Max nodded. 'And he was better than most of us, to be honest. A real team player – fair, never put anyone else down. That was one of the qualities he had that everyone, including myself, admired.'

'There were girls at school whose brothers weren't that nice to them,' said Lise, 'but Toby always had time for Emma.'

'He did. He teased her a lot from what I remember but you never doubted how much he loved her.' He thanked the waiter who came to take away their plates and Max looked to Lise for approval at the question of whether they wanted another bottle of wine.

'If we're here for a while?' she checked.

'I think that's a yes.' He handed the waiter back the wine menu without taking his eyes off Lise.

Lise felt her insides spiralling. Back when she had little concept of real life and long-term anything, Max's look was of the variety that would've told her they'd definitely be spending the night together. But things were different now. She was forty-four years old, she had a daughter, she'd changed so much. And yet she felt a bit fuzzy at the temptation and fought to get her mind back on track.

'I'm glad you kept in touch with Toby's family,' she told Max. 'The way Brendan talks about Toby has a definite sadness but there's pride and a joy at the memories.'

'My older brother had a similar experience.' Max paused when the waiter brought over the other bottle of wine. Once he'd poured and left again, Max explained, 'James lost his best mate and for ages, he didn't see the family. He stayed away, thinking it would be too painful. But it was the opposite.'

'I suppose in some ways, remembering is painful but in others, it's good for the soul. I think Mr Miller appreciates his family whether they're here or not, and is happy for any reminders.'

'You were almost a part of the family.'

'You were there at the house a lot too.'

'I was.'

'I was gutted I couldn't come to Toby's funeral.'

'It was sad, there was a lot of crying, but even then, we managed to talk about the joy as well as the pain. Emma did a eulogy.'

'She did?'

'She wasn't sure whether she'd manage it but she wanted to. It was her way of remembering her brother, she said, and she also said if he were there, he'd have been trying to make her laugh from the front row.'

Lise grinned. 'Sounds like Toby.'

'She had the congregation laughing, although a lot of the laughter dissolved into tears. She brought up the subject of his hair.'

Lise put down her glass of wine. 'What was wrong with Toby's hair?'

'Nothing once he'd matured, but when he started at the rugby club, he was obsessed with it. I gave Emma lots of information on that to weave into her eulogy and I knew Toby would've done the same in my position.'

'Actually, I think I remember way back – he must've been in his early teens. Wasn't he one for the wet-look gel?'

'Yep, and it was awful. But nobody could tell him.' The colourful, waxy candle in the centre of the table flickered between them. 'And what was with that earring he once had for about five minutes?'

Lise put a hand in the air. 'I take full responsibility for that one.'

'You told him to get it done?'

She shook her head. 'I did it. Pierced his ear.'

'No way.'

'Yes way!' Over more wine, she recounted the story of her and

Emma piercing each other's ears and Toby catching them at it. 'He thought we were making a big fuss out of nothing, that our screams were totally dramatic. So I challenged him, told him to put his money where his mouth was and get an earring. It didn't last long. He got fed up and took it out a week later.'

'He got told to take it out for the rugby-training session – no earrings allowed for obvious reasons.' Max caught the waiter's attention for the bill. 'Why don't we get a takeaway coffee from a place just up from here,' he suggested, 'then we can walk back through the city.'

'Sounds good to me.'

And it would give them a chance to talk, for her to say what she really needed to. She'd known when she came out tonight that she couldn't date someone without being totally honest with them.

As they left the restaurant, she shivered. He put an arm around her shoulders and once they had their coffees, they walked by the river, over the bridge. It was completely the wrong direction but Lise wanted to come this way; she hadn't seen many parts of the city at night-time since she got back.

'Did you miss Bath?' Max asked as they reached the middle of the bridge. 'I can imagine Paris, the City of Lights, is a tough competitor.'

'It is, but you know what they say...'

'There's no place like home.' His breath came out cold on the air as they looked out at the River Avon.

'I've had a really nice time tonight, Max.' Her hair licked against the side of her face and she hooked the strands over her ear, away from the lipstick she had reapplied in the ladies' bathroom before they left the restaurant.

'Oh no. This sounds like the brush-off. Go on, hit me with it.' His smile wasn't quite making his face crinkle in the way she'd got used to already.

'This isn't a brush-off, at least I don't want it to be.' She looked down to the depths of the water she could just about make out now it was dark. 'The thing is... before whatever this is between us goes any further, I need to be completely honest with you. About everything. About Paris. About my husband, my marriage.'

He rested next to her, his profile illuminated by one of the streetlamps. 'I'm listening.'

She felt his arm against hers and was drawn closer to him. She raised her head and waited for him to look her in the eye. She needed to see him when she said this, to know his true reaction.

Only then would she know whether they could ever have any kind of relationship.

14

NOW: 2023

Emma

Emma wiped down the two tables nearest to the counter in the Café on the Corner as her daughter came through the door, battling with her umbrella.

'Let me take that for you.' She grabbed the umbrella from Naomi, shook it off beyond the door and took it through to the back where she set it outside beneath the lean-to. In the café once more, armed with a big old towel, Emma dropped it on the floor and used her foot to go over the drips her daughter and the umbrella had trailed inside. 'We haven't had a storm like this in months.'

Naomi took off her coat and put it on one of the hooks on the coat rack at the side of the café. Often it was too full, but not today.

Emma looked at the big bag Naomi had hauled in with her, likely filled with schoolbooks, her laptop, notepads. 'Much homework?'

'Tons.'

'Are you going to stay here and do some for a while?'

'I thought I might.'

'After food?' She returned her daughter's smile. 'All right, what would you like me to get you? As you can see, I'm the opposite of rushed off my feet.' The café was empty, a sign of a quiet period combined with the ghastly weather.

'What about a chocolate mug cake with extra choc chips?'

'I'll see what I can do. Holler if someone comes in.'

Out in the kitchen, Emma took out a large, white mug with an embossed heart on the side. It took only five minutes to prepare the cake – the recipe was in the book she'd collated since she was in her teens and she knew this one by heart. As she popped the mug into the microwave and set the timer for seven minutes, she had just enough time to go serve Molly who lived at number nineteen and had come in soaked from head to toe. Molly insisted she hover at the door so she didn't wet the floors and handed her reusable cup to Naomi who handed it to Emma for the takeaway coffee she announced she was taking home to enjoy in front of the fire.

Alone again, Emma brought Naomi's chocolate mug cake out to her. 'Extra chocolate chips as requested.' She looked at the surface of the cake. 'They're almost bursting out of there.'

Naomi pushed her schoolbooks aside and as she ate, Emma sat with her and asked about school, a question that sometimes got a grunt; other times got an understandable answer.

'They load too much homework on us,' Naomi explained between mouthfuls.

'I always said the same when I was at school, but stick with it.'

'I thought I might go and hang out with Grandad once I've finished some of it.'

'That sounds like a lovely idea. You can take him the coffee and walnut cake I made earlier on. I made two, sold almost all of the first this morning but unless this rain goes away, I doubt I'll be selling much more of it. The weather forecast said a light drizzle.'

Naomi's eyebrows rose as she turned to look out of the door and windows of the café onto the street, as if she needed to for proof, even though she'd been out in it not that long ago. She scraped the last of the chocolate mixture from the edges of the mug. 'So good. Thanks, Mum. I'm glad you didn't throw away that ancient recipe book of yours.'

'It's a relic.' She wagged a finger. 'And don't even think of saying that so am I.'

'I would never.' She grinned.

'Do you know, when I was little and before I decided I was going to be a teacher, I was convinced that Uncle Toby wanted to take on the café one day? I was so jealous that a friend and I got together to do a pitch to your grandparents.' Her comment had been intended to pass as a flippant one but having to explain brought a sadness to her heart, another reminder of Lise and their friendship that had fallen apart. 'The pitch was a plan for where I saw the café going, what else we could make, how it could develop. I think we even went so far as sharing ideas for expansion to get more tables in although obviously the thought didn't enter our minds that planning permission, and space, were kind of necessary for that. We even wore business dress. I'm not quite sure how your grandparents kept straight faces through it all but they agreed that once I'd finished my education, I should come back to them because they were definitely interested in my visions – that's what they called them – for the café.'

'Do you ever miss being a teacher?'

'Sometimes. But mostly, I'm glad to be here. The café grew on me and I fell in love with it. Your dad supported me in whatever decision I made, but he was the first to comment on how much it felt like I belonged here. He said it with such a genuine smile, I knew it came from the heart.'

'Dad liked your cooking.'

'He was always on hand to do the taste test, wasn't he?'

Naomi nodded. 'I miss him.'

She reached out for her daughter's hand. 'I know you do. Me too. Every day.'

'What happened to the friend?'

'What friend?' She picked up Naomi's empty mug to take to the kitchen.

'The one you pitched with.'

'We lost touch. Hot chocolate?'

'Yes please.'

'And then you have to do more homework.'

She left her daughter rolling her eyes.

Naomi was still interested when Emma delivered the hot chocolate to her table. 'What do you mean you lost touch?'

Emma sighed. 'Only that.'

Naomi dropped her marshmallows into the milky drink one at a time, watching them bob on its surface. 'Was it Lise?' With a shrug, she added, 'Maisie says you and her mum knew each other a long time ago. That you were best friends.'

Emma's heart thumped. 'What else did she say?'

'Only that Lise never talks about what happened. That if Maisie brings it up, it makes her sad.'

Emma pulled a chair out and sat down. 'We were friends, for a long time. Since we were in primary school.'

'What happened?'

'That, my beautiful girl, is a very long story.'

'Which you won't tell me.' In full teenage mode, she pouted, sat back in her chair.

A rumble of thunder reminded them that this storm wasn't

over yet. 'I need to sort out how I feel first before I tell anyone else about it. Is that okay?'

The remark seemed to resonate with Naomi, who nodded.

Emma jumped when a bolt of lightning struck and the lights in the café momentarily dipped. She only had one other customer – a guy around her age who introduced himself as Liam, who was staying with his aunt and uncle at number nine. He was soaked through to the skin and only stopping to grab a fruit cake.

'Are you sure you don't need a coffee or something to warm up?' she asked him. It was thoughtful, picking up the fruit cake given how awful the weather was. 'You're wet through.'

'Can't stop today but maybe another time.'

'Another time,' she repeated as he left them to it.

After she closed the door, she noticed Naomi giving her an odd look. 'What?'

'He's interested. He's into you.'

'Oh, Naomi, stop it.' But she was smiling. It wasn't the first time he'd been in but it was the first time he'd told her his name and when he'd suggested another time, a part of her had wondered whether he was interested in starting something. But perhaps that was wishful thinking.

After another hour, she closed up early and made her way back home. Dating again? Not likely. She wasn't in her twenties any more; she was no longer that carefree, single woman who'd gone to Paris on an adventure. She was forty-four now with a daughter, a dad to look after and a business to run.

She didn't have time for much else at all.

15

THEN: 2005

Emma

'Can you believe we are here?' Emma closed her eyes and breathed in the night air at the top of the Eiffel Tower.

'This is our year, Emma. I can feel it!'

She couldn't see her best friend's expression given the gusting wind kept blowing her hair in her face the same way as it was doing with Emma's, but Emma knew Lise was beaming the same way she was. Their first night in Paris, the place they'd dreamed of coming to for an extended stay ever since they'd talked about it as young girls, felt surreal. The City of Lights was spread out beyond, there, ready and waiting, adventures to be had.

Since each of them graduated from university, Emma had moved home and begun teaching and Lise had been working as a public relations officer in the centre of London. When the firm Lise worked for closed their doors, it had been she who floated the idea that they follow through with the plan they'd talked about on and off over the years – to come to Paris together.

Emma had been resistant at first. She'd finally got a steady job

after a nightmare of a time doing her postgraduate teacher training. During her training, she'd made friends with another woman
on the course, Alison, and while Alison enjoyed smoking the odd
joint and Emma didn't, Emma didn't see any harm in the habit. At
least she hadn't until she was forced to prove that she was the original author of a written assignment Alison had plagiarised and
handed in as her own. The whole process was humiliating, having
her integrity questioned, and it was only the tip of the iceberg.
Alison was addicted to cannabis, something so many people saw as
harmless. Emma had witnessed and been a victim of the ramifica-
tions first-hand.

Alison began lying to Emma, making up stories for the hell of
it. Emma tried to distance herself but then Alison stole money,
spread a vicious rumour that Emma was sleeping with one of their
tutors. It had been hell. Emma's innocence was easily proven but it
was still a stressful experience she never wanted to have again, the
way Alison had changed, the way a drug could alter a person's
behaviour and personality like that.

Emma hadn't resisted the idea of Paris for too long. She'd soon
come to realise that if they didn't take the opportunity now, the
chance may never come around again. Lise would find a new job
and their lives would move on and that would be it. Maybe for
good. Lise had never said she wanted to settle down but Emma
wanted to eventually, and once she did, flitting off with her best
friend would be totally off the table.

Once Emma agreed, things moved along quickly. Emma sorted
out a twelve-month sabbatical with her boss, and she and Lise
made plans talking ten to the dozen about what they could see in
Paris, the experiences they'd have, how they could live like locals,
immerse themselves in the beauty of the language.

Emma had worried about finances. 'Paris is expensive,' she told
Lise. 'I'm not sure I can go for long.' She had savings – not as much

as Lise, but enough to see a bit of Paris and not have to work for a month or two.

'You can and you will. I'm paying for accommodation while we're there.'

'Oh no—'

'You can't say no. I've always had a ridiculous allowance from my parents and I never spent it all, no matter how much I tried. So this way, it gets put to good use. It'll mean more to me than if I frittered it away on clothes – well, more clothes.'

Emma had seen Lise's bank balance and although she knew Lise's dad did something to do with international banking, she was still gobsmacked at the money that got paid into Lise's account every month.

So now here they were. Really here. In Paris. They hadn't taken the ferry either; they'd taken the Eurostar, and sitting next to one another on board, they'd agreed it was fascinating how easy it was to get from London to Paris. They'd disappeared into a tunnel from their homeland and were spat out into a different country entirely, the land of the finest and fanciest pastries you'd ever seen, boulangeries with the freshest, buttery, melt-in-the-mouth croissants, the mayhem of beeping cars on the wrong side of the road, the whizzing of bicycles, the mix of foreign voices, and they were enthralled.

Emma needed this new adventure so much. Not only after her experience with Alison but after the problems at home. Her mum had had open-heart surgery, which had been more brutal than any of them expected. Her dad had needed help in the café so Emma's feet barely touched the ground since finishing her teaching position, and the only reason she was here now was that her parents had practically shooed her out of the door to go live her own life. Her mum was finally back working, albeit under her dad's watchful gaze and right now, Emma was glad of their insistence.

She'd half-expected a lecture on taking responsibility when she announced the sabbatical to her parents, stern words about not letting down her employer or the pupils she had under her wing. She'd been ready to defend the choice and point out the experience she'd gain, her ability to get another teaching job with a command of the French language under her belt, but she hadn't needed to. Her mum and dad had been excited for her. They'd confessed sometimes, they wished they'd done a bit of travel before they took on the café, which whilst it was their true love, now commandeered their lives.

Now, after one last embrace of the open-air section at the top of the Eiffel Tower with unobstructed, panoramic views of Paris, Emma and Lise took the elevator down and trekked back to their apartment in the 14th arrondissement. They'd secured a bijou one-bedroom for a good price, seeing as it was longer term than the usual one to two weeks people booked. Compact, with a double bed in the bedroom and a sofa bed in the lounge area, it would do for the time being. Once their eight weeks were up, maybe they could renegotiate or perhaps if they moved further out to explore wider Paris, they could get something bigger.

The next morning, their time in the City of Lights was off to a roaring start. And it didn't much change the rest of the week or the week after that. They crammed in as much sightseeing as they could, as though they were tourists with minimal time before they headed off again. It didn't seem right to do it any other way, their excitement taking over everything else.

They navigated the city on foot over the course of those weeks – Lise was terrible with a map and got them lost several times over, their pidgin French not much use with impatient Parisians who wanted to be on their way rather than help two young women who hadn't a clue. They boarded a cruise along the Seine when their feet were too tired to walk any more, ducked into cute

French cafés when the heavens opened and the downpour refused to let up. They ate buttery croissants, flaky pain aux raisins, croque-monsieur oozing with stringy cheese. A hop-on-hop-off bus tour showed them Notre Dame and the Eiffel Tower from a whole new perspective, and they gasped in shock at the mayhem surrounding the Arc de Triomphe roundabout with so many streets feeding into it, taking it to what looked like ten lanes' thick of traffic.

They hopped off the tour at the Champs-Élysées to stroll its length and bask in the late-summer sunshine. They crossed at Pont Neuf the oldest standing bridge across the Seine, explored the Île de la Cité, found the Palace of Versailles and embraced its opulence and endless gardens. They visited the Paris Catacombs and took a tour of Montparnasse. Paris was densely packed with history, food, a mecca for art and fashion lovers, and both Emma and Lise absorbed as much of it as they possibly could.

When they'd been in Paris for almost a month, the girls found themselves in yet another bistro taking the weight off their feet. It was a novelty to be without any responsibility and over a glass of wine and crêpes that Emma insisted were her treat one evening, it was Lise who suggested they might get more out of their stay if they found part-time jobs. 'I hate to say it—'

'You're bored of having no direction,' Emma interrupted before Lise could get the words out. She knew her friend so well. In England, Lise had given the final days at her job her all when most people might ease off, given they'd be out of that job soon enough. But not Lise – she liked to keep busy and an experience like this was amazing, but being out of work and not having a routine was something Lise didn't do well.

'I hate to say it but yes, I'm bored of no routine and I need some structure.' Lise rolled her eyes heavenward at the mouthful of crêpe. 'Why don't crêpes ever taste like this at home?'

'I want to know how they get them so thin,' said Emma. 'It's a real skill.'

'A French skill I wholly approve of,' Lise said as best she could with her mouth still quite full. 'So you're not freaked about the job thing?'

'Why would I be? It means I can treat you some more – no arguments. Although it'll be a challenge. Neither of us are fluent French speakers so that might limit our options.' A smile spread across Emma's face. 'If we have work, we'll really be living like Parisians.'

'Yes, we will... I mean, *oui, nous les ferons*.' She clinked Emma's glass of wine with her own.

'I don't understand how people can backpack for twelve months, moving around Europe from one place to another.'

Lise shrugged. 'The moving around part makes it different, so you've just about exhausted the sightseeing and the brand-new feel of it all and on you go to another place.'

'I'd rather do what we're doing.'

'Agreed. I mean, sleeping on a sofa bed in a lounge is something I'd take over six or eight strangers in a room at a hostel. Sam's stories of his trip around America are enlightening, as are your brother's stories of Asia.'

'I'll bet Sam is really patient with everyone. So is Toby usually, so for him to get pissed off with having little privacy, cold showers, cramped conditions, cockroaches and people snoring tells me it's not for me.' She mimed putting a crown on top of her head. 'I'm a princess.'

'You are not. You're easy-going and lovely... I'm more the princess.'

'True. Come on, Princess – crêpes were lovely but dinner at the apartment tonight.'

They finished their wine and headed off, making a pact that

tomorrow, they would start trawling the streets for casual jobs doing anything they could find with their limited, rather rusty French.

Three weeks later, neither of them were any closer to finding work. Emma unpacked the salad ingredients, fish and potatoes for dinner and they settled disconsolately at the table with a cup of tea each in the hope it might warm them up. Another thing their budget accommodation didn't have was decent heating and the pleasant temperatures of late summer had given way to the chill of the start of autumn that somehow never left the apartment.

When a potato tumbled off the kitchen benchtop, Emma swore. 'Paris apartments are so small.'

'Not going to disagree with you.'

Emma looked at Lise. 'I'm sorry, I shouldn't moan – you've paid for us to stay here. I'm so ungrateful.'

'You are not; it was a simple observation.'

She felt guilty for complaining but it didn't take away from the fact she hated the kitchen. Could it even be called that? It was more of a kitchenette – no wonder French women were skinny. There was nowhere to keep any food.

Lise went into the bedroom and came back with two hot-water bottles, one in each hand. 'Ta-da! Bought these today.' The water in the kettle would be the right temperature by now and she filled them.

'I did wonder why you'd filled the kettle so much for only two cups of tea.'

Lise handed her one of the hot-water bottles and she cuddled it on her lap.

'You're smiling.'

Emma was. 'It's like when you're little and your mum brings you a snuggly hot-water bottle in bed.' She gave it an extra squeeze in appreciation.

'I wouldn't know – my mum never did that. But I can imagine Keely doing it.' Elbows perched on the table, cup of tea between her hands as she took a sip, Lise caught Emma's look. 'Oh no you don't; don't go feeling sorry for me.'

'I'm not.' But her raised eyebrows attempting innocence gave away that's exactly what she'd been doing.

'It's all in the past, Emma. Mum is who she is; Dad is who he is. It's any wonder I turned out to be so put together.'

'You're right about that.' Lise was beautiful inside and out, the best friend who'd do anything for you, someone who'd talk you into coming on a crazy adventure totally out of both of their comfort zones. 'I'd better make a start with dinner.'

'You cooked last night – my turn.' Lise knocked back the rest of her tea and found the potato peeler after opening at least three of the drawers before she was able to locate it.

'Well if you're sure… I might take a shower then.'

'Go for it.'

The bathroom was at least decent with a tub and a separate shower and the bedroom was Emma's at the moment – they rotated every week when the bedding had a wash so it was fair and the same person wasn't always stuck on the sofa bed in the lounge – and by the time Emma emerged to the kitchen, the smell of the fish had her tummy rumbling.

'Are we sure we're not having wine?' she asked. They'd been trying to cut back on expenses or otherwise Lise's allowance she'd accumulated as well as both girls' savings would be wiped out in a city so expensive. 'I might go get us some.'

'Emma Miller. We've been so good with our cups of tea, which might I remind you was at your insistence.'

'And this is our reward.'

Lise turned and eyed her dressing gown as Emma picked up her purse. 'You going out in the street like that? Dare you.'

'Now if I'd had the wine, I might have done the dare but given I haven't had any for days, my daring side has done a bunk.' She went into the bedroom and pulled on a pair of tracksuit bottoms and a fleece. There was a small grocery store at the end of the street, which definitely sold wine.

Lise handed her a postcard before she went out. 'Could you pop this in the postbox for me?'

'Sure thing.'

Lise had written a postcard for Mrs Griffin, one of their neighbours back home in Bath, and it had a stunning mix of pictures of Paris on the front including the Eiffel Tower all lit up at night, the Seine in all its flowing beauty, the *Jardin des Tuileries*.

Postcard winging its way to England, Emma headed into the tiny grocery store and plucked a reasonably priced bottle of Sauvignon Blanc from a high-up shelf.

She turned to go and pay for it but smacked into someone in the tiny aisles of the cramped shop. She swore when her bottle went flying but the man she'd smacked into caught it just in time.

'*Excusez-moi,*' she said, somewhat embarrassed.

'*C'était fermé.*' That was close.

Emma knew she was blushing as she took the bottle from the man's hand that wrapped around the glass more than hers had. He probably wouldn't have been quite so careless.

'*Merci,*' she said to him.

'*De rien.*' It was nothing. 'English?' he asked with a smile that had her wishing she'd put on something better than scruffy clothes and had checked her reflection before she came out. She'd pinned her strawberry-blonde hair up into a messy bun for the shower and hadn't dealt with it since. She could feel half of it hanging down and knew she must look at state.

'It's a good choice.' His accent was beautiful, his English good and it took her a moment to realise he was talking about the wine.

'Thanks. I mean, *merci*. I've had it before.' And now she sounded like a bumbling idiot – sticking one random French word in a sentence as though that was as much effort as she needed to make. It was ignorant, assuming he'd speak in her native tongue when they were in his country.

He held out a hand. '*Je m'appelle Gabriel.*'

She met the gesture and the feel of skin on skin had her flushing. She knew she wasn't hiding the fact she found this random stranger in a supermarket attractive.

'And your name...?'

'Emma.'

'Beautiful.' He nodded to the wine again. 'Celebration?'

She could listen to the accent all evening, with its melodic quality. She corrected him, 'Actually, it's a commiseration.'

'Ah, *commisération*,' he said pronouncing the remarkably similar word in French. 'Same word in both languages.'

Now she felt silly but she was still smiling and in French, he asked why the commiseration.

She didn't feel she could explain properly unless she did so in English. There was too much room for error otherwise. 'My friend and I are looking for part-time work but we don't speak much French so neither of us have had any luck. We have money but it won't last forever and our apartment is too small, and it's really cold, with rubbish heating.' She felt herself colour again as she rambled on. 'And now I've said too much.'

'I can help you.'

She was about to ask how but shook her head. 'Thank you, you did. You didn't let this bottle smash on the floor so you saved me from wasting eight euros.'

But he was insistent. He called it fate that they'd met tonight. And she left the supermarket on a wave of excitement, as well as feeling a bit giddy at the attentions of a not-unattractive Frenchman, and almost floated back to the apartment.

'You took so long, I burnt the bottom of the fish!' Lise called out from the kitchen when she heard the door go, but if anything was burning, Emma couldn't smell it.

Emma set down the wine on the table and plucked two glasses from the cupboard. 'Shall I pour? It was in the fridge; it's semi-cold.'

'Ridiculous question, Emma.' Lise squeezed round her to open the top drawer, then the one below, then the one below that until she located the potato masher. 'Make it a large for me. And what took you so long? Was there a queue?'

'There was no queue.' She smiled to herself.

Emma poured the wine, Lise mashed the potatoes, Emma strained the mixed vegetables and Lise found a spatula to serve up the fish.

After Lise poured the herb sauce across the fish, they sat down and lifted their wine glasses to toast. But the 'Cheers!' was immediately followed by Lise with: 'All right, what's going on? Why are you smiling like that?'

'I took a long time at the supermarket because I met someone.'

'Your cheeks are almost the same shade as your hair was in primary school.' She gasped. 'That means it was a man. Oh, was he hot? You're going to have an affair with a Frenchman, get married and have lots of French babies.'

'Calm down – not quite.'

Lise had mashed potato loaded onto her fork but it went nowhere near her mouth. 'But he was cute?'

She let out a breath. 'Gorgeous.' She thought about his corn-flower-blue eyes, the light-brown hair, messy on top and receding ever so slightly in a way that made him look rather debonair. 'And that's not all.'

'You had sex with him in the alleyway down the side of the supermarket.' This time, Lise got stuck into her food.

'No I did not! That's crazy. Although I bet it would be amazing.'

'Not down an alleyway – you can do better than that.'

'I didn't mean down an alleyway. Anyhow, aren't you going to ask what else?'

Lise topped up both of their wine glasses. 'Well if it wasn't sex, I'm not really interested.'

'I got a job.'

'What?'

Emma explained how she'd ended up telling the stranger about their problems finding work. 'Gabriel's family own a café and they're short-staffed. They need a waitress. He said that French-speaking is preferable but they're desperate and so someone who at least knew a little of the language was better than having nobody at all. Gabriel thinks I'll pick up loads of French if I'm working alongside him and his sister who co-owns the place.'

Lise looked serious. 'Wow. Bet you didn't expect that when you went out to get wine.' She frowned. 'It all seems a bit good to be true. I mean, what if he's luring you to a random place and is spinning a story?'

'Then there'll be no job and I'll walk away. But I really think he's genuine.'

Lise shook her head. 'Here I was slaving away at a hot stove and you go get yourself a job, and a Frenchman. You are 100 per cent amazing.'

Emma sighed. 'Unfortunately, the job is near Montmartre.'

'That's a bit far away from here.'

'I know. An hour and a half to walk because Gabriel did it this evening to meet a friend of his near here. But he says he's travelling back by bus and the metro so that's an option.'

'You'll use all your wages on the travel.'

Emma hesitated. 'Unless we move. It might be cheaper up that way.'

Lise watched her carefully. 'Are we moving for the job or the man? Who, might I point out, you've known for...' She checked the clock. 'Less than forty-five minutes.'

'Lise, it's work, and you never know, there might be more opportunities up that way for you too.'

'I suppose we haven't looked around there.'

'Eat up, then we'll go online and have a look what's around apartment-wise, see if we can get a two-bedroom.'

Lise speared a piece of fish. 'Agreed. If you're going to start bringing a Frenchman back to the apartment, there's no way I want to see you going at it on the sofa bed.'

Lise's comment dissolved into lewd suggestions that had them in fits of giggles and over the rest of the bottle of wine, they began their search, taking them out of the 14th arrondissement and up to the surrounds of Montmartre and the areas beyond when prices were more than they were willing to pay. But they sent emails to five places, each a similar budget to where they were now, each with two bedrooms and, hopefully, decent heating.

And after ten days of hunting, they found their new apartment.

16

THEN: 2005

Lise

Three weeks after Emma started her job, the girls packed up and moved to their new apartment. Emma was working every day and falling head over heels for Gabriel. Lise was still looking for work.

Lise had enough funds not to worry too much as long as she wasn't overly extravagant but she wanted to immerse herself in French culture the way her friend was. She wanted to really live in Paris. What Lise really needed was a focus because the boredom and lack of routine as well as time on her own – given Emma was seeing Gabriel so much in her free time – was beginning to drive her slowly insane.

'I'm unemployable,' Lise groaned, her face in her hands in their albeit bright and much-bigger-than-the-one-before kitchen.

Emma looked up from cutting her apple into slices, pointing her knife unnecessarily towards her friend. Ever since she'd had one of her front teeth fixed, Emma was careful and never bit into a piece of hard fruit. 'You are not unemployable – you were actually gainfully employed for a whole day.'

Her remark roused a smile from Lise. She'd found a job two days after Emma had, within walking distance of their old apartment, but working as a kitchen hand, she'd lasted only the afternoon when on day one, she lost her footing and crashed into a shelf full of plates, which tumbled to the floor and smashed. The head waiter had shouted at her – in French, of course – so had the owner, and a couple of other workers had joined in. She'd yelled, 'I quit!' – pretty sure they all understood what that meant even though a couple of them didn't speak English and neither party had contacted the other ever since.

'Keep looking – something will turn up,' Emma sympathised. 'And tonight needs to be all about me, remember.'

'I haven't forgotten, birthday girl. I'll have a shower now, get out of the way so you can have the bathroom to yourself for a luxurious soak and a preen.'

Emma's voice followed her. 'You're definitely sure you don't mind if Gabriel comes too?'

'Of course not!' she hollered back, glad to shut the bathroom door behind her so Emma couldn't see her face.

It wasn't that Lise didn't want Emma to have a boyfriend but they'd come here to Paris on an adventure together. They were sharing an apartment and there weren't other friends to interact with. Lise wondered whether if she found work, she might make some new friends of her own, some that tolerated her still-developing, French-language skills. Perhaps then Emma doing her own thing wouldn't hurt quite so much. Since the night Emma had met Gabriel and started working at the family café, Lise had barely seen her friend. She was either working or seeing Gabriel or so knackered, she didn't want to traipse around discovering more of hidden Paris.

A couple of nights ago, when Emma came home from work, kicked off her shoes and fell back into the sofa, her strawberry-blonde hair haphazardly strewn across the material, she'd said to Lise, 'Can I ask you something?' When Lise sat down, she added, 'It's about my birthday dinner.'

Lise knew what was coming even before her friend said it.

'Would you mind if Gabriel came to celebrate my birthday with us?'

Before the night Emma met Gabriel, the girls had booked a meal at a posh restaurant to celebrate Emma's upcoming twenty-seventh birthday. They'd chosen somewhere ultra-fancy, regardless of the cost, because each of them would only get one birthday in Paris so it was the perfect excuse to treat themselves.

Lise mustered all the support she could. 'He's your boyfriend, of course you'd want him there. And it's *your* birthday.'

'I know, but we planned it for the two of us, a girls' night given we don't do it often.'

'There'll be other times. And I'd like to get to know Gabriel.' Perhaps it wasn't such a bad thing if he came – it would give her time to vet him, see if he was good enough for Emma. 'It's time I had a word with the guy who's taken away my best friend.'

'No!' Emma leapt up. 'That will *never* happen. We always vowed never to let a boy come between us ever since Jaimie Walker asked us both to the disco at the sports centre.'

Lise burst out laughing. 'We were kids back then!'

'It still meant something.' A crease of concern lined Emma's forehead.

She looked so worried, Lise spent the next half an hour convincing her friend that it was all fine, that she wanted to know some more about Gabriel.

And the booking had been amended from two to three.

Lise wiped the steam from the bathroom mirror when she emerged from the shower. Tonight's birthday dinner would be fine.

From what she knew of Gabriel, he was a decent guy and she'd get to see for herself, properly, rather than just in passing.

She smoothed on her moisturiser and smiled at her reflection, gave herself a stern talking-to that jealousy wasn't an attractive quality – or was it envy she was feeling? She never could remember the difference. One meant you wanted what the other person had but still wanted them to have it too, but that wasn't it – she wasn't desperate for a man. Sure, she could do with a man for a bit of fun, some sex – it had been a while – but other than that, she had no real urge in her late twenties to settle down for a long time, if ever. Right now, she wanted to have the time of her life in Paris with her best friend. And they'd done a lot of that so far. They'd walked the streets of the city as much as their energy levels and limbs would allow, they'd taken in the sights – famous and less-known – they'd enjoyed nightlife in the dazzling foreign place.

But the time of their lives had morphed into real life without much warning and slowly the excitement, the newness, the adventure had begun to fall away. When they'd first arrived, Lise hadn't thought about work or life in England much at all but lately, she'd begun to think about what came after Paris and could see herself heading back to England, maybe to London, finding a job in public relations and working her way up the career ladder.

Lise wondered whether she got her desire to work and a lack of desperation to settle down from her father who had never given the impression marriage and kids – or one kid even – suited him at all. It was as though his role had been mixed up with someone else's and he was stuck in it during Lise's years growing up, like being forced to do a job that had no redundancy or opportunity for retirement. Comparing herself to her dad didn't exactly warm her either – he'd been woefully absent emotionally to her as a kid, her mum had too albeit to a lesser extent, and she'd always been aware that she never wanted to be so one-dimensional as Randall Baker.

When Lise emerged from the bathroom, Emma was chatting on the phone to her parents, insisting she really did have to go, that they'd be late for the restaurant if she didn't get herself ready. Lise re-tucked the knot in her towel so it wouldn't come lose and held out her hand for the phone.

'Thank you,' Emma mouthed.

'Hello, Mrs Miller.' Her wet hair wrapped in a turban, she settled onto the sofa for a chat with her best friend's parents. It wasn't like she spoke to hers often. Rarely was a better description, although oddly enough, she'd been calling home every fortnight to check in. She'd started when they first arrived because she'd needed her mother to open some mail for her, then her mum had called her a week or so after that and as the weeks and months rolled on, they'd settled into a bit of a pattern. Surprisingly, they were finding more and more to talk about too, usually Paris and the sights Lise had seen, a bit about Bath and what her mother had been up to. There were no mentions of corporate dinners with Lise's dad but her mother had told Lise about solo trips to the theatre, a coach trip she'd done on her own to Devon.

Lise never spoke to her dad – if he was around, he never bothered to say hello – but in some ways, at last Lise felt as though she'd got her mother to herself, that maybe she was finally being noticed.

After a good catch-up with Mrs Miller, Lise did her hair, pulled on a little black dress and accessorised with jewellery. And off they went for Emma's birthday celebrations and a dinner for three.

* * *

Lise had to admit Gabriel was every bit as lovely, polite and kind as he'd seemed whenever they'd previously crossed paths. He was a gentleman who held open doors and did things like pulling out

Emma's chair for her to sit down and ensuring the girls ordered their meals first when the waiter came over.

After the appetisers, Lise decided she'd observed enough and with only tonight to get to know him, given he and Emma were in their own little world the rest of the time, she took over the conversation. 'So, Gabriel, tell me a bit more about yourself.' She was mildly satisfied that he looked a little uncomfortable. Not that she wanted him to feel bad but it did show he wasn't overconfident, nor too cocky.

As Lise got Gabriel to start by telling her about his family, even though she had some of the info from Emma, it gave her a chance to observe this man, who she'd describe as a gentle giant if she had to sum him up in two words. He had strong forearms, the rolled-up sleeves of his usual attire had been replaced by a very well ironed shirt and tie, given the occasion and the posh restaurant, which told Lise he was willing to make an effort for the woman in his life. Another tick. He spoke French eloquently to the waiter, English to the both of them. His blue eyes rarely ventured far from Emma and he brought her into the conversations even though Lise was conducting a decent inquisition.

'What do you think?' Emma asked when Gabriel went off to use the bathroom.

'I've met him before.'

'Yes, but now you're really meeting him.'

'Well to be honest, I'm not happy.'

Emma's face fell.

'Not only is he gorgeous, Emma, he's a perfect gentleman.' Lise leaned in to keep this between only them. 'Have you told him you love him yet?'

Emma's cheeks coloured close to the shade of the red hair she'd had as a kid rather than the strawberry-blonde hair she had now she was older. 'He told me he loved me when you went to the bathroom earlier. And I said it back.'

'I'm glad you're happy.'

In that moment, Lise knew her friend was smitten and it gave her a warmth inside she hadn't expected. There was no jealousy or envy or whatever it was that had her out of sorts. She couldn't be happier for her best friend. Gorgeous in a light-blue dress with sequins that they'd found together in a boutique the first week they arrived in Paris, Emma didn't just look happy; she was radiant.

Emma fiddled with the delicate silver bracelet Gabriel had given her for her birthday. 'I've never felt this way about anyone, Lise. Am I being crazy? Is this just a holiday romance?'

'Can't help you there but from where I'm sitting, it looks like a whole lot more than that.'

All three of them continued their meal and conversation over a couple of bottles of wine, and Lise had to admit she was having the best time. They finished up at the bar area of the restaurant there for people waiting for tables and anyone who wanted to stay for a *digestif* after their meal.

At the bar, Gabriel poured another red wine for each of them and Lise picked up the generous goblet. But she didn't get to drink the wine because she felt a hand on her bottom, a light touch followed by a big squeeze of her flesh and she whipped round to face the culprit, barely pausing she before she threw her drink in the offender's face.

Except either he had extremely good reflexes or had had this happen before and he moved to the side, which meant her drink left its glass all right but the red wine didn't get more than a drop on his shirt sleeve. Instead, it soaked a woman in a white blouse.

French expletives exploded from the woman's mouth. Lise was apologising profusely over and over although it seemed to do little to calm the woman down. Gabriel stepped in and tried to explain in his native tongue what had happened – he must have seen the guy do it. But it just made the woman even more furious.

The only defusing of the situation came when the chef appeared and took over. He spoke softly to the woman, and her face gradually began to lose its shade of puce, her breaths of fury eased off and finally, she walked away with nothing more than a flighty look in Lise's direction.

'*Je suis vraiment désolée*,' Lise began, but the chef held up a hand. Oh God this was worse than she thought – they were going to be thrown out and on Emma's birthday too. And the offender had already scarpered. He was nowhere to be seen. The police would be called; perhaps she'd be arrested!

'*C'était un accident*,' said the chef.

'*Oui. Et non.*'

'Explain, madame.' His muscular arms folded across his chef's whites and he looked slightly amused if she wasn't mistaken.

She launched into an explanation of the guy who'd grabbed her bottom, pidgin French and hand gestures only taking her so far before Gabriel stepped in again and said it all in French.

The chef switched back to English. 'What is your name?' he asked her.

'Lise,' she mumbled. When she met his gaze, she saw power, control, an ability to convey what he meant with a look rather than just words.

'Lisa?'

'No, Lise. It's short for Annalise. Except I didn't like Annalise, so my friends call me Lise.'

He seemed amused by her blithering. 'I can call you Lise?'

Did that mean he wasn't going to throw her out, press charges for assault if that were possible over a glass of wine? Was it? Perhaps it was in France and came with hefty fines or jail time? 'Yes, you can call me Lise.'

'*Je préfère Annalise. C'est un beau nom pour une belle femme.*' The stubble on his jaw continued down his neck and she knew beneath those whites, he would have to be as masculine as they came, with a muscular, broad chest covered in hair.

A beautiful name for a beautiful woman, he'd said. Dark-as-coal eyes didn't look away and she was beginning to wonder what he had in store for her.

'I will pay for that woman to have her dress cleaned,' Lise insisted, glancing around her. 'If she's still here.'

'I gave her dinner *sur la maison*.'

Even with her basic French, it was easy to translate. 'If you gave it to her on the house, then I will pay you.'

But he shook his head.

'I have to – it was my fault.' But on second thoughts, how much had the woman eaten and drunk? Some of the bottles of wine on the menu were well in excess of one hundred euros. And while Lise had a good bank balance, she drew the line at spending a small fortune because of an accident that happened when a stranger thought it was okay to grope her.

'*Excusez-moi*,' Gabriel began again, having come to join them. He said something in French to the chef and the chef's gaze shot up before he strode off in a way that suggested he meant business.

Lise looked in the direction he was heading and saw him intercept a guy coming out of the bathrooms.

'Oh my God, he's going to hit him!' Emma gasped as Annalise deduced that the man was her groper.

The chef took the man by the scruff of the neck and the next thing she knew, he was out of the restaurant.

She had no idea what to say when the chef came back over. He started speaking in French but changed to English as he calmed down. 'He won't be back here.'

No questions asked as to the man's innocence – the chef had

wholly believed Lise, even though he didn't know her any more than he knew that guy. For all he knew, she could have been making a scene on purpose.

Lise rallied. She pulled a card from her handbag – they were old business cards but she had some left over and with her email address on them she'd been handing them out when she applied for jobs. 'Take this. I expect that woman might come back and complain again. This way, you can let me know and I'll pay to replace her blouse or dry-clean it or whatever.' Although, as with the meal and the wine, she hoped the blouse hadn't cost the earth.

He took the card right before someone came from the kitchens and summoned him back.

The chef told her, 'Stay, you and your friends. Drink your wine.' He leaned over the bar and hey presto, another bottle the same as the one they had appeared, again on the house, which they found out when Gabriel attempted to pay for it.

What had started out as an effort to be a third wheel at tonight's dinner had turned into a wonderful birthday for Emma, a lovely chance to get to know Gabriel better, and an exciting encounter with a chef at a top Paris restaurant.

And when the chef – Xavier – emailed her the next day, Lise began to realise what it might be like to fall in love in Paris too.

17

THEN: 2005

Emma

It was early December in Paris. The temperature had cooled and the colours of autumn had faded as the nights grew darker day by day.

Since Emma first met Gabriel, she'd barely come up for air. Initially, she'd questioned whether the encounter in the supermarket had been too good to be true. Would she get to the street he'd given her directions to and find no café? Would there be no job at all and just a man who wanted to lure a young woman out of her comfort zone? But the first day she'd gone to the café dressed in a simple, plain shirt with jeans and seen him leaning against the wall out front with its red awning above, he'd looked up when she appeared and his expression said it all. He'd been waiting as much for this moment as she had. The café was very real and so was he.

So was the job. She was interviewed officially by his sister Delphine, for which Gabriel apologised, but Emma hadn't thought it was a bad thing. At least she felt she was earning the position rather than being handed it by a man who'd been attracted to her one night in a supermarket. She'd got straight to work that day; her feet barely touched the ground and she was exhausted by the end of it.

Apart from learning the job and a bit more of the language, nothing much had changed since Emma started at the café apart from it was increasingly difficult not to look at Gabriel and reach out to touch him when he was in such close proximity. But they managed it somehow, giving each other surreptitious glances, careful not to upset Delphine, who was strict with staff. Emma was a tiny bit scared of the sister of this gentle, kind and incredibly attractive man, but she made it to the end of every day and was even beginning to get the odd bit of praise from Delphine at what an asset she was.

'You can relax now.' It was an hour after the café closed for the night. Delphine headed off home and Gabriel said he'd walk Emma back to her place. 'My working day is much better with you there,' he told her and then repeated the phrase in French, whispering it in her ear. The melodic tone had her wondering whether her tired legs would give way at any moment.

She slipped her fingers between his, bringing their bodies even closer. 'Your sister is tough to impress.'

'Delphine is strict but as long as you work hard, she won't complain.'

Gabriel was younger than Delphine by ten years and with their parents having nothing to do with the business – they lived some distance away – Emma supposed Delphine saw herself as in charge.

She smiled up at him, his face illuminated in the streetlamp that cast its glow across the cobbles. It wasn't far to the new apartment she and Lise had rented but they walked slowly, Paris as much awake in the late evening as it was in the day.

'*J'ai tellement de chance,*' he murmured against her ear. I'm so lucky. 'If I hadn't gone to the supermarket, we wouldn't have met.' He looped an arm around her shoulders and it instantly took away the rest of the chill on the air tonight.

'And if I hadn't been desperate for a bottle of wine, we really wouldn't have met.' She reached up her hand to take his. They'd had this conversation many a time since they bumped into each other and it always made her smile, made her realise how lucky she was.

They slowed before the corner where they'd cross and he pulled her against him. 'I was watching you today as I do every day. You're beautiful.' He spoke in French. She was mesmerised; she never thought falling for someone could feel this intoxicating.

When his lips met hers, she melted even more. It lit a fire inside her, one that refused to go out and they stood, metres away from the crossing, lost in each other.

When they first got together, Emma had felt guilty spending so much time away from Lise. She'd tried to invite Lise out with them when she could but Lise hadn't wanted to be the third wheel and insisted she was too busy looking for work anyway. And since Lise met Xavier and spent much of her time with him, it seemed they were both beginning to fall in love with more than just Paris itself.

Gabriel was not only a hard worker in the café he co-owned with his sister; he was a talented artist. He could paint, particularly people, with a remarkable accuracy, capturing their character and mannerisms in oil with layers, shadows, details, and in such a way that it felt like staring at the real person on the canvas. He took Emma to the magnificent Musée D'Orsay, the Louvre, the Centre Pompidou and explained the controversy of when it first opened with its exterior of pipes and tubes on display. They shared wine and cheese together at his apartment on rare evenings off. He always walked her home after a shift, and they talked about the parts of France he'd never been to and wanted to take her to some day.

Their time together was a whirlwind right from the start and she never wanted it to end.

The next day, Emma and Gabriel weren't working in the café until later and so they'd taken advantage of the daylight hours and strolled hand in hand up to Sacré-Coeur. He wanted to take photographs and had her posing on the steps leading up to the iconic monument. She larked around, running up two at a time to keep warm and pausing at the top of each section to face him. When he caught her up, he'd put his hands around her waist, lifted her up in the air and twirled her around. 'I love you, Emma, you know that?'

She nuzzled the warmth of his neck, just about burying her face beneath the high collar of his coat. The weather necessitated extra layers, hats and scarves and keeping close for extra body heat. 'I'm so happy. But do you know what would make me even happier?'

'Let me guess: a hot coffee?'

'A good cup of coffee and some crêpes.' She grinned.

They ate, then walked around Montmartre, strolled along Rue du Chevalier de la Barre, widely known as one of the prettiest streets in Paris. Absolutely nothing could take away the love she was feeling, nothing.

At Gabriel's apartment, he loaded up the photographs he'd taken to his computer. He settled on one in particular of Emma, walking away from him but body turned as though someone just said her name, a smile and an excitement captured on her face. He'd taken it when she hadn't realised so rather than on the steps leading up towards Sacré-Coeur, it was on the pretty, Paris street as a car whizzed by in the opposite direction, her hair whipped around with her body, her smile genuine and sure.

He set up his easel, got his paints ready, the brushes, every-thing he needed and with Emma desperately trying to hang around in the background and not disturb him, he painted her from the photograph.

She watched him as he worked, the fierce concentration on his brow easing off now and then but returning frequently, him pushing his shirt sleeves up when one of them dared to fall as he reached over for a different brush. His strong jaw tensed and then relaxed alternately as whatever came to mind as he worked passed.

After sitting on his bed for almost an hour, she couldn't stay quiet any longer. 'What do you think of Xavier?'

After she asked her question again, he set down his brush on the small lip of the easel and wiped his hands on a rag. 'The myste-rious Xavier.' It was neither an answer nor a conversation-thread starter. He shrugged. 'He came out of nowhere.'

'That doesn't answer my question.' She lay on her stomach, legs bent up at right angles, her feet waving in the air. They hadn't spent much time with Xavier and Lise but had all snatched brief moments in passing, enough to get an idea of the man in her best friend's life. What she did know was that Xavier clearly adored Lise, or Annalise as he insisted he call her. The fact that she let him when she'd been Lise to everyone for so long niggled Emma. It didn't sit right and neither did the edge of possessiveness she wasn't sure her friend even noticed. He wasn't obvious with it; he was clever. He made the decisions about where they ate and when but made it sound as though Lise was a part of that decision-making process. When Lise had wanted to go to a fashion exhibi-tion, he'd organised a night off to take her. Lise had seen a man who wanted to escort her and keep her safe in the big city; Emma had seen a man who didn't want to let her out of his sight in case she found she had a whole life without him.

But it was Lise's choice. And she seemed happy.

Gabriel looked at the canvas on his easel. 'What sort of frame do you think would go with your picture?' He asked it in English. Their conversations were a mix of both languages these days – she was understanding more and more French but Gabriel was perceptive enough to know when to switch between the two. The fact he didn't help her out straight away when she struggled was good; it gave her time to try and for her brain to switch languages. But his love, the way he treated her, the way she felt as though they belonged together just served as a reminder that this wasn't going to last forever. She was getting closer and closer to the twelve-month mark of being here and then she'd be due to return to England, back to her teaching job, as though none of this had been her life at all.

She looked at the painting. 'It's yours – you should decide.'

'*Non, ma cherie*, it'll be yours when it is finished.'

'No way, I do not want a picture of myself.'

'Why not? It's beautiful.'

She didn't want to debate this now. She wanted to talk about Xavier, see if she was the only one who had her doubts about him. 'I don't know what to make of him.'

'Who?'

'Xavier,' she reminded him, amused at how easily he could let go of a conversation thread when he was absorbed in his art. 'He just appeared in her life and now she's consumed with him.'

'You could describe us in the same way.'

'We're different. You're genuine… there's something about Xavier I don't trust.'

He came over and made her giggle when he went to touch her, hands maybe wiped clean but still covered in artists' remnants. When she admonished him, he relented and went over to the kitchen sink to wash his hands properly. 'I just appeared in your life. I went to the supermarket and there you were. *Une apparition.*'

'Hey, no complaints here.' And when he came over to her on the bed, she rolled onto her back and wrapped her legs around him. His lips were warm when he kissed her but she was distracted, and when he picked up on it, he stopped.

He propped himself up on one elbow. 'Are you worried about your friend?'

'She can handle herself. So, not really.' Emma wondered whether the language barrier between them wasn't quite letting him know how concerned she was, or maybe it did and he thought she was overprotective. Lise was a grown woman and from what Emma had seen so far, she was head over heels.

Gabriel trailed his finger down the side of her face, her neck, lower towards her breasts. 'Don't think of him; think of me, of us.' He followed it up with a kiss that didn't let her think clearly at all.

'I've got a weird feeling about him,' she said when she came up for air.

'Have you talked to her? Perhaps you need a dinner, a bit like the birthday dinner. Then you can ask all your questions, the way your friend interrogated me.'

Emma laughed. 'Maybe. But he's very intense. I'm not sure how that would go.'

'Intense?'

'With her.'

'So she's having lots of sex?' He grinned, leaving little doubt as to what was on his mind. 'We could have more if we stop talking about Lise.' He looked at his watch. 'We've got one hour until we're in the café.'

She kissed him tenderly, whispered in French, 'One hour?' And with a look between them, he knew he'd got his way.

Their lovemaking was tender. Gabriel murmured in French, which fuelled her passion, and they didn't waste a single minute of their remaining time together before they left for work.

* * *

Gabriel walked Emma home in the evening before going back to finish up at the café, their goodbye short given Delphine wasn't in the best of moods after she'd caught Emma and her brother kissing in the kitchen earlier today.

Emma had been home for almost an hour, snuggled up on the sofa with a book and a blanket, when Lise came in the door.

Lise was still smiling when she sat down next to her. 'Can't stop. Xavier is picking me up once he's finished at the restaurant.'

Emma buried the disappointment. Her friend had never once made her feel guilty about the time spent with Gabriel and she should do the same. Lise looked tired though and Emma told her, although she suspected the exhaustion erred on the side of satiated, which meant it was probably down to Xavier.

Lise had a smile plastered on her face that was going nowhere. 'You have no idea how hot Xavier is in bed.'

'That's what you've been doing this evening?'

'Yes... well no, it was in the store cupboard.'

'Oh my God, Lise!' Emma laughed despite the graphic declaration. 'At work?'

'It wasn't meant to happen. I was there at one of the tables job-hunting online and went to tell him I had to come back here to get my things and it just... happened.'

'I'm going to need details.'

And so Lise shared everything, Emma peeking through her fingers half the time at the descriptions as though shielding herself from the reality.

Lise reached over and grabbed Emma's hand. 'I've missed this.'

'Me too.'

'We've both got men in our lives. Which, might I add, is hard to believe sometimes. I *never* thought I'd come to Paris and fall in love.'

Emma sat up a little straighter. 'Wait, you're in love?' She thought Lise might be but hearing her friend say it was another matter entirely.

Lise sat up herself. 'Shit, yes, I think I am. God, I've not told him yet. What if he doesn't feel the same? What if he's only in this for the sex? Shit, how did I ever let myself get like this?'

Emma couldn't quite believe it either. Lise wasn't the sort to seek out a sweeping love affair. Short and sweet and on to the next was more like her style while she was young and maybe forever. But Xavier appeared to be changing all of that.

'It's not just the sex,' Lise admitted once she'd finished sharing the juicy details with her friend. 'He makes me feel special, like I'm the only person who matters to him. He takes me to the nicest restaurants, he took me shopping on the Champs-Élysées, he's always interested in me.'

Emma put her arms around her friend. 'I'm pleased you're happy.' Lise was fast becoming Xavier's world and despite her misgivings, Emma knew Lise deserved a chance to be happy. She berated herself inwardly – perhaps she'd made a snap judgement, maybe she didn't know Xavier well enough yet to judge him.

'Xavier saw me trawling through more job ads tonight and he came up with a plan. He suggested I work for him.'

'In the restaurant here in Paris?'

'In a PR job – he actually has two restaurants so he has his own PR team,' she beamed. 'I'll need to learn the ropes, improve my language skills, but it's what I do and do well.'

'That's amazing, Lise.'

'I can enrol in evening classes to get better at French and if I work hard, I could see myself being a real part of it, Emma. A part of the business as well as a part of Xavier's life. I'll have to start as a basic assistant so not much responsibility but as I improve my French, I don't see why I can't work my way up the ladder. Oh, and it'll be interesting, much more interesting than any of the jobs I've applied for. I'll have a chance to work with a restaurant business, build their brand awareness to keep them at the front of the marketplace, target audiences, help make the restaurants visible.'

Passion oozed from Lise's soul. She had always loved her job and if Xavier could give her that, how could Emma not be happy for her? She pushed aside her doubts that this man viewed Lise as more of a trophy, someone he wanted to own and show off. She'd seen it the night they watched him deal with the customer who'd touched Lise. In a way, it had been admirable, impressive, but the way he'd looked at Lise when he'd come back to them was as though he'd won a contest. But perhaps that's exactly how it should be. Because Lise was a prize to any man who got her. She was gorgeous, gregarious, a gem in Emma's life as well as that of others.

'Lise, your idea, the job, it sounds really long term.'

Her friend met her gaze. 'It does, doesn't it?'

'We didn't predict Frenchmen being a part of this year.'

'We didn't. I was planning a fabulous year with my best friend in Paris before I returned to England, got a cracker of a job and worked my way up the ladder.'

'Are you saying that's all off now?'

'I've no idea.'

'Well I suppose it's a good thing Xavier offered you a job,' Emma admitted finally. 'You're having way too much sex to make time to look for one elsewhere.'

Lise laughed but soon turned serious. 'I've missed this – me and you having an evening together.'

'Me too.' She grabbed her friend's hand and gave it a squeeze. 'So let's plan one. How about tomorrow? I finish by 7.30 p.m.'

'I can't. Xavier could only get one early finish and it's tomorrow so we're going to the theatre.'

'I'm working the night after that. How about Sunday night?'

'*Dimanche. Oui!*' Lise spoke with a flamboyant French accent.

'Oh you are so French.' Emma giggled, giving her friend a shove before Lise disappeared into her bedroom to grab some more clothes for her stay at Xavier's apartment.

After she left, Emma, happy she'd soon have another evening with her best friend, snuggled up on the sofa again to read a few more chapters of her book.

The girls' landlord had been happy to install a phone line providing the girls paid the bills and both Lise and Emma jokingly called it the Miller hotline because most calls that came and went were from Emma's family. And so when the phone interrupted her reading, Emma answered the call fully expecting to hear her mother's voice on the end of the line.

But it wasn't. It was Shelly Baker and she needed to talk to her daughter.

Emma explained that Lise was out. 'I can leave a note that you called. She'll be back tomorrow.'

'I need her to come home.'

'Mrs Baker, is everything okay?'

Emma knew at once that it wasn't when Mrs Baker said, in a very soft voice, 'It's her father...'

18

THEN: 2005

Lise

Lise loved staying at Xavier's place. He'd done well for himself, came into money as a young man, which allowed him to make a splash in the restaurant business, and he owned an apartment in *Le Marais*, plush, with all mod-cons. The kitchen was out of this world and gleaming. Everything was perfect, even more so now it was decorated for Christmas with garlands strung across the top of the fireplace, a six-foot-tall fir tree standing in the corner adorned with ornaments that rebounded light from all angles. And what Lise loved all the more was that with just the two of them, she didn't have to worry about them being interrupted, that they'd disturb Emma with their lovemaking. They'd barely got through the door tonight before Xavier had lifted her up and carried her into the bedroom. It didn't matter they'd had wild sex that afternoon; he was hungry for more and so was she.

Lise sank into the slipper bathtub filled with luxury lavender bath salts Xavier had bought especially for her to use when she was staying here. He always thought of the extra touches – a white waffle robe on the back of the bedroom door for her when she was here, her favourite chocolates with mint in the big cupboard in his kitchen, her preferred cereals and fruits and brand of coffee, a car service to a spa hotel on the outskirts of Paris twice when he'd been working and so was Emma, leaving her at a loss for what to do now she was no longer job-hunting. And it wasn't only the things he bought or gave her; it was him. She never once felt invisible; she never once felt unheard. It was as though she'd changed from that girl who had fought so hard to have her own family notice her and become someone else entirely.

The water enveloped her. Though a little on the hot side, it left her skin tingling in a good way. The water was cloudy from the salts and she watched the patterns created when she ran her hand back and forth, listening to the gentle swooshing sound, as well as the classical music soundtrack playing from the speaker in the corner.

She luxuriated in the tub and every time she thought about stepping out onto the chenille bath rug and reaching for the towel, she decided against it. At least until she heard a voice she recognised.

She sat up, the water sloshing violently as she leapt out to grab her towel. 'Emma? Is that you?' For her friend to be here, there had to be something wrong. She emerged in the towel, her hair at the back dripping water between her shoulder blades, her skin red from the water temperature and not in the least bit cold.

And that was when Emma told her.

Her dad was gone. Randall Baker had had a heart attack. Just like that, he was dead.

Lise felt numb. Her emotions were with her mother, on her loss, but as for her own grief, she had no idea.

Since the moment she found out, the only time Xavier had left her side was to take Emma home in the early hours and then he'd been back, curled around Lise on the bed as though wondering at what point she'd break down and fall apart.

She still hadn't done that and now here she was on an early-morning flight bound for England.

'Another drink?' he asked.

Had she already had one? She couldn't remember.

'No thanks.' She turned, looked at Xavier. He was dressed in dark jeans, a dark-grey, knitted sweater with a French designer's name she didn't recognise on a leather tag at the bottom. 'You came with me.' It was as though she'd only just realised.

Emma had offered to go home for the funeral too but Xavier had assured her that he would look after Lise. And Lise hadn't had the energy to argue. She'd thanked Emma for the kind offer but added, 'I don't even know if I want to go myself, let alone put you through it. We weren't exactly close.'

'I couldn't let you go alone.' His dark hair, cut short, was the same colour as his eyebrows, thick but not too thick. His facial hair was kept just so. 'The restaurant can survive a few days without me.'

She rested her head on his shoulder. Lise had fallen hard for Xavier since that night at the restaurant when she'd thrown her wine all over a random woman who, as it turned out, had been more furious about the groper being her husband than she was at Lise for throwing the drink, a fact hard to deduce when you didn't speak the language. With Xavier's work hours, it had taken a few days for their first date to eventuate but in the meantime, the emails had flown back and forth, the flirtation building, the attraction growing and by the time he took her to dinner followed by a romantic stroll across the *Pont des Arts*, with its view of the Seine and the twinkling lights of Paris all around them, they were already comfortable with each other.

Lise had almost gone home with him that first night – it was what she'd assumed would happen if she met anyone in Paris, that it would be a brief fling, a moment of mutual enjoyment, and then she'd be back to her year away from England living in an apartment with her best friend. But it had been so much more than that. By the time they slept together, they were hungry for each other. The waiting had almost become painful. She'd spent a lot of time with him since. She'd kept up with her job search but he'd always been a distraction. If she was at the laptop searching online, he was nuzzling at her neck until she gave in to temptation. If she went out looking for adverts in windows of cafés or anywhere else, he wanted to know when she'd be back because he missed her being around. She'd sit in the corner of the restaurant with a book sometimes just so he could sneak out and spend time with her on a break.

Xavier had taken her away for a weekend in early December, to a chateau with a roaring fire – they'd eaten room service, fed each other strawberries dipped in chocolate. It had been a forty-eight-hour escape from Xavier's manic life and it was bliss. A week after that, he'd introduced Lise to some of his friends, all charming, all successful in their various jobs. She'd been a little lost with the French even though they'd done their best to adapt between English and French to help her out. But she hadn't really cared – it was good to feel a part of Xavier's life, for him to feel so proud to have her on his arm, to take her out and about to meet the people from his world.

Their love affair wasn't like any Lise had ever had before. Emma could see it; so could she. She'd fallen hard.

And nobody had been more surprised than Lise when she blurted out that she loved him to Emma earlier that night, the night before she found herself packing for an unexpected return to England.

* * *

The funeral was, for want of a better description, a morbid, miserable affair. Randall's sister had come over from Jersey, his brother down from Scotland. Her grandparents had died years ago so apart from a handful of work colleagues, Shelly and Lise, it was a compact party. The funeral had taken place a week after Lise had got home to Bath and so Xavier had had no choice but to fly back to Paris and his business after seven days away already. On the day of the funeral, Lise had taken charge of the wake at number twelve and it had given her something to focus on now she didn't have Xavier. Because if anyone was expecting her to fall apart with grief, they'd be disappointed.

The day after the wake, Lise had had to get out, anywhere, as long as it was away from Honeybee Place and the walls that had begun to feel as though they were closing in around her. She'd donned jeans, knee-high, all-weather boots and a big coat with a hat to cover her dark, wavy hair, and she'd set off for the city.

Bath was beautiful in the run-up to Christmas. The streets were filled with glittering lights and festive spirit, the shops were bursting with Christmas shoppers, the big tree at The Royal Crescent was there as it was every year, and the nip of cold in the air mixed with the sounds of carols emanating from services eased Lise's sadness. As it grew dark, she continued to wander. Lit-up entrances of shops beckoned her inside but she kept walking until her legs ached and her tummy groaned for a warming winter meal. Tonight, she'd be at number twelve rather than the hotel she'd stayed in with Xavier when they first arrived, and the thought of being at the house made Lise realise that despite the connection formed with her mother since she left for Paris, and their phone calls that had developed over time, she still had no idea how to talk to her properly.

Emma's mum was straight out of the Café on the Corner when Lise tried to pass by on the pavement on the opposite side of the road. Lise was about to wave but Keely held out her arms and Lise found herself crossing over. She'd seen the Millers at the wake but she hadn't been on her own until now and the minute Mrs Miller wrapped her in a hug, she felt the tears coming. Lise had cried with Xavier more because she had no idea how to feel – it was a loss but of what kind? And Xavier didn't really get it. How could he? He hadn't seen her growing up; he didn't know what her family were like. The Millers had seen it all; they'd know that her tears weren't for her father necessarily but for a life she'd never quite fitted into, for the grief of what had never been for Lise: the belonging to a family.

Inside the warmth of the Café on the Corner, Brendan brought out a big oval plate with waffles and maple syrup along with a scoop of vanilla bean ice-cream. 'Stay here as long as you like, love.'

She nodded, she ate, she didn't talk. And the Millers carried on around her, this café more of a home than number twelve ever was.

After she'd eaten, she felt calmer, ready to talk without falling apart. She set her cutlery together as Mrs Miller came over. 'You two are wonderful, you know that?'

Mr Miller whisked her plate away and winked at her in a way not many men could carry off without looking sleazy.

'You're pretty wonderful yourself,' Mrs Miller told her. 'We're here for you whenever you need us. And your mother is, in her own way.' Lise must've looked confused because Mrs Miller looked uneasy as she admitted, 'Your mum came to see me this morning. I don't think she really wants you to know, but I think you need to. She's hurting, Lise. Not just from losing your dad but from almost losing you.'

'She said that?'

Mrs Miller nodded, wiping her hands on the apron in her lap. 'She knows it's been hard for you, that she didn't give you the best upbringing. But I will tell you how glad she was that you came back here when she called to let you know about your dad.'

Lise ran a finger down the side of her water glass, wetting her skin with its condensation. 'I thought about not coming, you know.'

'I'm not surprised.'

'It was Xavier who booked the flights without me having to say a word. The next thing I knew, I was on my way.' As another customer went up to the till, Lise said, 'You're busy. I should go.'

'Brendan will see to it. I'm here with you.'

'I'm fine, honestly.'

'You're a strong woman.' Mrs Miller smiled. 'But you still lost your dad.'

'He wasn't much of a father.'

Keely reached out to touch Lise's hair so tenderly, Lise only just managed to swallow without bursting into tears again. 'Oh, love, I can see why you think that way. Don't be angry – it'll hurt you more if you are.'

With a nod of acceptance, she said, 'I'm trying my best.'

'I know.'

'Can we talk about something else?' she sniffed.

Keely handed her a tissue. 'Of course we can.'

So Lise found herself talking about Paris even though Mrs Miller had heard it all on the phone before from Emma's updates and her own. She told her how happy Emma was, how they'd approve of Gabriel. She told her about her work with Xavier for the restaurant. And she went back to number twelve Honeybee Place with the knowledge that her mother had admitted weakness by going to see Mrs Miller and talking about Lise, and that in itself was something Lise never could've predicted.

* * *

The next few days were strange. Lise heard her mum crying at night, saw her wiping tears away during the day, and while she wasn't able to give much comfort in the way of words over a man she'd had no idea how to connect with, she'd been drawn to stay with her mum and even changed her flight back to Paris to give her another few days.

'You've done enough already,' Shelly had told her when Lise let her know she'd stay a while longer. 'You did everything for the wake; I did nothing.'

The day before Lise was due to leave, they cooked a roast-chicken lunch together. It was the first time they'd cooked along-side each other since Lise was so small, she'd had to stand on a step stool to be able to stir anything on the stovetop.

With the kitchen still warm from the oven as it cooled, the clearing up all done, and a cup of tea each, they sat at the kitchen table.

'I didn't know whether you'd even come back, you know.' Shelly pushed a plate of biscuits across to Lise.

Lise shook her head. 'I'm too full. And of course I came back. He was my father; you're my mother.'

'So you came out of duty.'

'Yes.' The admission fell from between her lips before she thought about it, but it was the truth. 'Although it was Xavier who booked the flights. I knew I *should* come but without someone else taking control, I might have stayed away, avoided it even though I knew I should be here.'

Her mum let the information settle. 'Well, I'm glad you came.'

Lise felt an odd whirl of emotions, like this was the start of another change between the two of them, the honesty they'd touched upon over the phone calls but which was different face to face. 'So am I.'

Shelly looked vulnerable in a way she never had before. She still wore the same buttoned-up blouse and smart trousers that made her look ready for a day at the office, the way she'd always dressed, but deep down, she was a different person to the one Lise was used to seeing. What would her mother do now she was no longer a wife, a role she'd excelled at and was the mould she'd been in for years? Lise thought about asking, but her mum got up, made another pot of tea, and they were on to talking about Bath and Christmas and what Lise planned to do when she got back to Paris.

They were still talking in the kitchen when the skies grew dark and as Shelly put the lights on beneath the wall cabinets, a knock at the front door saw Mrs Miller delivering a lasagne with a black-berry crumble for their dessert. She assured them there was no need to rush to return the dishes and to Lise's surprise, Shelly invited her inside. Although she insisted that wasn't necessary, Mrs Miller eventually conceded and two turned to three around the little kitchen table at number twelve Honeybee Place.

Now that Lise knew her mum had talked with Mrs Miller, it made sense. The pair were forming an unlikely friendship of sorts. Lise couldn't ever see them spending a lot of time together but rather than her mother flitting around doing things for her husband and keeping the house spick and span, it felt good to know she might well start to become a part of things here. Perhaps she'd get to know more people and have neighbours she could turn to if she needed.

The fairy lights surrounding the kitchen window made the atmosphere cosy as the three women talked about Paris, the girls' adventures, about Toby's new job as a disability support worker, the café, Christmas. During their conversation that shifted from topic to topic, there wasn't a single mention of the man they'd buried so recently, the man who was now absent from Shelly and Lise's lives. To outsiders, it would be easy to assume that was because it was too difficult and painful to acknowledge but Lise knew better. This was the start of a very different chapter in the Bakers' lives.

The following day, as Lise hauled her suitcase downstairs, her mother answered the door to what they both assumed was Lise's taxi. But when Lise saw it was Mrs Griffin, she set down her case and launched herself at the woman for a hug.

'I didn't think I'd see you, Mrs Griffin.'

'I got back this morning, had a lovely time with my son. I wasn't supposed to be back until this evening but I couldn't let you go without seeing you first. How are you?' Her head tilted and Lise knew she meant the question with regards to her dad.

'I'm fine, honestly. Under the circumstances, Mum and I have had a good week, haven't we, Mum?' She turned but her mother had disappeared into the kitchen, perhaps to give them a chance to talk.

'Look after her, won't you?' Lise whispered to Mrs Griffin.

'I promise I will,' she said, equally quiet.

'She's different.'

Mrs Griffin put a hand to Lise's cheek. 'She's missed you. Keep in touch.'

'I will. I'll keep sending those postcards.'

'Not just with me, dear. Keep in touch with your mother.'

Lise nodded.

A beep outside announced the taxi and Lise was surprised that a part of her felt disappointment. 'I have to go.' She hugged Mrs Griffin one more time.

'Will you stay for morning tea?' her mother asked their neighbour as she emerged from the kitchen. Her mother really was coming out of her shell as a widow and Lise couldn't say it was a bad thing.

Mrs Griffin smiled. 'Well that would be lovely.' She took off her coat and hung it on the hook in the hallway and Lise got the impression this had happened before. 'I'll be in the kitchen, let you two say your goodbyes.' And with one more squeeze to Lise's arm, she left them to it.

Outside in the winter chill, Lise thanked the driver who loaded her suitcase into the boot.

'Safe trip.' Shelly stood beside the open back door to the taxi and Lise was about to climb in when her mother wrapped her in a hug. 'Call me, won't you?'

Lise gulped. Hugs had never been on the agenda before and it took her by surprise. 'I will.'

'Thanks, Lise.'

Lise started at her mother's use of her shortened name.

Shelly smiled. 'I know you prefer it. I thought I might use it from now on. If it's all right with you.'

Lise couldn't get the words out. Instead, she gestured to the taxi's warm interior. 'I'd better...'

'You go – safe flight.' She set off down the path to the front door.

'Mum...' Lise's hand rested on the top of the taxi's open door. 'I'll call soon, I promise.'

With a nod, Shelly Baker went inside, Lise got into the taxi and it was time to return to her life in Paris, a life she'd paused to come back here for the funeral.

And when she got to her apartment in Paris and found it empty, no sign of Emma, she dumped her luggage and went straight to Xavier's place.

And he welcomed her home with open arms.

19

NOW: 2023

Lise

Since their date when Lise had told Max everything – the whole truth about her marriage to Xavier – they'd seen each other a handful of times before he'd gone away on a business trip. In truth, it had been good to have some distance. Lise wanted him to work out how he felt about things now he knew and she could always use the extra space, especially given she was no closer to being able to talk properly with Emma.

No Emma and no Max had meant that Lise had a chance to really progress with doing up number twelve. She had the tradesmen come in and quote for the staircase refurbishment – she wanted it sanded back to the original wood and given a good coat of varnish. She found out the costs of repairs to the flooring and the replacement of the bathroom fixtures and fittings, and she chose paint colours for some of the other rooms.

Painting was hardly Lise's forte but today, she got going with more in her bedroom. She stood back – narrowly missing the tray she'd poured the paint into to allow good coverage of the roller – once she'd put the second coat on the walls. Passenger blared from the Bluetooth speaker set on the floor in the corner as she admired the heather-purple shade she'd chosen rather than the lilac she thought she'd wanted. The colour was fresh, went well with the other walls in Chantilly Lace, and she'd already got both sheer white curtains on order for the windows along with a set of deep-purple, heavy drapes with tie-backs to keep in the warmth and block out the dark. The colour scheme was Lise through and through, but in all likelihood, she'd be selling the place and she was sure whoever ended up buying the house would love it too.

'Looks good,' Maisie's voice came from behind her.

'I thought I heard you come in.' She'd got used to it already, how little you could really hear from up here if you had music on. 'Badminton?' She eyed the jogging bottoms and hoodie.

'Yep, it was a tournament. I was out in the first round.'

She held open her arms and wrapped Maisie to console her. 'Better luck next time.' Lise had always loved badminton although had never played seriously and they'd played a bit in Paris, enough that Maisie had caught the bug.

'Still had fun,' she trilled, heading off for the shower.

'How was school?' Lise called after her but she was met with silence. She smiled. School was never as exciting to recap on as anything extra-curricular.

Lise went downstairs to wash out the brush and the roller and by the time Maisie came downstairs too, she'd set everything to dry. 'Could you get that please,' she asked her daughter when the doorbell rang.

Lise dried her hands as Maisie came back into the kitchen with Naomi in tow.

'Hello again.' Lise smiled. She did her best not to be awkward now she was well aware that this was Emma's daughter.

'Hey.' She even spoke like Emma once had, a little unsure of herself and very polite.

'It's okay, right?' asked Maisie.

Lise shook away her worries. 'Of course. Naomi, you're welcome any time.'

As Maisie poured them both a drink of juice, the girls talked about what was on at the movies but had no luck deciding what to see.

'Why don't you stay here and watch something,' Lise suggested. 'And don't worry, I'm heading out for a while anyway. I won't cramp your style. Need anything from the shops?'

Popcorn was the only request and so Lise showered and changed, done with painting for today. Little and often was the best approach as far as she was concerned. She collected the flowers she'd bought this morning from a local florist and left in the utility room, their stems drinking up the water in the base of a bucket, and with Maisie too preoccupied to notice her mother carrying the blooms, she went out to the car and drove to the cemetery not far from the city.

The rain of the last couple of days, the impressive storm that had marked the start of the week, had given way to clear skies and a fresh breeze as Lise walked from her car. She stopped at Mrs Griffin's graveside first, which wasn't far from the entrance. She pulled out a couple of the pretty yellow blooms from the bouquet in her arms and pushed the stems into the pot for the purpose, which already held delicate white flowers but welcomed the company of something fresh. Lise expected this gravestone was visited frequently – Mrs Griffin was such a favourite, she'd never be short of visitors. Lise smiled. *I miss you,* she tried to convey somehow as she thought about the kind woman who'd been there to talk to whenever she needed, who she stayed in touch with by postcard for years.

Lise moved on, further into the cemetery until she came to another plaque:

Randall Baker
Beloved husband and father
May he rest in peace

Apart from the dates of his existence, there was nothing else. The flowers that had maybe once been here had gone, most likely taken away when they shrivelled and died. This was the first time she'd come here since she came back from Paris for the funeral. That had been her final goodbye to a man who'd been, at best, disinterested.

'You were never a part of my life,' she said out loud but without malice, as though he was there in front of her. 'Even when I lived at home, where were you?' She waited but her only response was the rustle of leaves from a nearby bush. 'I never wanted that for my kid.' She pulled out a single yellow flower and laid it on top of the stone plaque before she moved away. She knew then that she wouldn't visit his plaque ever again.

Lise followed a different pathway to her next destination. And this time when she arrived, she got down on her haunches and set the flower arrangement at the front of Toby's granite memorial stone marker. 'Hey, Toby.' The petals of the flowers fluttered in the breeze and she took a few moments to find her voice. 'I still can't believe you're gone. It's all so unfair. Nothing is the same any more, Toby.' She gulped. 'I dug up the box we buried in my parents' veggie patch.' A soft catch of her breath accompanied tears she hadn't expected as her eyes scanned the words of his epitaph:

Toby Miller

Beloved son of Brendan and Keely, dear brother to Emma, gone before your time and missed forever more.

A woman who had been walking past looked as though she might stop and ask whether Lise needed her help, her comfort, but Lise turned away and she moved on.

'You were right to tell me to hold on to those diaries, Toby.' She spoke through another sob and if anyone was listening to her, they wouldn't be able to decipher what she'd said. Thinking of how muddled she sounded had Lise smiling through her tears, remembering Toby had once said that crying made all women incoherent. 'I found your note in the box too. It was like hearing you speak from beyond the grave. It took me right back to that night. You must've written it when you went to get the tin so we could bury my diaries. I'm so glad you did it. I really am.'

Lise had found a note inside the old tea caddy storage tin written in Toby's handwriting and she'd laughed when she read it, cried, clutched it against her chest and kept it safe. The note had read:

If you're reading this now, Lise, and Toby is not flying planes, slap him. And if he's sitting behind a desk in an office, for goodness' sake drag him out of there, his life must truly suck. I hope we're still making each other laugh and still good mates, Lise. Who knows, we might both be grown up and totally serious by now but part of me hopes we're still those young people of Honeybee Place with a sense of fun and adventure. Toby xx

Remembering the way it had made her feel to read the note for the first time, she wished more than ever that they were those two people, that they could have opened the box together.

'You never found yourself in an office, you know.' She grinned.

'You did good, Toby. Really good. Apart from dying – that was a pretty crappy thing to do.' She could imagine him looking down on her and agreeing with that one. 'Your sister and I aren't friends either. Maybe your ghost could come and visit her one night and tell her to give me a chance?' She hooked her hair behind her ear when the wind blew it across her mouth and as the sky above grew unexpectedly dark and she felt a few drops of rain, she laughed. 'Damn weather can't make its mind up. That's my cue to go, Toby. Just one more thing before I do – I really need to put things right with your sister so whatever divine intervention you could come up with would be great.'

She blew a kiss to his memorial stone marker and hurried away as the drizzle turned to a more definite pitter-patter that threatened to worsen. Already, she knew he'd done something unwittingly that might help her and her best friend get things between them back on track.

She just hadn't had the chance to explain any of it to Emma yet.

20

THEN: 2006

Emma

Emma had barely seen Lise since she returned from England. There'd been Christmas Day, which they'd shared before Emma went to Gabriel's, Lise to Xavier's, but over the last few months they'd been living very separate lives. And Emma hated that they were drifting apart in their friendship. They had dinner in the diary for tonight though, and despite having to share Lise with others, she couldn't wait to see her best friend.

Emma had also begun to wonder about the long-term – something she hadn't given much consideration to yet. It was times like this she wished Lise wasn't quite so caught up with Xavier, that they could talk late into the evening and she could get advice from her best friend. Last month, they'd managed to squeeze in a night, just the two of them, at a small bistro and, before they talked about anything else, Emma had tried to be a good friend and find out how Lise was really doing since her father died.

'I'm busy with work,' Lise had told her when Emma asked her how she was. She'd picked up a piece of crusty baguette and dipped it into the baked camembert. 'I'm learning the basics in a different language and it's been a big challenge that's keeping me busy.'

'That wasn't entirely what I meant.' Emma broke off a piece of bread and dipped it into the gooey mixture.

'You mean family,' Lise deduced. 'Well, my dad isn't a factor any more so I guess I'm okay about him.'

Emma noticed the next piece of baguette was dragged more forcefully through the Camembert. 'Lise—'

'But he's not. Never was really. He was never interested in me; why should I be sorry that he's gone?' She topped up her own glass of wine but Emma declined.

'He was still your dad.'

'You know what my childhood was like. My teenage years weren't much better, even the days before we came to Paris. That man had no business being a dad.'

'Lise—'

'No, I mean it, Emma.'

Emma knew Lise well enough to see she was either about to lose her temper or burst into tears and she wanted neither to happen. 'I'm sorry...'

'No, I'm sorry.' She sighed, sitting back in her chair. 'You're being nice and I'm... well I'm avoiding talking about him.'

'How's your mum?' Lise had told her that staying with her at Honeybee Place after the hotel she and Xavier stayed in at first had been better than expected. She'd described to Emma the little things they'd done – the cooking together, talking over cups of tea, watching television – all the things Emma had taken for granted as a young girl with her loving family. Her dad had once told her that for all the money the Bakers had, it hadn't brought them much happiness, something Emma was all too aware of. But it sounded now like Lise and Shelly were in a much better place.

'It's weird,' said Lise. 'Mum seems really together. Ever since my dad died, she hasn't fallen apart. She was upset of course – she loved him – but it's as though she never realised before that she could have a life outside of her marriage. I haven't said that to her. I don't want to upset her when it's still delicate whenever we talk, but she probably sees it for herself.' She proffered the wine again and this time, Emma relented.

'Have you been talking to Xavier about everything?'

'Of course I do.' She frowned. 'He's there for me.'

'I'm glad.' Emma had been surprised Xavier took off from his restaurant and went to England with Lise but it had given her pause when he did.

When the time came to leave the bistro, Emma was disappointed. 'When can we meet up again? You're so rarely at the apartment.'

Lise pulled a face. 'I was supposed to talk to you about that.'

And Emma knew what was coming. 'You're moving in with Xavier,' she said.

'Not yet, but it's on the cards. I mean I'm practically there all the time anyway.'

'Things are changing.'

Lise pulled her friend into a hug. 'Why don't the four of us have dinner? Soon.'

Emma smiled. 'Okay.'

And so that was how the four of them found themselves at Xavier's apartment on a Tuesday night, sitting around his thick, oak refectory dining table and delivering compliments to the chef for the main dish he'd introduced as *Le Gigot d'Agneau*. The tender roast leg of lamb was placed in the centre of the table in all its glory, the scent of rosemary and garlic lacing the air, and Xavier served the meat along with gratin potatoes and *haricots verts*. It was a simple meal – meat, potatoes, green beans – but as a chef, Xavier carried it to a new level that had his guests, despite being involved in the food business, curious as to how it tasted so good.

'The key is in the slow roasting of the lamb,' he told them confidently. 'This time, seven hours.'

'Well at least it's winter – it warms the kitchen,' Gabriel put in, accepting another glass of red wine from Xavier.

The entire apartment was enormous in its proportions and the ceilings in the kitchen soared above them, vaulted, with different angles. Hanging from the section of ceiling over the table were exposed lightbulbs encased in glass globes all hanging down at varying lengths in an arrangement that looked more artistic than practical. A generous island bench sat parallel to the table with stools along one edge, all arranged with perfect spacing between them. Exuberant foliage in a vase of crystal-clear water stood at one end of the island's stone top, a sink sat slightly off-centre, a knife block at the other end. The kitchen surfaces were sparse with very little clutter but one tap on the sleek, modern, walnut-brown cabinetry would likely expose every possible gadget and utensil you could ever need.

'Annalise loves this place,' Xavier announced with an undeniable underlying boast in his words. 'Especially my kitchen. And the bedroom, of course.'

Lise laughed. 'Okay, that's enough of that sort of talk.'

'I don't see much of her any more,' Emma complained.

Xavier fixed his eyes on Lise. 'She's almost moved in. I just want her to go the whole way.'

Emma swallowed hard. It wouldn't be long. Still, could she deny she'd move in with Gabriel if he asked her? They hadn't had the conversation yet but it might happen soon; Emma could feel it.

As they talked, Emma watched Xavier swirl the contents of his wine glass to agitate the contents. Perhaps it tasted different if you did that first. Although Emma suspected if she tried it, she'd likely slop red wine all down the royal-blue top she'd worn tonight.

The men were very different. Where Xavier exuded confidence, Gabriel was more wary. Emma knew deep down he believed in himself, he was content with his life, but she could see how someone like Xavier could tap away at a man like Gabriel and leave him feeling lacking. She didn't know whether Xavier did it on purpose, maybe it was a quality he didn't realise he had, but it was there nonetheless.

Lise smiled over at her, eyes widening slightly as if to say how well it was going. Which it was, kind of. All four of them had chatted and laughed all evening over their delicious meal but at the same time, Emma couldn't wait to slip out of her clothes and into her comfy pyjamas and snuggle against Gabriel, who was staying over at her place tonight. He'd kiss her worries away, her concern about her friendship with Lise now Xavier was on the scene and they barely saw one another. He'd tell her as he had before to stay the course. She couldn't remember the French phrase he'd used, only that that was what it meant.

Emma shifted uncomfortably in her seat as the conversation between the men got a little more heated. They were talking in French and she didn't fully grasp all of it, just that they were debating the merits of various wines, reds and whites. Lise had obviously lost track too and cleared the plates, insisting Emma stay seated. Although she really would rather be with her friend, perhaps it was a good idea to stay at the table in case she needed to help Gabriel out.

'This is a good wine,' she put in, in perfect English, to try to bring the men back to the party of four rather than two.

The interruption worked and Gabriel mouthed the word *merci* in her direction when Xavier looked away and urged Lise to leave the dishes and come join them.

'So, Gabriel, how's the café business?' Xavier asked as Lise came back to his side and he put an arm around her waist before she could sit down.

'Can't complain.' Gabriel was wearing a smart shirt this evening, his light-brown hair was freshly cut that morning and he had a little nick on his jaw where he'd shaved. He'd never looked sexier despite his discomfort and him making an effort for Emma meant the absolute world to her.

'You own the business with your sister?' Xavier asked.

Their conversation was in English thankfully – Emma had learned to recognise that a flip to French usually meant trouble and a heated exchange, which might need intervention. She'd never been so on edge at a simple dinner before but tonight, it was in the back of her mind that this had all been a huge mistake.

Gabriel answered the question. 'That's right. Before that, the café belonged to our grandparents. It does all right, nothing like your restaurant, but enough for the two of us.'

'What about expansion some day?'

'Neither myself nor Delphine have thought about doing so.'

'But you must want to grow long term.' He topped up Lise's wine without her having asked. 'We have plans in place for a third restaurant.'

'You already have two?' Gabriel enquired.

'One in Paris; the other is in Chaumont. You'll have to visit, both of you. The head chef, Jacques, is *magnifique*, I can assure you. Let me make a reservation.' He looked around, presumably for his phone.

'I'll need to check my work schedule first,' said Gabriel with more humour and acceptance than Emma could muster herself. Xavier was pushy and Lise didn't seem to notice it.

'But you're the boss, *non*?' Xavier used a wide hand gesture as though the thought of having to check a schedule when you owned a café was unbelievable. 'Give yourself a night off, take your beautiful girl for dinner – it comes with a generous discount. Any friends of mine are welcome.'

'Thank you but we'll have to let you know.' Gabriel kept his voice level.

Emma put a hand on his knee beneath the table. She knew how uncomfortable this must be for him. And it didn't stop there. Xavier moved the conversation on to the menu at Gabriel's café, the types of customers it attracted. Perhaps small talk about business was common ground so Emma went with it, joining Gabriel in his replies, asking more questions about Xavier's restaurants and whether the menus differed between the two – they did but only slightly – and whether seasons dictated much change.

'Who's ready for dessert?' Lise sprung up.

'Let me help you.' Emma left the conversation to simmer and followed her friend to the kitchen.

At the counter behind the bench, Lise brought out a tub of vanilla ice cream from the integrated and very hidden freezer. Even now Emma would have to guess again as to which door it had been.

'You made a crumble.' Emma smiled.

'It's your mum's recipe.'

'Don't tell Xavier,' Emma whispered, 'but I bet it'll be the star dish of the evening.'

'It's going well, isn't it?'

Emma murmured agreement, thankful Lise was busy portioning out the crumble with the large serving spoon and then the ice cream, too focused to look for any meaning in Emma's lacklustre response.

'There's a lot of shop talk about the food business,' Lise went on, 'but I don't mind; at least the men have something to chat about.'

'Definitely.' Emma whisked a couple of the bowls away before Lise could pick up on anything more – partly to not leave poor Gabriel being grilled about his business, wine, food, whatever. Xavier was unpredictable; they could be onto anything by now.

Lise brought the remaining two bowls over and announced, 'It's a simple crumble, very British, apple and blackberry. Emma's mother's recipe.'

Gabriel picked up his spoon. 'Traditional British food – looks and smells wonderful, Lise.'

'Thank you. Dig in,' she urged.

'Wow, this looks just like Mum's.' Emma smiled across at her friend. At the enormous square table, which was the opposite of intimate, her friend was next to Xavier; Emma was next to Gabriel.

But at Xavier's first mouthful, he began to cough.

'Did you burn your mouth?' Lise's face fell. 'I'm sorry, I should've left it to stand out of the oven a bit longer.'

It took him a while to recover, after a sip from the glass of water she handed him. 'How much sugar did you put on it?'

'The right amount.' Slighted, Lise looked around the table to see whether the others had an issue. 'Is it really terrible?'

Gabriel was the first to insist that it wasn't. 'It's delicious, not too sweet for me.'

Xavier didn't seem to have a volume switch now. 'Oh come on,' he said in French, 'you own a café; you must be able to taste it's not right.'

Lise clearly had a better grasp of the language than her boyfriend realised and immediately tried to take the bowls away. But Emma clung onto hers. 'Lise, it tastes like my mum's. I'm having every last mouthful whether you like it or not.'

'Me too,' said Gabriel.

Xavier staggered off to the bathroom, leaving an awkward Lise at the table with their guests.

'I think he's had a lot of wine tonight.' Lise spoke without looking up.

Emma wasn't sure whether to console her or stay quiet. She chose the latter and thankfully, Gabriel leapt in by saying perhaps the wine made the dessert taste funny and then totally changed the subject by telling them about his outing last night to the new bowling alley for a friend's birthday. Emma could've hugged the life out of him for it, for being so perceptive about the discomfort.

Xavier wasn't much better company when he plonked himself back into his seat. 'I think I'll stay home if you lot go bowling.' He sloshed the rest of the bottle of wine into his glass.

'You're no good at bowling?' Gabriel asked the question in French. Up until now, Emma had to hand it to him: he'd been courteous and polite, patient and let things go when he could've retaliated. But he wasn't a saint – the man was getting to him. Plus he had ammunition and explained that the guys he'd played against were heavily into the game, much more serious than anyone he knew and he'd gone along for a catch-up rather than a win.

Xavier stiffened at being put in his place; Lise looked uncomfortable.

'I never said I wasn't any good,' Xavier said quickly. 'I just don't enjoy the game. It's mostly for kids, isn't it?'

Gabriel, to give him his due, didn't laugh in the man's face but instead began to regale knowledge of tournaments, tours, championships and the European Bowling Federation. He threw in names of past winners, cited reports from the World Tenpin Bowling Association. But when he moved on to talking about the friend of his who played in America, Xavier saw his chance to interrupt.

'*Nous sommes en Paris!*' Xavier declared with a flamboyant raise of an arm. And then he disappeared off to another room.

Lise topped up everyone's glass of water and Emma noticed she gave her boyfriend a nice full glass. But Emma was also pretty sure Xavier wasn't going to drink it.

When Xavier emerged from the other room, it seemed he had another plan in mind other than wine, because he took out a little box, a packet of rolling papers and a lighter and, as though he was doing something as regular as making them all a cup of tea at the end of a meal, he set everything up and began to roll a joint.

Emma's jaw dropped. She'd seen enough of Alison smoking dope during their year of postgraduate teacher training and watching Xavier now reminded her of why she detested the stuff. Some thought it harmless; she knew otherwise. She wanted to walk out, leave right there and then with the perfect excuse that she couldn't be around it, but Lise had invited her here and she couldn't do it to her friend.

Lise also knew all about Alison and the effect it had had on Emma. She shifted in her seat and muttered something quietly to Xavier, and judging by Lise's face, he'd completely misunderstood her when he uttered his apologies for being rude and not offering his guests the same option for after their meal.

There were shakes of heads, murmurs of refusal, Xavier carrying on as though this were perfectly normal. And poor Lise looked panicked that Emma was going to get up and walk out.

When Gabriel's phone rang and he excused himself to take a call from his mother, he went all the way down the hallway towards the apartment's front door so he could hear better – or maybe he wanted to run through it like she did and never come back.

Xavier made some remark, in French of course, as he likely hoped Emma would miss it, about Gabriel being a mummy's boy. Emma could feel her anger beginning to surface but she put a lid on it. As soon as Gabriel came back, they'd make their excuses and leave. They had to be at work early – that would do.

Xavier put an arm around Lise, the joint between his fingers. He planted a kiss on her cheek. And as he apologised to her over what he'd said about the dessert, Emma just cringed. She'd gone from wondering whether she'd misjudged the man before tonight to feeling like she'd judged him in exactly the right way – arrogant, possessive, and not right for her friend.

Xavier sucked the joint dry. Emma couldn't even bear the smell – it was such a reminder of those days with Alison and her addiction. He picked up the spoon from his bowl still in front of him and ate some of the crumble. He didn't even wince once, which had Emma convinced he'd made a whole song and dance about his girlfriend's cooking because he was trying to show off.

Gabriel at last returned to them and assured Emma that his mother was fine. She'd not been well lately, although Gabriel hadn't elaborated much but he was worried enough that he'd left his phone on during the dinner, which he didn't do unless it was important.

Lise served coffees following yet another apology to her friend for Xavier's behaviour and the fact he'd smoked a joint. Emma had told her it was fine – it wasn't. She couldn't wait to leave. This evening had gone from mildly uncomfortable to practically suffocating.

When Xavier got a knock at the door and jumped up to go and take delivery of a couple of cases of wine he'd been expecting, Emma took the chance to give their excuses.

'No, stay a bit longer,' Lise pleaded. 'Is it the joint? Because I promise it's only recreational – he hardly ever does it.'

'But he still does it, Lise. And you know how I feel about it.' So did Gabriel – she'd told him all about Alison not long after they met.

'I'm so sorry. I didn't think he'd do it when we had guests.' She put a hand on Emma's arm. 'Please stay. I like you being here.'

Any remaining doubt about leaving was soon erased when Xavier came into the kitchen again, wallet in his hand and demanded, in gruff French, whether Lise had taken out fifty euros.

When she told him no, he turned on Emma and Gabriel, or at least Gabriel, and demanded the same.

A sinking feeling told Emma she knew where this was going – Gabriel had been out in the hallway answering his call. He had the perfect opportunity to take the money.

Gabriel denied it, more than once when Xavier wouldn't let it go. In the end, Lise found her purse, gave Xavier some cash and he went back to the door to tip the delivery guy.

And that was it, evening over.

21

THEN: 2006

Lise

It was a rainy morning in mid-April, the rain coming down so hard, Lise wasn't sure she'd even venture beyond the apartment today. She put the heating up higher and did her best to concentrate on learning more business French to distract her from thinking about Emma. She lasted less than an hour before she picked up the phone to call her best friend, only to get the answer machine again. She put the receiver down and slumped back onto the sofa.

Since the night of the dinner, Lise had barely seen anything of her best friend. She'd moved into Xavier's apartment and Emma had kept their place, which was paid for in advance. Lise had picked up the last of her bags but Emma had been aloof and Lise was tired of trying to make sense of it. Lise knew all about Alison and her addiction and the things she'd done to Emma, but Xavier wasn't Alison. This wasn't the same.

When Emma and Gabriel had left the apartment the night of the dinner, Lise and Xavier had fought about the accusation of the missing money – Emma was undeniably still mad about that too even though Lise had apologised to them both after Xavier subsequently found the cash down the side of the stand in the hallway. It had likely fallen out of his wallet when he was trying to pull out some euros and he hadn't noticed. Lise and Xavier had argued about the joint, about how much he'd drunk. They'd yelled at each other, and Lise had burst into tears when she'd seen all her belongings she'd only just brought over to his place, the beautiful Parisian apartment she'd seen herself as calling home one day.

Back when she was at school, at university, even in the workplace, she'd see other women with men who were clearly bad news. Men who treated women badly, who expected to control who they saw, spoke to, spent time with. She'd thought the women were crazy to be putting up with it but when she realised that here she was doing the same with Xavier, she realised how easy it was to slip into a life and stay there. And before she could think too deeply about whether Xavier was really a man she wanted to live with and have in her life long term, he'd surprised her with an enormous bouquet of red, velvety smooth roses, an apology so heartfelt and honest that she'd seen him as a man with flaws rather than someone to get away from.

When he came in from work that evening, she'd been focused on her textbooks, trying to learn a lot more of the jargon for her job choice. Some of it was sinking in; some of it went in one ear and out the other.

He came to her side, took her hand and made her stand next to him, her body pressed against his. But rather than kiss him as she expected, he said, 'I need to apologise to your friends, Annalise.'

She put a hand against his chest, her fingertips brushing the hair of his chest at the top of his unbuttoned shirt. 'You'd really do that?'

He took her face in his hands. 'For you, I'd do anything. I hate that I upset you.' He kissed her once, firmly, muttered more and more apologies in French, the beautiful language having its effect.

Lise smiled across at the silky roses standing proudly in their vase. 'You already apologised.' She'd put a vase in here, one in the kitchen to add a bit of colour, another in the bedroom.

'And I'll keep doing it. Please, let me say sorry to Emma, to Gabriel.'

She wrapped her arms around him, held him tight. He was a good man, wasn't he?

Lise had wondered whether Gabriel would even give Xavier the time of day when he called the café but clearly he had because they were invited to the café near Montmartre after hours the following week. Lise went in feeling sheepish because even though she hadn't been in the wrong, Xavier very much was. He'd accused Gabriel of stealing, he'd used drugs in front of their guests, he'd been rude.

Gabriel and Xavier seemed the only two who weren't awkward. Whatever they'd said in that phone call, obviously it had cleared the air. Perhaps it was a guy thing, a bit like the boys in the playground at school – girls would carry on with the bitchy looks, the vendettas, the undercurrent forever more; boys would land a few punches on each other and that would be it. Time to move forwards. There was a lot to be said for it.

Xavier expressed his apologies for accusing Gabriel and making the both of them uncomfortable but as the men went over to the counter to share another beer, presumably to talk in their native tongue and leave the girls to have their time together, Emma didn't seem willing to move on.

'Emma, please, Xavier apologised. He really is very sorry.'

'I'm sure he is.'

'What's that supposed to mean?'

'He didn't apologise about drinking too much.'

'Oh come on, have you *ever* apologised to anyone when you've been drunk? No, you have a good time, you move on.'

'What about the joint?'

Lise had known Xavier was never going to apologise for that specifically, only that he'd made his guests uncomfortable, but she told Emma, 'He's sorry he did it in front of you both, said it won't ever happen again.' Actually, it was she who'd said it wouldn't, that it couldn't.

'I'm worried about you, Lise.'

'You're acting as though I'm living in a crack den.' She kept her voice low although the men looked as though they were in deep conversation about something so likely wouldn't hear them anyway.

'I'm not worried about the cannabis. Although maybe I am. But is that all he's into?'

'Yes, of course.' The fact was, Lise didn't really know but she was put out by her friend asking as though she needed a guardian angel on her shoulder when it came to men. 'If you're not worried about the cannabis, Emma, then what are you worried about?'

'I'm worried about you being with *him*.' She said *him* like he was a rodent that needed exterminating.

And now there was no softness in Lise's reaction. The chair Lise was sitting on scraped across the floor as she stood up. 'I don't have to listen to this bullshit, Emma. You're taking this way too seriously. He apologised so you need to move on. What's done is done.'

'Yeah,' said Emma, clearly not believing anything of the sort. 'What's done is done.'

* * *

Lise rolled off Xavier onto her back. They'd got home from the café, gone straight to bed and just when she thought she'd seen all his moves, he surprised her again. She'd wanted to ask him about what he and Gabriel talked about, how they'd managed to go from barely tolerating each other to as if they were brothers all in the space of a phone call and an evening over beers. She'd wanted to tell him about Emma but at the same time didn't want any more tension between them than there already was.

Xavier's eyes were closed. She leaned over and kissed him, picked up his discarded shirt from the end of the bed and loosely wrapped it around herself before she went into the kitchen. With an ice-cold glass of orange juice, she was about to go back to the bedroom when she noticed her phone on the island bench.

The display showed ten missed calls. From Emma.

And Lise doubted she was calling her to tell her how much she didn't like her boyfriend.

Lise called her back. 'What's going on, Emma? Are you all right?'

As Emma spoke, Lise could barely understand her.

'Calm down, Emma; talk slowly. What's happened?'

Sobbing, Emma got out, 'It's Gabriel. He was stopped by the police.'

And while Xavier slept on, Emma told her that Gabriel had been pulled over on their drive home from the café to her apartment. He'd failed to stop at a stop sign. One of the officers had breathalysed him, they'd asked to see his licence and when he'd rummaged in his bag to find it, a tin fell out and they must've sensed something was off by the way he grabbed it and shoved it back in so quickly. The tin had contained a large quantity of cannabis.

As soon as she got off the phone, unable to calm her hysterical friend, Lise went to wake Xavier. When he didn't stir, she shoved him harder than she usually would and he swore in French, the words easy to translate.

Lise lost it with him; she knew the drugs must have come from him. 'What the fuck were you thinking? You know Emma and Gabriel aren't into smoking dope!'

Xavier shrugged and had the audacity to open up the bedside table drawer and take out a packet of cigarettes, light one up. 'He obviously does it.'

'He does not! Emma wouldn't be with him if he did.'

He blew out rings of smoke and shrugged. 'Then why did he ask me for some?'

Her shoulders slumped. 'What?'

'That's right.' He grunted, put the lit cigarette between his lips and let it dangle as he got out of bed and yanked on his pyjama bottoms.

'I don't believe you.'

He ripped the cigarette from his lips. 'Before you blame the evils of the world on me, maybe ask him about it.'

Lise didn't sleep a wink that night. She sent umpteen messages to Emma, all of which went unanswered. And she didn't speak to her friend until the next day when she showed up at Xavier's apartment.

But Emma hadn't come for her.

'Where is he?' Emma demanded.

Lise closed the door and followed after her friend, who looked like a hunter ready to close in on their prey. If she kept going from room to room, she'd find him eventually, in the shower.

'Where is he, Lise?' she yelled yet again.

'Emma, calm down.'

'Do not tell me to calm the fuck down!'

Lise held up her hands. 'What's going on? Just tell me that.'

'Gabriel is in trouble. And your boyfriend played a big part in it, but Gabriel being Gabriel won't give up who sold him the drugs even though it might make things better for him. You know why? Because he's a better man than Xavier ever was.'

'Stop yelling at me.' Lise wasn't sure whether she should argue back or just let Emma have her say but the matter was taken out of her hands when Xavier emerged from the bathroom, just his lower half wrapped in a towel, droplets of water cascading down his chest.

'Thought I heard voices,' he said as if this were just an ordinary day.

Emma rounded on him and Xavier took it all, the hurling accusations, the shove of Emma's hand against his chest, the name-calling from Emma who had lost her mind.

'Emma...' Lise interrupted, trying to bring some calm to the situation. 'Talk to me: where is Gabriel now?'

'He went down to the police station again, said he had to.'

'And what's going on exactly?'

'I don't know, Lise. I really don't know. Delphine won't look at me unless it's with contempt.' She rounded on Xavier again. 'Why can't you admit the drugs were yours?'

He clutched the knot in his towel as though suspicious Emma might tug it off just to make an example of him. 'What good would it do?'

Emma didn't answer. She couldn't; she must know it wouldn't help Gabriel with whatever he was facing.

Lise wished Xavier would keep his mouth shut but he seemed up for an argument when he goaded Emma, adding, 'I didn't make your lover buy the cannabis. He asked; I gave.'

Emma turned to Lise again, her venom coming her way. 'So he's a drug dealer now?'

Xavier shook his head and went off to the bedroom, presumably to get dressed.

Lise put a hand to her friend's arm. 'Emma, please talk to me. What's really going on? Has Gabriel been cautioned? Fined? Arrested? Will he have a record?'

Tears filled Emma's eyes. 'I don't know, Lise. He won't see me. He left before I woke up this morning. I went to the café and Delphine is barely uttering a word apart from to bark orders at me.'

'Oh, Emma.' She pulled her friend to her and for a moment, Emma let herself be comforted.

But Xavier made it worse, again, when he came out with jeans on and wrestling a T-shirt down over his bare chest. 'Time for you to leave,' he growled at Emma.

Lise moved in front of her friend, separating her from Xavier. 'Emma, let me come out with you and we'll go somewhere, talk about this. Let me help you.'

'Annalise,' Xavier warned from behind her.

Lise turned and looked at him. Was he seriously asking her to choose between him and her best friend?

But before she could react, Emma did. 'The both of you have done enough. You're welcome to each other.' Her fury left Lise speechless. Emma looked her in the eye. 'You probably don't realise this yet but you've picked a man who is just like your dad.'

Lise was about to deny it, say that of course she hadn't, but Emma walked away before she could say anything else.

In this moment, her best friend hated her and she had no idea how to fix it.

As soon as the door slammed shut after Emma, Lise turned on Xavier, his nonchalance right now infuriating. 'You just made things so much worse. Why couldn't you stay out of it?'

'How is this my fault?' he yelled back. 'Nothing I said was a lie.

And you brought me into it by accusing me in the first place.' He added a few swear words for good measure.

'Gabriel might be in serious trouble!'

'It's not something we can fix.'

'Don't you even care?'

His voice rose louder than ever before as he yelled in French about how he'd done the man a favour and now he was in the wrong because Gabriel was stupid enough to get caught.

'You're an arsehole!' He was acting as though this was a minor inconvenience when what had happened had blown her friend's life apart.

'I don't have to take this,' he hissed. 'If you don't like the way I am, Annalise, then leave. Move out, go, do whatever you like.' And with one more trip into the bedroom, he grabbed a shirt, car keys and, muttering more than one or two insults, was out of the door within minutes.

22

THEN: 2006

Emma

Delphine set down a pile of plates next to the sink with a crash loud enough to startle the whole of Montmartre, never mind Emma, who jolted. She barked an instruction in French, something Emma didn't even understand, but she was beginning to realise that was likely Gabriel's sister's intention.

When Delphine wasn't looking, Emma tried yet again to call Gabriel. He wasn't taking her calls, he wasn't answering the door to his apartment and, when she'd asked Delphine where he was, she blatantly ignored the question and told her to get to work with an additional muttering in French that no doubt had a few insults buried in it.

The night Gabriel had been pulled over by the police, they'd both thought it would be a simple traffic stop, he'd get a warning or a fine and they'd drive away and he'd tell her he should've been more careful.

Emma would never forget his face when the police officers found the cannabis. Most of their conversation had been in French but Emma knew enough to get the gist. And in the time the officers spoke to Gabriel, he never once looked her way; he avoided her gaze no matter how many times she said his name or reached out for his hand.

The following afternoon, she'd gone to the police station when there was no answer at his apartment but they weren't helpful. She felt a nuisance. She'd sat there waiting for someone to take her aside and all she'd got was a dismissal when it turned out Gabriel wasn't there and they couldn't help her. To them, he was just another man who'd done the wrong thing; to her, her life was falling apart.

Emma had been back every day to his apartment, in the morning before work, at lunchtime, in the evening. She'd sat on the step to the apartment building until she began to draw unwelcome attention from men piling out of a nearby bar.

Gabriel had disappeared from her life almost as quickly as he'd come into it.

And so Emma kept showing up for work. This was partly his business. Surely he'd have to come in sooner or later and she wanted to be there waiting.

But at closing time, after Emma had mopped the floor, doing everything she could to be a help rather than any form of hindrance, Delphine came over with a small, brown envelope.

And this time, she spoke in English. Funny, in all this time, she'd never really used English. A stranger could be forgiven for thinking she didn't know any but now it was crystal clear.

'That's the last of your pay,' Delphine said, hands on hips, talking above the rain that came down so hard beyond the awning that it sent splashes onto the edges of the nice clear floor. 'Today is your last day.'

'But you need the help.'

Delphine guffawed. 'I do not need your help.'

'But—'

'Goodbye, Emma.'

Emma didn't move straight away. She let the rain splash the backs of her legs as she stood on the periphery of leaving the café, stepping away from this world she'd found.

'I need to close the doors now,' Delphine snapped.

'I'm not going until you talk to me.'

Delphine slammed a set of keys down on the nearby table. 'I have nothing to say to you other than you ruined my brother's life. I curse the day you even came into it.'

'Where is he?' The words were out without acknowledging the hateful comment that had come her way.

'Gone. You don't need to know. All you need to know is he never wants to see you again. Go, leave my family alone. Go!'

Emma started at the last order, delivered with such hatred.

She grabbed her bag from the hook out back and ran through the café, out of the section of door Delphine hadn't yet closed, into the rain and almost into the path of a cyclist whose hand gestures and yelling were never going to make her feel worse than she already did.

There was nothing left for her in Paris. Nothing. No boyfriend, no friend, no job and no yearning for adventure.

And it didn't matter that she was in her twenties – the little girl was still inside of her and she'd never wanted to go home to her parents more in her entire life.

23

THEN: 2006

Lise

In the week that followed the awful dinner party at Xavier's apartment, Lise didn't see or hear from Emma. She hadn't left Xavier's apartment straight away; she'd wanted to see if they could work this out. But the rows continued, both of them so angry for very different reasons. Xavier had expected her to be in his corner and not question him; Lise had hated how blasé he was about the whole affair, the absence of any guilt on his part that he'd supplied the cannabis in the first place. And when their arguing reached new levels both in volume and insults back and forth, Lise packed a suitcase and headed for the apartment she shared with Emma. If she was there then her friend would finally have to face her; they'd have to talk this through. She'd do anything to help, whatever she could.

What she didn't expect when she was fumbling for her keys outside the apartment was for Emma's brother Toby to open the front door.

'What are you doing here?'

'I could ask you the same thing.' He hugged her tight.

Her smile faded as they pulled apart and she hauled her suitcase inside. 'This is where I live.'

'Emma says you moved out.'

Shirtily she replied, 'And now I'm back.' She wheeled the case into her bedroom and found the sheets rumpled before she turned to Toby. 'You've moved in?'

He pulled a face and dashed past her to hastily pick up a few clothing items from the floor and shove them into a sports bag. 'Didn't think you'd mind me crashing in here for a few days, especially given the circumstances of my visit, but I apologise – it's out of order.'

She slumped down onto the bed and lay back, arms above her head. 'I don't mind, not really.' And then she propped herself back up onto her elbows. 'Wait, you're here because of what's going on with Gabriel?'

He came over to join her. 'Emma called Mum in a right state. I offered to be the one to come to Paris and see if she needed help. She wasn't making much sense on the phone. You know what you women are like when you're crying – incoherent at best.'

'Shut up,' she said through her own tears, which had begun to flow so much, she felt his arm go around her.

After a few minutes, while she tried to talk about what had happened, he said, 'See, I've no idea what you're saying. Like I said, incoherent.' He nudged her in jest, which had her laughing but did nothing to stem the tears. He pulled her into another hug. 'What a mess.'

'Total fucking mess.'

'You always were good with words. How's that PR career going anyway? I assume you use those phrases in your promotional materials?'

He'd made her smile more than she had in days but the smile

didn't last long. 'Where is she, Toby? She won't take my calls; I daren't go to the café to try to find her.'

'I think she's gone to work or to try to see Gabriel at his apartment again.'

She sat up, her tear-stained face looking at him. 'Try?'

'He's refusing to see her. He's not working at the café either and his sister is keeping schtum about everything. Emma is pretty much cut out from whatever is happening.'

'Delphine was never the kindest to Emma. But I don't understand Gabriel. Why would he push Emma away?'

'No idea. I don't know Gabriel, never met him.'

'Oh God.' She sat forwards, arms resting on her thighs.

'She sounds a mess, Lise. And by the sounds of it, Gabriel's sister blames her.'

She got up, started to pace. 'This is all my fault. Xavier sold him the cannabis.'

'So how is that your fault?'

'Because...'

'You know the thing Emma doesn't understand is that Gabriel never did drugs. I asked Emma if he thought they'd been planted but she said no, that he'd admitted he'd bought them.'

Lise picked up her bag.

'Where are you going?'

'I have to go find her.'

'Lise, this is Paris – you don't have any idea where to start. At least let me come with you.'

'No, you stay here in case she comes back. I need to know she's okay. I'm going crazy not hearing from her.'

It was ridiculous to go searching, a bit like the proverbial needle in a haystack, but it didn't stop Lise from heading out onto the streets to try some of their favourite haunts – the little bistro they'd been to whenever they could afford it, the cosy café next to the launderette where they'd taken their washing when their machine broke, the crêperie at Montmartre, the streets surrounding Gabriel's café. She even hovered outside the café itself but didn't get closer when she saw Gabriel's sister and no sign of anyone else. She already had Emma mad at her and Xavier; she didn't need it from her too.

She tramped back to the apartment and when she let herself in, Toby got to his feet.

'Lise, she's gone.'

'What are you talking about?'

'She came here, filled a suitcase, asked me to pack everything else up for her and send it on. Back to England.'

'No...' She ran into Emma's bedroom in disbelief, but all the signs were there that her friend had said goodbye to a significant part of their lives, the part that had changed their friendship forever. Her trifold mirror was still there but none of the little necklaces were draped over its tallest points; the wardrobe was open but bare except for wire hangers, a lot of which were bent out of shape; the bed was made but the soft teddy bear on top had gone.

Toby was at her side quick enough to hold her up as she cried, 'She's really gone; she left.'

Had she lost Emma for good?

* * *

Lise spent days sobbing into her pillow, wallowing as Toby packed up the rest of Emma's things and arranged for them to be returned to England. She didn't go to her job working for Xavier; he didn't call to ask her why not. It was such a casual arrangement, she had nobody to answer to. She was the boss's girlfriend, British and on the outer of the team in so many respects.

Toby stayed in Emma's room, giving Lise hers back and allowing her space to get her head more sorted if that was possible. A few days after the boxes of her best friend's belongings had been collected and were on the way back to Bath, Toby asked Lise whether she was going to leave Paris given they'd come for a year and there were only a few months left.

'And go back to England?' she asked him. She was putting make-up on for the first time in almost a week, glad her eyes had lost some of their puffiness now the tears had dried. She and Toby were going out to a bistro this afternoon, given it was his last day here before he got on the Eurostar tomorrow and it whizzed him all the way back to London.

'Yes, your home.'

She pushed the wand back into the mascara tube and screwed it on tight. 'Is it? I'm not so sure any more. Maybe Paris is my home. And Emma left *me* here, remember.'

'Well her boyfriend doesn't want to know her; her work conditions became intolerable with Delphine. You can hardly blame her for wanting to get away.' He held his hands up in defence to ward off another argument.

After a few strokes of trademark red lipstick, Lise felt the most human she'd felt in days. She'd spent a long time crying, time trying to contact Emma on the phone, but now she felt sad and a part of her was angry that Emma hadn't hung around and talked to her. It made her feel as though Emma placed less value on their friendship than she did, and what happened wasn't Lise's fault. Neither of the girls had done anything wrong.

At the bistro, they ordered a platter to share and over cheddar croquettes, squid fritters with a creamy tartar sauce and tender chicken, slowly Lise began to feel a bit better and more like herself.

After Toby's third attempt to eat the escargot – he gagged every time it touched his tongue, which Lise found hilarious – he asked, 'So, where does this all leave you and the chef?'

Lise plucked the escargot from his fingertips and put it out of its misery. 'He has a name you know.'

'Easier not to use it. I've never met the guy but...'

'Emma told me I'd picked a man just like my dad.'

'Really?'

Lise shrugged. She supposed Xavier had money, a touch of arrogance, indifference to anyone he wasn't really interested in. And if she was honest, Emma's comment got to her so much, her mind had been churning over and over trying to come up with ways that Xavier was nothing like Randall Baker. One thing was for certain: she was the centre of Xavier's world, whereas for her father, she'd merely been a blob on its circumference.

'I'm sorry,' said Toby, 'maybe with this being my last day, we should make him and everything that happened a no-go area for now.'

'Amen to that.' She lifted her glass to his, clinked and drank. She was happy to avoid all talk of the past week and a bit. She wanted to get some of her sanity back.

They talked about Bath a lot – what they loved about living there, Honeybee Place.

'Honeybee Place does have character,' she said. 'I always loved that.'

Toby nodded. 'Homes are transformed behind their closed doors but the exteriors remain pretty much the same. Take your home and ours...' He plucked the last piece of chicken. 'They're both vastly different inside – although I've only seen the ground floor of number twelve – and yet from the front, they look the same. Always did.'

'Vastly different...' She raised her eyebrows. 'That's one way of putting it. Different in appearance, in the families behind them.'

His face fell. 'Lise, I'm sorry, I didn't think. I didn't mean—'

'Don't you dare apologise. I'm not some poor little girl lost. I dealt with it the best way I could. By coming to your place.' She grinned, picked up the drinks menu. 'We need to do some shots.'

'Kind of working on the wine still.'

She caught the waiter's attention and Toby downed the rest of his glass as she ordered tequilas for them.

After a throat-burning shot of tequila, she told Toby, 'Your family mean a lot to me you know.'

The waiter had pre-empted the request for more shots by hovering nearby and he responded quickly and efficiently.

'I know they do,' said Toby. 'And you mean a lot to them.'

'Well I did...'

'This isn't the end, Lise.'

'No?' She picked up the next shot when it was delivered and downed that one too.

'How's your mum doing?'

'We get on better these days.'

'That's a good thing.'

'Or disturbing... My dad died and she found how to talk to me and spend time with me. Kind of sad really.'

When the waiter delivered a third round of shots, Lise paused. 'You're lucky, you know, Toby. Don't ever take your family for granted.'

'I don't.' He watched her down her drink but when she went to raise her hand to get the waiter to bring more, he held it down on her knee. 'Emma will come round, you know.'

She looked at him, his face full of mischief and concern at the same time. She put a hand to his cheek, her palm against the well-clipped beard, the feel of it surprisingly soft. 'Toby, you always were Mr Glass-Half-Full.'

'And so are you, Lise.'

She dropped her hand. 'Yeah, maybe. At least I was.'

'You guys have been best friends forever.'

She lolled against him. 'This wasn't the way things were supposed to go in Paris.'

'I know.' She felt him kiss the top of her head. 'Come on, let's get you home.'

'One for the road?' Head still on his shoulder, she reached out for the shot glass in front of her and found it disappointingly empty.

Toby shook his head the waiter's way, paid their bill and had her out of there quickly enough. She winced when the bright sunshine hit her eyeline like a slap – she'd sworn in the depths of the bistro that it was night-time but they'd emerged into broad daylight.

When they got home, Toby wouldn't let her flop into bed until she'd downed a couple of big glasses of water. She acquiesced and then fell into a heavy sleep.

Emma was gone. Where she went to from here was anyone's guess.

* * *

Lise heard from Xavier a week after Toby returned to England. He called her and said he was sorry, asked her to go back to him. She told him she couldn't, that too much had happened. Her head was all over the place and yet a part of her wanted to so badly. He was an anchor; he wanted her and worshipped her. He'd keep her safe in a ready-made home with a job and as much affection as she could ever ask for.

Xavier persisted over the coming weeks. He called her over and over again, said he missed her, left messages in English and in French. He asked her to go to the restaurant, said the team needed her to discuss strategy for opening the next restaurant. He assured her that she was indispensable and she was a real part of his life. He told her he'd do anything to repair what was broken, although she knew that wasn't possible because he'd never be able to put her and Emma back together.

Lise pushed him away every single time.

Lise called Emma. She tried to catch her at home or at the café, but either got the answer machine or the phone rang and rang until she gave up. Lise sent emails but they went unanswered too and one evening when Xavier knocked on the door to beg for another chance, her resolve to sort her life out once and for all took a turn she didn't expect when she burst into tears in front of him. He wrapped her in his arms and held her. They didn't speak, but the comfort was there for Lise and she didn't feel quite so alone.

She didn't agree to go back to Xavier that night, nor the night after. But a couple of weeks later, she went to his restaurant and through to the kitchen where he was run ragged as usual with orders, zipping this way and that, her strong man, the man who wanted her and wanted to give her a life here in Paris, the City of Lights.

This man, the father of her child.

She'd found out that morning. She'd sat in the bathroom, on the floor with her back resting against the bath tub, waiting to see whether one or two lines appeared in the little plastic viewing panel on the test stick.

When she saw the test was positive, she'd put a hand to her stomach. This baby was meant to be; she was sure of it. And in that moment, she knew she would never let it have the unhappiness she'd felt in her childhood or teenage years, the loneliness and isolation despite having two parents around.

No, her baby would have all the love in the world.

And that meant her life was here, in Paris, with the baby's father.

* * *

Xavier was thrilled to have Lise back. He rallied and took care of her and her pregnancy, forever fussing that she was all right, cooking her food for the baby and her health. And although she wanted to mention Emma, she wanted to mention Gabriel, she didn't talk about either of them. Because she knew it would only cause friction. And this baby deserved parents who were present, who cared.

When she was thirty-eight weeks pregnant and missing her best friend more than words could say, came the devastating news via her mother that Toby Miller had died. He'd been killed in a helicopter crash.

Lise called the Millers' house in Bath, she called the café and still Emma wouldn't speak to her. Brendan and Keely were too devastated to talk and Lise had no words that could ever mend their broken hearts. For months, Lise had been writing emails to Emma, she'd sent letters, but her efforts were futile. Lise realised it was time to accept that Emma didn't want to know her anymore, that that part of her life was over.

Lise gave birth the day of the funeral, her tears for the labour, for the joy, for the pain of Toby, for losing her best friend. And when she cuddled her newborn baby in her arms, she knew all that mattered now was that this little girl was happy, safe. With two parents who loved her more than anything else in the world.

24

NOW: 2023

Lise

Lise made sure she'd pulled herself together by the time she got home, dried any tears after visiting the cemetery. Her head was constantly flitting back and forth from past to the present and managing her emotions at the same time wasn't an easy task.

'This weather sucks,' Maisie declared as she and Naomi came into the kitchen back at number twelve where Lise was emptying the popcorn she'd got at the supermarket into an enormous bowl.

'The rain is really coming down now.' Lise looked beyond the window as she unpacked more of the shopping. 'But it's good for the garden.'

Maisie groaned. 'Mum, that's such an old person thing to say.'

'But it's true!' Lise secretly loved it when her daughter reminded her of the generation gap; it made her feel like she had a certain wisdom with the years that had rolled on by.

'I love the weather no matter what it's like,' Naomi declared and at Maisie's surprise, she shrugged. 'I do. I've always wanted to become a weather forecaster.'

'Good, then you can tell me what clothes to select every day,' said Maisie. 'I'm always getting caught out and I'm sure the weather app is only updated *after* I leave the house. What? It is,' she said at her mum's look of doubt. 'A few days ago, it had no rain symbols and ended up pouring with rain twenty minutes after I left here with no umbrella or rain coat. And last week, the app said cloudy all day, then I was caught without sunglasses.'

Lise liked having Naomi here; she was a great kid. 'So you like science?' she asked her. 'Because it was my least favourite subject at school.'

'Mine too,' added Maisie. 'Especially physics.'

'I *love* science,' Naomi admitted.

'Well good for you,' said Lise as she separated a bunch of bananas and put them in the fruit bowl.

'I don't know if I'm clever enough to become a weather fore-caster,' said Naomi, although Maisie leapt straight into the argu-ment that of course she was and it gave Lise a pang for a blossoming friendship, one that was strong, where you stood up for one another. It was exactly what she'd had and then lost.

'I'm sure if you work hard, Naomi, then the world is your oyster.' Lise folded up the last of the reusable shopping bags and stowed them in the cupboard.

'Dad told me I could be anything I wanted to be when I grew up.'

Lise would've heard no such comment from her own father. 'That's lovely. Was your dad into science too?'

A smiled beamed across Naomi's face. 'He was always fasci-nated with meteorology. He worked with companies to provide weather data to help them plan for the future and make decisions.'

'Sounds complicated.' But as she said it, something in Lise's brain clicked over like a cog in a wheel that got a little bit stuck before it was able to move to the next place. 'He must've been clever.'

'He was.' And when Naomi smiled, another cog in the wheel cranked over at the resemblance of a smile she'd seen before.

'Is your dad around?' Lise's heart thudded. 'Does he live with you guys?'

'Mum!' Maisie groaned.

But Naomi answered. 'I don't mind people asking. My dad died when I was eight and I miss him every single day.'

'I'm sure you do.' Lise's insides plummeted but she had to keep probing. 'What was your dad's name?'

The final cog of the wheel cranked into place when Naomi replied.

'Sam,' she said. 'His name was Sam.'

* * *

Lise's hand smacked against the closed café door and pushed it open, sending it back on its hinges.

'Sam died, and you never told me!' she yelled over to Emma at the counter.

Lise had left the girls with popcorn, cans of fizzy drink and with a smile and a close of the lounge door, they were none the wiser to her fury. But judging by Emma's face now, she had expected this moment to come.

'I have customers,' she bit back, smiling at the three women on the only occupied table, another cluster of customers having coincided their leaving with Lise's whirlwind arrival.

Lise followed her into the kitchen. Emma kept her back to her, dumping plates into the sink, sending a few bubbles flying carelessly into the air.

'Sam died.' She said it again, hands on hips. 'You married Sam.

Our Sam. Our friend.' She wasn't sure what was the worst part: the fact she never knew they got married or the fact her friend had kept his death a secret from her.

'You weren't around; we weren't in touch.' Emma left her post at the sink and grabbed a tray of clean cups to take out to the café.

Lise's voice softened in disbelief. 'But Sam. We were friends, all of us.' Gradually, the three of them had lost touch as university ended and the rest of their lives began, and Lise had often wondered what had happened to their friend. Well now she knew.

She followed Emma into the café as she set the tray on top of the coffee machine at the very back. 'You kept it from me, Emma.'

'You know, Annalise, it's funny... when my husband died, my first thought wasn't you and how you'd feel about it. It was how I was going to go on with the rest of my life without him, how Naomi would cope without a father. You weren't at the forefront of my mind. Hard to believe, I know!' She threw her hands up in the air. 'Now if you don't mind, I have customers.'

Lise waited for Emma to serve the party of three and make their drinks, deliver their slices of cake. All the while, tension mounted and her fury almost got the better of her.

'I get it, Emma,' she said, hot on her tail out to the kitchen again. 'I'm a rubbish friend after what happened in Paris. I stayed with a man you clearly didn't like, we drifted apart and I wasn't there for you enough. And then I couldn't get my boyfriend to somehow rescue yours from the trouble he was in. I'm well aware of all of that. But you know what? You're the one who ran away, who stopped all contact. That was you! We both made mistakes so when are you going to stop putting all of this on me?'

She couldn't bear to wait for an answer and stormed out of the café.

She was getting nowhere fast with Emma.

She snatched up her phone when it rang and snapped a hello,

mellowing at the voice of the estate agent who'd organised the house's rental prior to Lise's arrival. She apologised for her abruptness. And when he talked about the townhouse's potential price, how many people he had on his books itching to get into Honeybee Place, it seemed the logical next step.

She agreed a day and time for the first viewing.

* * *

'Mum's in there,' Lise heard her daughter say after she answered the door while Lise was making pasta arrabbiata for dinner. She was in a total mess – the pasta had boiled over on the stove already, the sauce splashed as she stirred and she'd grated off a fingernail in the cheese and had to bin the entire lot.

She wondered who her visitor was but a deep murmur and she knew it was a man; a peek around the kitchen door and she saw it was Max.

She set the washed grater onto the draining board. 'You're back.' She met him on his way into the kitchen and put her arms around him. She hadn't realised quite how much she'd needed a hug right back. After her run-in with Emma, she was torn between anger, frustration and falling into a heap on the floor and crying all over again.

'I missed you,' he said with his irresistible smile.

She realised Maisie had left them to it and told him, 'I'm glad you did.'

'Something smells good.'

'Is that a hint?' She went over quickly to check she wasn't going to do the same thing again with the pasta, having mopped up the water and set it on high to get it back to simmering.

He shook his head. 'No way, wouldn't intrude.'

'You're not intruding,' Maisie announced as she appeared again

– so she hadn't left them to it – and told him, 'You can stay. Keep Mum company.'

'Approval from the teen,' said Lise with a nod of appreciation. 'She's a tough audience too.'

'She's right, I am. But she hasn't dated anyone in *years*—'

'Maisie…' Lise knew her cheeks weren't only hot from standing so close to the stove.

'Well it's true.' But lucky for Lise, in typical teenage mode, Maisie was already on to the next concern. 'Me and Naomi thought we'd go to the café for a coffee.'

'But dinner will be ready soon. There's enough for Naomi if she wants to stay as well.'

'I'll only be an hour.' Maisie put her hands together in a pleading gesture. 'Can you keep mine warm? A couple of girls from badminton are this way this evening, so we said we'd go and meet them. Please, Mum.'

Naomi must have been in the bathroom but joined her new friend and said a confident hello to Max. Lise sometimes forgot that Max saw Naomi's grandad and Emma all the time. He was already in their lives.

'Go on then,' Lise relented. It was easy to forget how fast teenagers' social lives moved. 'Naomi, are you coming back for some dinner?'

'No thank you, I'm eating with my grandad.'

As soon as the girls left, Max pulled Lise to him. 'You smell good, you know.'

'I do not. I stink of food prep – onions mostly.' Things between them were moving fast but it felt easy; it felt right.

'Then my sense of smell must be off.' He pressed against her, interrupting her cooking to kiss her before he murmured, 'I've been waiting days to do that.'

When they finally took their hands off each other, Max

commandeered the grating of the cheese while Lise found three bowls. 'Naomi and Maisie are getting closer, becoming friends,' he said.

She didn't have to glance his way to know that he was looking at her. 'It's nice, although let's hope Emma doesn't banish Maisie from the café when they go in there.'

'Why would she do that?' He set the bowl of grated cheddar in the centre of the island bench and when she told him the sauce was arrabbiata, he said, 'Isn't it supposed to be Parmesan cheese with a pasta sauce?'

She laughed. 'Not in this house it isn't.'

When she'd come back for the funeral, she and her mother had cooked Bolognese together and when Lise asked where the Parmesan was, the cheese her father insisted was the correct one to top any pasta dish, her mother said she couldn't stand the sharp taste and preferred regular cheddar from the fridge. They'd laughed about it that day and it was the first hint Lise had had that perhaps her mother was pushing herself out of the cocoon she'd been in in her marriage and that perhaps that cocoon had shaped her not only as a wife but as a mother too.

Max wrapped his arms around her waist as she finished spooning some of the sauce into the three bowls on top of the dished-up pasta. 'Back to what you said a minute ago, before I interrupted you with my totally important cheese concerns... Why would Emma banish Maisie from the café?'

Lise moved away from his grasp and covered one of the bowls with a spare saucepan lid. She took the other two over to the island. 'There's plenty more in the pan,' she told him, shuffling her chair in beneath her.

'Stop avoiding the question.'

'I'm not. Well, I am. But that's because I'm still trying to get my head around the fact that Emma was married to Sam.'

He sprinkled a good helping of cheese on top of his pasta. 'And...'

'Sam,' she said again. 'I knew him.' And he clearly had no idea of what she was talking about so as they ate, she went back to the day the girls had first met him, the days they'd hung out as a three-some, the strong friendship until university and life took them all in different directions.

'So you really knew him. Wow, I never realised.'

'I don't suppose Emma talked about me much after Paris and Sam probably knew enough to stay quiet as well.' She frowned. 'I can't believe Mr Miller – Brendan – never told me about Sam being *Sam*.'

'Perhaps he didn't know; I mean, I never knew.'

She wasn't sure the Millers ever met Sam in the days when it had been the three of them in a friendship group. They were so busy with the café and as the girls were older when they met up with Sam, they tended to hang out away from Honeybee Place. His presence would've been fleeting back then and given what had happened between the girls and the way Emma was now, there was every possibility Emma had never told her parents that the three of them had once been close. Sam would've been introduced as someone Emma knew and then the man she was dating. Emma had likely kept Lise's name well and truly out of it, and out of decency and understanding, Sam had probably done the same.

'I heard from Brendan that Sam sometimes talked about you and Emma, how he wished you could somehow work out your differences.'

Knowing that gave Lise a bit of comfort. 'Sam was always fair. And he always liked Emma. Never admitted it of course, but all the signs were there.' As she ate, her comfort gave way to disbelief again. 'He was friends with both of us. He died and she never told me. I found out from Naomi and went over to the café to confront her.'

He stopped chewing momentarily. 'I don't need to guess how that went, do I?'

But she told him anyway, the words that flew back and forth.

'How did he die, Max?'

He set down his fork. 'A brain aneurysm, sudden, unexpected.'

Her own fork clattered into her almost-empty bowl. 'Shit. Poor Emma.' And then she couldn't help it; she started to cry. 'I was her best friend. All the times she needed me and I haven't been there – it hurts, Max, it really hurts.'

He came around to her side of the island and wrapped her tight in his arms. 'She did need you, her best friend. But what about you? You had a baby without her around, you had a crappy marriage and a divorce. There were times you needed her too, Lise.' He ran a thumb beneath her eyes on one side and then the other. 'You're strong but everybody needs someone in their corner. Emma was your person.'

She nodded. 'You know I've done more crying since I got back to this country than I've done in years.'

'Well as long as I don't make you cry, that's all right with me, and I'm always here for a hug you know.'

When they heard the door go, she pulled away, wiped her eyes, puffed out her cheeks and he assured her she looked just fine as Maisie came in to have her own dinner. And with no reference to a drama at the café, at least Lise could be thankful that neither she nor Emma were letting their own troubles impact their daughters' unexpected friendship.

25

NOW: 2023

Emma

It was a few days after Lise had confronted her about Sam, and Emma had thought of little else since. Her anger and her grief were strange bedfellows and yet they still climbed beneath the covers together, especially where Lise was concerned.

'Dad, I'm going to the shops. Do you need anything?' Tara was opening up the café this morning so Emma had time to run some errands and take her dad to his hospital appointment.

She found her dad in the kitchen nursing a mug of tea.

'Dad... need anything from the shops?' she repeated. Perhaps he hadn't heard her. 'Shall I close this?'

'Please.' He nodded to the window he'd opened up behind the sink. The kitchen was aired and bordering on the side of too cold. 'Come, sit down, Emma.'

'Dad, I only have the morning.'

'You can sit for five minutes.'

Her breath caught in her throat. 'What's going on? Are you all right? Dad?'

'I'm fine. Apart from getting older and the usual aches and pains. Now stop fussing.' He set down his tea, about a quarter of an inch left, the way he always left it, disliking the *dregs* as he called them. She and her mum had always found it funny, told him he was wasting half of his tea doing that.

'Then what is this about?' She sat down next to him.

'Lise.'

'What about her?'

'Have you talked to her yet?' When she didn't answer, he told her, 'I saw her again yesterday. She smiled at me as she climbed into the car, apologised she couldn't stop as she had an appointment, but I can sniff an avoidance tactic a mile off. Your brother used to do the same, that shifty look, the claim you have something else on your agenda.'

Emma remembered. 'Toby never carried it off very well, did he. He was way too honest to lie to you. He got away with a few things with Mum, though.'

'I don't need to know about that.'

Silence descended until Emma admitted she'd seen Lise at the café, that Lise found out about Sam.

'We were all friends, Dad.'

'She knew him too?'

Emma explained about the day they'd met Sam, the friendship that had evolved. 'Nobody here knew Sam. He kind of floated in and out of our lives quite seamlessly.'

'Probably a good thing.' The creases around his eyes deepened with amusement. 'At that age, any boy floating in with an almighty thud spells trouble.'

She'd never brought too much trouble to their door, had very few boyfriends before Gabriel, which made losing him all the harder to bear because it had been so real, so consuming.

'I deliberately didn't mention to you and Mum that Lise knew him too.'

'You didn't mention her much at all when you came home.'

'I know.' She gulped. She could still see the pain on Lise's face when she'd confronted her and it gave her no pleasure. 'Not long after I returned from Paris, he came back to Bath from Scotland and by chance, we reconnected.'

'He was a good man, perfect for you.'

While her parents had been upset that something went on in Paris involving a man, a man Emma had been completely in love with, she knew that deep down, they were glad their girl was home. They never would've said. They wouldn't have told her this was where she should stay, but having her own daughter now, she knew how much they would've craved the family being close by.

Brendan realised the true repercussions. 'If Lise didn't know you married a mutual friend, she never knew he died either.'

'No, and that's made her pretty angry with me.'

'I can understand why.'

She'd never admitted it before but when Sam died, the first person she'd thought of after their daughter was Lise. She'd questioned whether she should try to contact Lise to tell her, but their falling-out had been so long ago, Lise had no idea Sam was in Emma's life, let alone as her husband and the father of her child. And then the wondering had turned to monumental pain at her loss of Sam and so Emma had blocked out further thoughts of Lise. She'd got out of bed every single day and done her best to learn how to be in a world where her husband and the father of her child no longer existed except in her memories.

'Emma, I don't know exactly what happened in Paris – I'm not sure I want to or need to – but I do know that when there's a falling-out, there are usually at least two sides to a story, sometimes more than that. Was Lise's part in it really so awful that you don't want to give her a chance to talk with you? She says she's here to do up her mum's place, get it ready for sale, but I can see through that in the same way I see through an avoidance tactic. She came here for you, Emma. Plain as day, she wants to fix things between the two of you.'

And as Emma drove to the supermarket, she knew deep down that he was right.

* * *

'Thanks so much for managing on your own.' Emma arrived at the café mid-morning, ready to let Tara go on a much-needed break.

'No worries and I've done it before. It's all good.' She picked up her bag and coat. 'I'll be back for the lunchtime rush.'

Liam, who was staying with the Cavendishes at number nine, came in with his aunt and uncle and Emma felt a flutter of nerves as they sat down at one of the tables. He was definitely looking her way and she needed to stay professional, not act like a giggly schoolgirl, which was exactly the way she felt right now.

At the counter, Liam ordered three slices of Victoria sponge and three cups of tea. 'You have a wonderful café here.'

'Thank you.' She smiled. 'Are you enjoying Bath?' Her heart thumped.

'I am. I'm hoping to see a lot more of it too.'

She didn't miss him glance over once or twice after he was settled at his table with tea and cake. He was intelligent-looking, handsome with dark hair longer on top, and round-framed glasses he carried off well.

With a sigh, Emma shook away the feeling she hadn't had in a very long time, the feeling that perhaps she might be more than a mother, a widow and a café owner, that maybe she still had a lot of living to do.

Emma talked and laughed with Mrs MacFadden from number twenty, Mr Sewell who had lived at number six for decades and still remembered Emma as a little girl with scraped knees as he was fond of reminding her. Between customers, she juggled the task of making a couple of quiches, two sponge cakes and a fruit pie. And from late morning to early evening, it seemed the Café on the Corner was the hotspot in the city and even Tara hung around until 6 p.m., their usual closing time.

'You go,' Emma assured her. 'I'll finish up. And enjoy a lie-in tomorrow – you've well and truly earned it.'

Out in the kitchen now the sign on the door at the front was turned to closed, Emma finished the last of the washing up, scrubbing hard against the tin to clean off the part of the pie crust that had stuck. She hadn't had a chance to wash it straight away and now, much like every other time that happened, she was paying for it with twice as hard a job. Still, she couldn't complain – the café was thriving and it gave her a flicker of a reminder at Sam's encouragement on some of the toughest days at the start.

On the last day of her first week working in the café pretty much solo, Sam had come in to see her and she'd confessed, 'I don't know how my parents did this day in, day out.' Her mum popped in when she could, her dad too, and even if it was only with moral support, she welcomed it.

'You do know,' he said, turning a chair in the café around so that he was straddling it but resting his forearms on the back of it. 'They did it for the love of this place and much as you were adamant teaching was for you and that would always be the way, I see the same fire in your eyes running this café as I saw in theirs.'

'It doesn't feel like fire; it feels like exhaustion.' She had her head resting on the table, the table that still had crumbs on it and was in desperate need of a wipe.

'If I thought this wasn't for you, Emma, I'd have talked you out of it when you made the decision to jump in and help.' He wrapped his arms around her when there were no customers left.

She felt herself relax in his embrace. He'd always been able to calm her down with the power of a hug. Less stressed, she told him, 'I remember when I thought my brother was after this place. God I fought for it, tried to sell my parents on the idea that I should be the one to take over. And then I changed my mind, never thought I'd be back here.'

'The question is, Emma, are you here to stay?' he murmured against her ear, putting them in danger of being completely inappropriate in the workplace. 'Whatever you decide, I will support you and you should know that your parents will too.'

At first, she'd taken the café on for their benefit. She didn't want them spending the last of their days watching a stranger take on their legacy, changing it in ways they hated, there on the corner tormenting them. But since she set foot in here on day one and became her own boss, she'd felt a connection tug at her so hard, she wasn't sure it would or could ever sever.

The last of the crust floated off in the hot, soapy water now and Emma set the tin on the draining rack. She squeezed out a cloth, picked up the surface cleaner and took it out to give the counter a once-over. She finished wiping around the base of the till and was about to dump the cloth in the kitchen, take off her apron at the end of another day and switch the rest of the lights off when she looked up and saw beyond the doors to the café. Lise. With Max. They were walking on the opposite side of the road.

Emma went out to the kitchen so she wasn't spotted. She steadied herself against the sink. Was her dad right? Had Lise come back for reasons other than to sort out her mum's house? She felt terrible at how much anger she still harboured and threw in Lise's direction. She'd acted terribly about Sam, not getting word to her somehow, at least eventually. Naomi had talked about her dad yesterday and that was when Emma realised how Lise had found out, that Naomi had been talking about him when she was over at number twelve. It should never have come out that way. It was a hurtful thing to do, and Emma was the only one responsible for that.

She took a deep breath, hung up her apron and switched off the kitchen light followed by the one in the small hallway area that led out to the café itself.

But as she emerged into the café and reached across to switch off the light behind the counter, a movement in the corner of her eye made her stop.

Lise. There in the doorway, the palm of her hand pressed against the glass as though she'd been thinking about knocking and changed her mind.

Their gazes met and for a moment, neither of them moved.

'We're closed,' Emma mouthed eventually.

Lise pointed up at the sign she could clearly read. 'I know,' she mouthed back.

Emma went over to unlock the door. If nothing else, she knew she should apologise about Sam.

When Lise came inside, it felt almost natural to go and stand back behind the counter, never mind whether the café was open or not. 'I was about to leave.'

Lise tentatively walked a little closer, hands in the pockets of a beautiful, faux-fur, black coat that suited her well.

'I saw you, with Max,' said Emma before Lise could say another word.

Lise nodded, looked at the floor. 'It's early days.'

'I'm happy for you.'

Lise's gaze snapped up. 'Really?'

Emma smiled. 'Really.' The café wasn't in total darkness but near enough, the air between them filled with tension. 'Lise, I'm really sorry about the other day, the way I reacted. I was wrong to do that to you, wrong not to tell you about Sam.'

'That he died or that you married him?'

'Both.' She gestured to one of the tables, the light in here enough for a conversation, her dad's words very much coming back to her now. 'Sam came along in my life at a time when I thought I was broken,' she began. 'I've had so much grief, for Gabriel, for Toby, for Sam and for my mum.'

'It's a wonder you're still standing,' Lise said softly.

'Yeah, well I am, and sometimes it's easier for me to be a total bitch than try to say sorry and see my own part in any of what happened between us.'

Tears pricked at the corners of Lise's eyes. 'You're not a bitch.'

'Oh I think we've all got a bit of bitch in us.'

Lise wiped beneath her eyes, mouth open as she stemmed tears and her fingers did their best to save her mascara. 'Fuck, now you've got me crying.'

'Please don't swear in my café.'

Lise looked around. 'There's nobody here for fuck's sake.'

'There you go again.' But she was smiling too as she went to each of the windows in turn and pulled down the blinds. She switched off the light closest to the door and left only the light behind the counter, ample for them but not so much that anyone would be mistaken that the café was still open for business.

'How did you and Sam get together?'

Emma smiled, the memory warm and comforting. 'I bumped into him outside the abbey one night. I'd been to the carol concert, so had he. Oh, it was so lovely to see him. I was there with some girlfriends and he asked me out to dinner. We didn't stop talking all evening. It was amazing. He walked me home, kissed me good-night and we arranged to meet up the next day, then the day after that, and then I'm not sure we went more than a couple of days without seeing each other. It moved fast.' She added, 'I didn't tell him about you, not then anyway. I let him believe you were living it up in Paris, which to be fair you might well have been and I always hoped you were. I never wanted you to be unhappy.'

'I'm glad you had Sam.'

'Do you mean that?'

'Of course I do.'

'Gabriel was my first true love. He was the one, or so I thought at the time. And I was always honest with Sam about him. But when Sam proposed, I realised how much I'd changed, how much I'd fallen for him without ever expecting to. Sam made me really happy. We were pregnant before we even set a date for the wedding and things were wonderful between us.

'When Sam found out what happened between you and I, he wanted me to return to Paris. He did his utmost to convince me, but I dug my heels in. I just couldn't do it.'

Lise looked around the café. The tables empty, bereft of any beverages or food waiting to be enjoyed. 'So you stayed, you took over this place.'

'I think this place was partly my saviour as well as Sam. After Toby died, life was never going to be normal again and Sam knew before I did that this was what I needed.' She looked down at her lap briefly. 'He had a way of seeing the real me.'

'That's nice. That's love,' said Lise so honestly, it made Emma's heart break just a little bit. 'I'm really sorry for everything that happened in Paris, Emma.'

'So am I.' She was running her fingers along the edge of the table but looked up. 'I never took the blame for any of it. The falling-out between us took two. I think it was happening long before that night. We were having to fight to stay in each other's lives and we both let it happen.'

'We should've prioritised our friendship and maybe it would've given us a better chance.' Lise gulped. 'You couldn't stand the sight of me in the end.'

It pained her to hear those words. 'I couldn't stand the sight of Xavier.'

Eventually, a slow smile crept onto Lise's face. 'Neither could I eventually.'

Emma's lips curled into a similar smile, which soon faded. 'I couldn't forgive Xavier and I blamed you by association. I lost Gabriel just like that. He wouldn't talk to me. He wouldn't see me. He wasn't at his apartment, he didn't show up at the café and I never ever found out what had happened to him. His sister was terrible. She hated me. I lost my love, my job and I felt like the only option I had was to come home.'

'You really never heard from Gabriel again?'

'Never.'

'I can't believe that that was it. I mean, I always thought he'd get in touch. Even if it wasn't to work things out between you, I thought he'd contact you and you'd both talk. He was so decent. I'm really sorry, Emma.'

'Me too. But if we hadn't split up, I'd never have got together with Sam, I wouldn't have Naomi and I wouldn't have spent all that time with Toby before he died.'

Lise let the information settle. 'I don't want to dredge it all up but I have to say this...' She paused but Emma urged her to say what was on her mind. 'Xavier always said that Gabriel bought those drugs.'

'He did.'

'What I don't understand is that if he bought them, why close himself off from you?'

'I don't know. I never understood it either and I think that's what hurt me the most – that none of it made sense. Sam said he probably did it to protect me but perhaps that was Sam trying to be positive, see the best in everyone.'

'I remember Sam being that way. And he always liked you. It took him the best part of a decade to make a move but at least he got there in the end.'

Emma felt a connection she'd pushed aside in all these years, someone else who knew Sam back then. 'I'm very sorry I never told you he died. It was a mistake to do that to you and you have every right to be angry.'

'I understand why you didn't,' said Lise. 'Max said his death was very sudden.'

Emma felt her voice tremble as she began to speak. Even though she'd picked up the pieces, telling Lise, given their history, was still hard. 'It was. He kissed me goodbye in the morning when I came here to open up. I went home late morning when he didn't come in to see me the way he usually did.'

'You found him?'

She nodded. 'It was terrible. I'm only glad I did and that it wasn't Naomi.'

Taking it all in, Lise told Emma, 'Naomi is a great kid, you know. I can see Sam in her. I can see his smile.'

'And she's kind, like him,' said Emma. 'She inherited his love of meteorology much in the same way as she got my hair colour. It's nice that she got a bit of the both of us.' She met Lise's gaze, which every now and then dropped away as though she wasn't sure whether being here was right and any minute now, she might be given her marching orders.

'Do you mind Maisie being friends with Naomi?'

'I haven't minded it at all. It's been nice to watch.'

'I did wonder whether it would be a problem.'

Emma sat forwards, resting her forearms on the table top, toying with her nails. 'I think that maybe deep down, I needed something to pull me to you.' She looked up tentatively, her honesty stark in the emptiness of the café.

'I could've got someone else to deal with the house,' Lise admitted.

'Dad said the same thing to me. He told me you weren't just back here because of property.'

'Nothing much gets past your dad. He's the dad I never had.' Her smile faded. 'I resented you, you know, when you once said to me that I'd picked a man just like my father.'

'I don't remember telling you that.'

'You said it the night you came to the apartment, the last time I saw you.'

'Oh, Lise. My mouth was out of control that night. I didn't know half of what I was saying.'

'You know the worst thing?' She waited a beat. 'It was completely true.'

Without a word, Emma got up, went into the kitchen and came back with two glasses and a bottle of red wine.

* * *

Lise told Emma everything about Xavier, the way he wanted her at his side, and she loved it mostly but also how she felt she couldn't have much of a life outside of their relationship.

'It was fine for a while. I basked in the attention. I felt special, noticed, worthy.' She thanked Emma for topping up her wine glass. 'He made me feel beautiful every day.'

'Nobody would ever deny he was in love with you, but maybe he loved you too much.'

'Do you think that's possible? To love someone too much?'

'In his case, yes. He wanted you from the moment he laid eyes on you, Lise. That night at the restaurant, Gabriel and I could see it. We talked about it as we watched the both of you.'

'I was flattered. He was handsome, successful, confident. I felt like I was his world. But without realising, I began to forget the importance of everyone else, the importance of our friendship. That was the worst casualty.'

Emma had seen it for herself but never realised Lise ever saw it that way.

'Another way my own father impacted my life, I suppose. My own dad never noticed me, was never pushing me to be better. He was absent despite living in the same house. I never had to fight to be seen with Xavier. Maybe that's why I wanted him so much.'

'I'm still sorry I threw those words in your face, about your dad.'

'It hurt but maybe I needed to hear it. The thought that Xavier was anything like my father came back to me often enough in the following years; perhaps that's how I finally saw it for myself.' She paused. 'Do you remember that big book Sam took camping that time?'

'The one about the weather? I do. It was one of many he collected and it now sits on Naomi's bookshelf.'

'No way!' Lise began to chuckle. 'Rather her than me. But my point is, do you remember me reading it and finding those sections that described tornadoes? I do because it scared the hell out of me. I'd planned to go to Florida to see my cousins and that put me off big time.'

'What do tornadoes have to do with Xavier?'

'It was when I left him that an analogy, description, reference, whatever you want to call it came back to me from the book. I can't recall the exact words but it was something along the lines of how a tornado comes along, picks up everything in its path and twirls it around in confusion before it lets the pieces fall in a way they weren't before.'

'And that's how you'd describe Xavier?' Emma had never known him that well but now that she thought about it, those descriptors weren't too far off the mark.

'I didn't expect to meet Xavier that night in the restaurant. I didn't expect the attention and before I knew it, I was carried away and then it was up to me to pick up the pieces after our falling-out, once I was pregnant and when I became a mother.'

'You're a good mum. Maisie seems happy.'

'I came back before now,' Lise admitted.

'What do you mean?'

'I came back here, to England, to Bath, to Honeybee Place. Ten years ago.'

Emma narrowly avoided missing the table altogether when she put down her glass and pushed it to safety.

'I left Maisie with Mum who was in London by then. I stayed in a hotel, but I came and stood outside this very café.'

'Why didn't you come in?'

'Come on, seriously?'

She pulled a face. 'Yeah, not sure how I might have reacted.'

'I don't know why I thought it a good idea. But I'd just split up from Xavier. It was a knee-jerk reaction to come and so I did.' She turned and pointed to the window farthest from the door, the window you could see through from the opposite side of the street. 'I stood over there on the pavement and watched you. You looked happy. I saw you had a child with you and there was a man hugging you both. I didn't recognise him as Sam because he was there one second, gone the next, but you all looked so content. A complete unit. And so I walked away. I didn't want to mess with that. I returned to Paris and tried to carry on with my life. I thought that was where I was meant to be. Without you, I wasn't sure I wanted to be here.'

'What changed this time?'

'A few things.' She sat back in her chair. 'Maisie was the linch-pin. The timing was right for her and she wanted to come here, finish her schooling. I was out of work, which made it easy and it gave me time to do up number twelve. The house is actually in my name, which was Mum's decision.'

'Do you think she transferred ownership to make you come back?'

'Yes.'

Emma couldn't believe it. 'I never would've thought...'

'I know – surprising, isn't it? But Mum and I have worked on our relationship over time. She's not the same person as she was when she was with my dad. We get along quite well now; we talk often. She's remarried and living in the south of France, and she adores Maisie.'

'I'm pleased for you, Lise. But may I ask, what made you leave Xavier for good?'

'It's a very long story.'

'I've got time.' She looked at the bottle of wine. 'And plenty more where that came from, if we need it.'

When Lise took a while to compose herself, Emma realised how hard this was for her too. Their friendship had shown no bounds, had the strength many admired and then all of a sudden, it was gone. And that had had a long-lasting effect on both of them.

'It was a little after Maisie's fifth birthday when it all went downhill. When I was pregnant, Xavier was exactly the way you remember him: attentive, put me first. I was his whole world. But once I had Maisie, he became more and more like my dad. It wasn't that he was a terrible father. He provided, he was there with us, but spending quality time as a family never seemed to happen. He wanted me to himself; he didn't understand why that wasn't possible. I told myself he was mourning the life we'd had as a twosome and I understood because sometimes, I'd have given anything for a night or two as a couple, free of responsibilities.'

'I totally get that. Motherhood is hard. It's full time, it's overwhelming.'

'That's how I felt a lot of the time but loving Maisie was the easy part – it kept me going on the tougher days. Xavier opened up another restaurant and we saw even less of each other. Business came first, and the less time we had together, the more difficult it became. Maisie had started school. I had the urge to get back to work. But Xavier insisted it was too hard. I'd been out of the industry for too long to catch up he said, and while my French was good, he told me it wasn't fluent enough to understand everything and not miss the nuances in the business world. I called him out on that one, said it was bullshit. I knew he had another British worker who spoke less French than I did and yet they seemed to be doing just fine. It caused so many rows.

'I was missing England more and more. Although, if I'm totally honest, I don't think it was that in isolation. I think I was missing being myself, a professional as well as a mother, a woman with a best friend who'd come with her to France on an adventure and was nowhere to be seen.'

'I left you.' It was another reminder that as hard as she'd had it, Emma had blinkered herself and not seen her friend's pain too. How could she have been so unable to see it?

'You had your reasons. And I stayed, I didn't come running after you begging to sort this out. I gave up when you ignored my emails and letters and I let our friendship go.'

'Both of us were wrong to do that. It's just taken a while to see it.'

Lise returned a tentative smile and carried on. 'The fighting between Xavier and I was exactly the way our relationship always was – dramatic and passionate. But it got worse and worse. We fought more than anything else. And then one night, he yelled at me that everything was my fault. He told me that I'd made this life for us all, as though it was terrible, as though he begrudged being a part of it. And then he told me he'd never ever wanted to have kids. He never wanted to be a father.'

Emma's heart went out to her.

'He'd never said it to me before.'

'Oh, Lise. That's so hurtful. To you, to Maisie.'

'Since the divorce, I've made sure to tell Maisie in my own words that children weren't in Xavier's future plans. The thing is, he's not so much of an arsehole he ever would've said it to her – they actually get on pretty well. I don't think she suffered and she's known ever since she was around five or six years old that Xavier isn't her biological father.'

Emma sat up straighter. 'He's not?'

'The night he spat out that he never wanted to have children, he told me something else... that he was infertile. He had a chronic health condition as a kid and he knew from an early age that he'd never father a child. The way I was manipulated was all part of the reasons why I had to leave.'

It took Emma a while to get her head around the facts. 'Did you know all along that he wasn't the father?'

'No! I honestly thought he was. I didn't have an affair. It was one night and we used a condom. I never used protection with Xavier, not apart from the pill I was on, so I was convinced Maisie was his. I sometimes think what an idiot, how could I not know, not ask the questions, but I didn't. Until that moment.'

'Fuck.' Emma grimaced. 'Sorry, I tell you off for swearing in my café but this is a fuck moment. Shit just wouldn't cut it.'

'No, it really wouldn't.'

'So... you had a one-nighter? Did you ever tell the biological father?'

Lise looked right at her. Her chest rose high, fell and on a breath, she said, 'I never got the chance. He died.' Tears filled her eyes when she added, 'The one-nighter was when I found out you'd come back to the apartment, packed a suitcase and left Paris for good.'

Emma imagined Lise distraught that night, going out, getting wasted, hooking up with a total stranger. 'Wait... but you were with Toby that night. He told me when he came back to England that you were a mess when you found out I'd left, that you were doing shots at the bistro...' Her voice trailed off as she grasped what this meant.

Toby was Maisie's father.

26

NOW: 2023

Lise

Emma's hands shook as she brought two mugs of freshly brewed coffee over to the table. She'd taken her time making it but Lise wasn't surprised. Emma had to absorb the fact that her brother Toby had been a father, that she was an auntie, her dad a grandfather for a second time.

'This is a lot to take in.' Emma's voice came out small.

'I know it is. It wasn't something I ever saw happening, not really.'

Emma said nothing. She looked so shocked. And so, barring the details a sister didn't really want to know about her own brother, Lise recounted the night she'd spent with Toby, her head right back there in Paris with him on the night she'd needed him more than ever.

The shots at the bistro after their food and wine had gone down quickly but when Lise woke up, she was glad Toby had stopped it when he did and made her drink water when she got back to the apartment. At least she felt semi-human after a sleep.

She emerged bleary-eyed into the lounge and warned Toby, 'Do not say a word.'

'Wasn't going to.'

She didn't need to look at him to know he was grinning from ear to ear. In the kitchen area, which was at the side of the lounge with a big window stretching all the way across, she filled a glass of water, downed it, got another. 'I'm going to take a shower.'

'A bath might be a better idea.' He had the remote control in one hand and had been flipping through the channels but gave up at the lack of shows he'd have a hope of understanding.

Actually, he had a point. Standing up seemed a bit energetic and perhaps a bath would bring her fully back to the land of the living.

She went off to run it, adding in a big squirt of bubble bath for good measure.

It was nothing like Xavier's bathroom in here. His tub was free-standing; this one was against the wall. His had a fancy, shiny mixer tap that sat along one edge in the middle; this had two taps, the cold one only a trickle so you had to remember not to turn the hot to full or you'd end up with a temperature you could never get right.

She was about to climb in when she heard a knock at the door. 'You need to use the bathroom?' she called over the sound of cascading water. She pulled a fluffy towel around her torso and opened the door.

'No, just checking on you.'

'Thanks to the water police – you – I'm not too bad.'

'I'm bored, Lise. There's sod all on television.'

'Well, that's not strictly true. There's plenty, but it's all in French.'

'I hated French at school.'

She laughed. 'Stay there, talk to me. Through the closed door.'

'Are you sure?'

'Of course.' She closed the door, turned off the taps and with her towel back on the hook, she climbed in, slipping down into the water with an enormous sigh.

'Are you sure this is okay? It feels odd,' his voice said from the other side of the door.

'Just stay there and talk, Toby. You can make sure I don't fall asleep and drown in here.'

'Deal.'

The bubbles enveloped her skin; the temperature made her prickly in a good way.

Through the door, which had a bit of a gap at the bottom and carried their voices easily, they talked a bit more about Paris, what the girls had seen, and Lise recounted all their best times from the start, the laughs they'd had, the thrill of it all. She covered the days after Emma met Gabriel, how she'd met Xavier at the restaurant. She asked Toby whether he was seeing anyone special but he wasn't. Instead, he was on his way to obtaining his pilot's licence, working as a disability support worker and at the same time heavily into wildlife photography.

'I'm impressed.' She lifted the bubbles on her hand up in the air, watched them slide down the skin of her arm.

'With which part?'

'All of it. I knew about the job as a disability support worker – perfect for you, might I add. You always did care about other people. And the pilot's licence? Can't say I'm surprised, mostly because Emma told me you were doing it. And the wildlife photography... well, that came out of left field.'

'It did for me too.' His voice came under the door. 'Although I was always fascinated by the beehives at number twenty-eight.'

'You were obsessed with those. Remember when you got caught sneaking into the garden and then reprimanded for being a complete imbecile?' Her laughter echoed against the tiles. 'That was what Mr Raker called you, wasn't it?'

'It was but he invited me back, let me put on the special suit and showed me the bees properly.'

'How come I never knew that?'

'I like to keep part of me quiet, Lise.'

He was such a gentle person, always thought of others. 'What was your first ever photograph of wildlife?' She imagined tigers in Africa, dolphins leaping out of the ocean, a snake coiling around a tree trunk in the Amazon forest.

'The spiders in the shed at the bottom of the garden.'

She gasped. 'That framed photograph in your parents' hallway, the one of the intricate cobwebs and all the frost, that's yours?'

'I'm surprised you didn't know.'

'Maybe they said and I missed it. Too self-absorbed, that's me.' She sloshed the water one more time as she stood up and reached for her towel.

While she dried herself and pulled on a big, fluffy robe, Toby kept talking about photographs he'd taken, the places he'd been. He was going to Botswana soon and was hoping to take good enough photographs to sell to a wildlife magazine. He talked about the solitude in some of the countries he visited, how he'd immerse himself in a hobby he was in love with.

She emerged from the bathroom and tugged the knot firmer around the waist of her robe. 'So basically you're looking to cut yourself off from the rest of the world.'

'Kind of,' he said with the same cheeky smile he'd had ever since she'd known him. 'And right now, I really do need the bathroom.' He passed her and got hit with the wall of steam.

In the lounge, she flopped onto the sofa, curled her legs beneath her and got comfortable. She'd had so much to drink earlier but thanks to the water, the sleep and the bath, she felt almost normal already.

Toby came and sat at the other end of the sofa and she laughed when he picked up the remote control again out of habit. He put it down, rested his head on the back of the sofa, turning to face her. 'You'll be all right you know.'

He'd be a natural in his day job she bet, with his soft voice, sense of humour and a demeanour that exuded empathy and understanding. 'I'm sorry I fell apart this afternoon.'

'Don't be. And today was fun – although I really hate tequila.'

'You do not!'

'I do – only had them so you wouldn't drink my share too.'

With a sigh, she admitted that's exactly what she would've done. 'Thank you.'

'My pleasure. You tired?'

'I've been to sleep, remember.'

'Yeah, and you snore like a trucker. Came in to check on you earlier.'

She gave him a shove. 'I do not snore!'

'Well you'll never know, will you.'

'You should probably get to bed.' She caught sight of the clock. 'You're travelling tomorrow.'

'It's Paris to London – pretty sure I could do it if I stayed up all night.'

'You want to pull an all-nighter?'

He shrugged. 'Why not? I won't see you for a while.'

She reached out to touch his earlobe, the mark still there from when she'd pierced his ear. 'It's been great having you here, Toby. I didn't realise how much I've needed you the last few days.'

'Happy to be of help.' She saw him swallow, his gaze dip to her lips. 'Lise, I—'

'You've always been nice to me.'

'Not always...' His smirk had her laughing.

'The diaries, well apart from that, and you did make it up to me if you remember.'

'Oh I remember; my naked tush remembers.'

She made a face and puffed out her cheeks. 'I've got a bit of a confession to make,' she admitted coyly.

'Don't tell me you've got evidence, photographs.'

'No! I promise! But... well, I looked. You know.'

He merely shrugged. 'I figured you would. And... verdict?'

'I'm not going there.' She laughed. 'No way.'

'Worth a try.' He put a hand out and rested it on her knee, a friendly gesture but one that had her mind going in a completely different direction.

'You're a good man, Toby. And apart from that one time with the diaries, you *have* always been nice to me.'

'Comes with the territory of you being my sister's best friend.' He took his hand away, maybe with the reference to Emma.

She pulled the robe across her knees again and leaned back, looked at the ceiling, at the old strip light they'd joked about when they moved in but now she rarely noticed, she was so used to it. 'Yeah, well I think that's changed.'

'I hope it hasn't, Lise.' This time, he shifted closer and picked up her hand again, his fingers slipping between hers.

'I wish she would've at least talked to me before she left.'

'She's upset, lost. You guys will work it out in the end.'

She looked up at him, their closeness making her breath heavy in her chest. She knew she was leaning closer to him, sure he was doing the same.

The next thing she knew, they were kissing, his hands were in her hair, both hungry, both wanting. She climbed onto his lap. His groans were met with her own as though this was what they should've been doing all along but had somehow missed it.

He picked her up and carried her against him into the bedroom, her legs wrapped around his waist. And they collapsed onto the bed, the knot in her robe still there but not for long when Toby looked at her, questioning, his fingers against it, and she urged him not to stop. She barely had time to tell him there was a full packet of condoms in her bedside table drawer – she and Xavier hadn't used them – and he barely had time to ask her again whether she was sure.

'Toby, I'm sure. I promise.'

Toby was tender, gentle and yet passionate. He was unexpected and it felt right.

They fell asleep in each other's arms, only stirring once to make love again in the early hours of the morning.

'I'm a mess, Toby.' Lise rested her head against his chest, the morning light only just beginning to peep through the sides of the curtains in her bedroom.

'I know,' he whispered into her hair as he held her.

Just like that: *I know*. No question of where this was going, where this left them.

'Are you sorry about this... us?' he asked, Lise still in his arms.

She looked up at him. No matter what happened from here, she really couldn't say that she was. 'No, I'm not sorry.'

'Me neither.'

In the café now, Lise looked at Emma. This was huge, the biggest confession she'd ever had to make.

'We both agreed that it was one night and one night only,' she told Emma. 'I was in a state. I didn't know whether I was coming or going. I knew I needed time and I wanted to be fair to Toby. He was understanding, kind, respectful. We said goodbye. He said he'd get in touch after Botswana to see how I was, and I closed the door and fell apart even more. I knew I had to work out how to pick up the pieces on my own before I could really let anyone else in.

'I spent the next week wandering in and out of small bistros. I trawled job pages to see whether I could find anything. Part of me questioned whether to jump on the Eurostar and head back to England too, but I didn't feel ready for that. I'd needed Paris, to go there and be someone else, do something different.

'I thought a lot about Toby in the days after he left. I knew that if I ended up going back to England then I'd want to see him again. But circumstances changed; I had to make a choice.' Her voice caught. 'Toby was one of a kind. I couldn't explain to anyone the pain I felt when I found out that he'd died. I told Xavier Toby was gone and he comforted me. He knew how close I'd been to the both of you, but I never admitted that Toby was the man I'd slept with when we were apart for that short time. I couldn't do that because I needed my baby to have the home life that I'd never had. It was the real reason I'd stayed in Paris. I needed to keep things together. My baby wasn't going to have the upbringing I'd had – I was sure of that. And so I grieved behind closed doors, when Xavier was at work and I wasn't, when I was in the bath, anywhere but in front of Xavier.'

'When did you tell Xavier that you slept with someone else?'

'When we were still broken up. I was living in our apartment and he kept calling me, kept trying to get me to go back to him. I guess I told him because I thought it might make him leave me alone but it didn't. He still wanted me. It was only when Xavier admitted his infertility that I realised exactly how I'd been manipulated. I fell pregnant, assumed it was Xavier's; he knew it couldn't possibly be and yet he wanted me back. He married me; he became a father. And it was a cold move on his part, one that I've never been able to forgive. I think I might have understood had he *wanted* the baby to be his, but he didn't. He just didn't want to lose me to anyone else.'

She growled. 'I still can't believe I never questioned it. I felt so stupid. Although it made me realise why Xavier never insisted we use protection. He was blasé about it. Stupidly, I put it down to him being French. I thought maybe it was a typical thing that they did. What a dumb thing to assume. As if all Frenchmen think the same way. And I was on the pill, had been for a long time, but I was also very bad at remembering to take it. Some days, I'd forget and I hadn't been caught out before so I guess naively, I assumed I never would be. Looks like fate had other plans.'

'Anyone who uses a condom expects it to work,' said Emma. 'I can see why you assumed the baby was Xavier's, not Toby's.' She shook her head. 'I'm so angry that Xavier lied, that he did that to you, to Toby.'

'Believe me, so was I when I found out and I've never forgiven him, just reached a point of peace and acceptance.'

'Tell me he was at least a good enough parent for Maisie some of the time?'

'He was better than my own father as time went on. But he still lacked a true interest. She was never a priority the way a kid should be. I hated that I'd chosen a man who couldn't fulfil the role of a father the way Maisie deserved, but it made me all the more determined to be a good mum.'

'How did you leave things with Toby?' Emma's eyes glistened with unshed tears, tears that threatened to spill over at any moment. 'Did you have contact after he went to Botswana?'

Lise hated that she hadn't ever seen him again since that night. 'I sent an email and told Toby that I was staying in Paris. I kept the details scant. I said I'd never regret the night we had together. He replied – Toby was a good man – he wished me all the best, which was almost worse than no email at all. I only hoped he'd find someone, fall in love and be really happy.'

Both of their coffees had gone cold; neither had touched a drop.

Emma went to make fresh coffee, leaving Lise the chance to gather her thoughts. Lise had no idea how her friend was feeling. Was this worse than before she knew Toby was Maisie's father? Had Lise ruined things all the more now she'd told Emma the truth?

When Emma set the coffees down and took a seat, Lise picked up her spoon ready to scrape off the froth on her coffee the way she always did before she stirred the rest into the depths below.

She looked across at her friend. 'Please say something, even if it's bad, even if you yell at me. I don't care.'

'Does Maisie know about Toby?'

'No. I wanted to tell you first.' She took a deep breath. 'She thinks her biological dad is called Thomas.'

'You lied to her?'

'Thomas was just a name – all the other details I shared such as what he was like are true. But I couldn't risk you finding out any way, other than having me tell you.' She watched Emma do the same as what she was now doing, using her spoon to scrape off the foam from her coffee. 'I knew that once you found out, I could tell her the whole truth.'

'Everything?'

'Yes. I think the truth is probably the only way forward for me, for you, and part of facing the truth is telling Maisie the details.'

'You're close.'

'We are. I think single parenting made us closer too, but she's also got Toby's kindness, his attentiveness as a friend.'

Emma sighed but smiled. 'I still can't believe it. Toby, a dad.'

'Emma, I also plan to tell her that she can be involved with you and your family even if I'm not. Even if we never manage to be friends again, I don't want her to feel like she can't be a part of the Millers' lives, if that's what she, you and your dad want.'

Her last remark had Emma looking up from the coffee she was peering at as though it might take on a life of its own.

'Please tell me how you're feeling, Emma.' She'd rather be yelled at than the withdrawn, not-saying-much treatment.

'I'm still processing.'

Lise ran a finger up the side of her coffee mug to gather some of the froth that had escaped without her noticing. 'When I found out about Maisie being Toby's, I was too. I felt stupid for a start, an idiot for not seeing it. I mean, she has Toby's eyes, the same cheeky smile.'

'It makes more sense that you took flowers to the cemetery now. I knew it was you; I saw you carrying them out to your car.'

Lise smiled. 'I would've done that even if Toby and I had never been involved. Your brother was quite a guy. He always had time for me. Remember all those badminton games we played?'

'I remember the one where you belted a shuttlecock all the way into Mrs Griffin's tree and he had to climb up to get it out.' Emma laughed.

'He wanted me to try getting it. Mrs Griffin came outside and told him that if he was a gentleman, he wouldn't make a girl climb a tree.'

'Sounds like Mrs Griffin.'

'I always liked your brother. I just never realised how much.'

'I'm sorry, I didn't mean to dismiss your feelings with what I said about the flowers.' She looked up at the ceiling to stem any tears. 'I'm making a hash of this.'

'No, you're not. There's no roadmap here, or if there is, nobody handed me a copy. I'm clueless at what to say, how to react. All I knew was that I had to come here, I had to bring Maisie, and the rest... well, the rest will be what it will be. I only wish...'

Emma knew exactly what she'd been about to say and finished the sentence for her: '...that Toby could've met Maisie.'

Lise nodded. 'I cried when I was at the cemetery. It hit me again, like a ton of bricks. I wished he could've been around to meet his daughter and see how beautiful she is, with a big heart just like he had.'

Emma pulled a packet of tissues from her back pocket and passed one to Lise.

'Thanks.' She wiped her eyes and tackled a mouthful of coffee before this one went cold too, although the bitterness didn't sit well at all. 'Do you think you'd like to get to know Maisie?' This was what she was afraid of: another reason not to tell anyone about the paternity until she knew how Emma was going to react.

'Lise, of course. Maisie is family. I'd love nothing more than to get to know her.'

'Thank you.'

'No need to thank me. I should thank you for bringing her into our lives. I should say thank you for sleeping with my brother.'

Lise laughed through tears. 'Imagine if he could see us now.'

'He'd be glad we were talking.'

'I think so too.'

'Toby would've made a great dad but he would've been up to no good half the time I bet, letting them get away with more than you or I would.'

'Most probably. He always was a bit mischievous, especially as a teenager. Did he ever tell you about my diaries?'

'No, what happened?'

Lise reminded Emma of the time she'd kept her diaries in her bedroom so that her parents never saw them and that Toby had snooped at the contents.

'I can't believe he did that.'

'I was embarrassed, expected him to shout about it and take the mickey out of me, but he didn't. He apologised and all he was worried about was making amends to show me how sorry he was. He really never told you?'

'About the diaries? No. I mean, he would've known how furious I would've been that he'd done such a thing to you.'

'I don't mean about the diaries; I mean about what I made him do as a punishment.' When Emma began to smile, Lise told her exactly what had gone on. 'I knew the only way I could forgive him was if he was as embarrassed as I was. So I told him he could apologise by running around the grass square in the middle of Honeybee Place, an entire lap, totally naked.'

'No!'

'Yes.'

'Wait... you're not telling me he actually went through with it, are you?'

Lise nodded. 'Totally naked, not even a pair of shoes. He cut his foot. I felt terrible about that, but we agreed that we were even.'

'I can't believe he did that. Except maybe now I know about the two of you, perhaps I can. I had a suspicion he liked you.'

'You never said anything to me.'

'No, I didn't. I was guarding my friendship. I didn't want my brother getting between us. And sorry, but imagining you and he...'

'All right.' Lise laughed. 'I don't think we need to go into too much detail. He admitted to me that night that he'd wanted to say something to me for a long time.'

'I wonder what would've happened if he had.'

'Me too.'

'You and Toby would've made a great couple,' said Emma after a beat.

'I like to think so too. And I wish I could turn back the clock.' In so many ways, not just the staying with Xavier, but in their friendship too, the fact she hadn't fought for it.

'I still can't believe he ran naked around Honeybee Place.' It was a bit of humour necessary in the seriousness of the moment. 'What did you even do with those diaries?'

She explained how she'd wanted to burn them so nobody else got their hands on her innermost thoughts. 'Toby persuaded me that one day, I might like to read them. And so we buried them in the back garden at number twelve, in the veggie patch.'

Emma sat up straighter. 'Do you have them now?'

'I do. I dug them up. Do you remember what we agreed?'

'I remember.' She smiled tenderly. Perhaps she was back there on the day they'd had the conversation, two best friends thinking they'd be that way forever. 'We said we'd read them when we were at least forty...'

And at the same time they chimed: '...with wrinkles and saggy boobs.'

Lise's laughter pealed inside the café's walls and she looked across at her friend. 'Do you think we should go and read them now?'

'Let's do it.' Emma collected the cups. 'We're in our forties; I've got a few lines on my face.' She looked down at her own chest, then across at Lise's. 'Neither of us have saggy boobs but I'd say we've waited long enough.'

27

NOW: 2023

Emma

Emma knocked on the door to number twelve and when Lise opened the door and she stepped inside, she was catapulted back in time, remembering the last time she'd been within these walls.

'This place is still much like I remember.' She followed Lise into the kitchen.

'It's tired. Renters haven't been kind – put it that way.'

'I doubt it'll take too long to sort it out.' She sat down next to Lise at the island bench and accepted the offer of a hot chocolate. 'Thanks. I don't think I'll sleep tonight if I have any more wine or a coffee.' She eyed the pile of diaries. 'They look like they survived their years in the garden.'

'Your brother was clever enough to use a good container plus a plastic bag for extra protection.'

'Lise, before we look at them, I need to say how sorry I am... yet again... for the way things turned out.' Emma hadn't even taken her coat off yet as Lise poured the hot milk onto the chocolate and began to stir the first cup to melt it. But she felt that for so long, she'd put the blame on Lise and she knew why – it was easier that way than admitting her own part in the failure of their friendship.

'I think we're both very sorry. We can't keep saying it, can we?'

She felt an immense surge of relief. 'No, I don't suppose we can.' Her lips twisted. 'We let a man, or men, come between us, something we vowed we'd never do.'

Lise brought over two mugs of hot chocolate. 'I just wish it hadn't gone on so long between us.'

'Lise...' She paused, fingers on the edge of the mug. 'I'm really glad you came back.'

'I'm glad I came back too.'

Their words felt like a start. They were an acknowledgement of what had passed, what was ahead of them.

Emma eyed the diaries again after she blew across her hot chocolate to cool it and took a tentative sip. 'Shall we?'

They started with the first diary and Lise flipped through to find the section where they met at primary school.

'It's like being catapulted back in time,' Emma declared after only a few pages. 'I can almost feel the chair beneath me in the classroom, the big desk in front of me, being terrified of getting picked on.'

Lise read out the page where each of them had had a crush on Cody Graham one Easter. 'I wonder where he ended up.'

'Probably in trouble somewhere. Wasn't he always getting hauled into the head teacher's office?'

'I remember that now – funny how much you forget.'

They laughed over the memories, the recollections, some of which they could remember vividly, others not so much.

When Lise got to the pages detailing her homecoming one summer when Emma was out at a sleepover, she didn't really want Emma to see it.

'Please, Lise, let me see.'

Lise relented and after Emma read the entry, she looked up at her friend. 'I never realised you were so hurt that I wasn't there. Disappointed, yes, but here it sounds like you thought I'd abandoned you.'

'I did. I was devastated. I thought, *Emma has moved on.* I realised that perhaps that summer might be the year everything changed.'

'But it didn't.'

'No, it didn't.'

Emma laughed at some of the next memories, the first time the girls had got drunk on a bottle of gin they'd found in Lise's mum's drinks cabinet, fixing themselves gin and tonics and feeling grown up until they spent the entire night puking, taking turns for the bathroom. They'd kept it hidden from Lise's parents too, not hard when she was left up to her own devices a lot of the time.

When they reached the section in one of the diaries about Sam, Emma shifted in her chair. 'I think when I fell for Sam, I pushed out the friendship we'd *all* had,' she confessed. 'I feel even more of a cow for not telling you about him now. It was unforgivable, Lise.'

'You didn't do it to be spiteful.'

'I promise you, I never did.'

Lise read out the part about Sam, how she thought he liked Emma as more than a friend and that she really didn't mind. Emma read the part about Lise observing how Sam looked at Emma, how his face changed when she was around.

'This is like having him tell me his feelings back then.' Emma put a hand against her chest. 'It feels so real.'

'Well that's my skill as a writer, obviously,' Lise claimed. 'We destroyed our letters to each other as agreed but aren't you glad your brother made me keep these instead of burning them?'

'I really am.' Emma reread the section about Sam bringing flowers for her when she was off school and down with a heavy cold, miserable as sin. The flowers had been from both Sam and Lise but Lise had made him do the delivery.

'I never knew you'd insisted it was him who came over,' said Emma.

'I wanted to see if he'd have the nerve to tell you how he felt. I wondered if he'd see you so helpless that he'd finally admit it.'

'Not likely when I expect I looked a total state.'

'He wouldn't have noticed.'

Lise found a funny section about one of their sleepovers when they'd sneaked out and gone to a club underage with fake IDs.

'You were determined to go to that club,' Emma recalled. 'Nothing I could say was going to put you off.'

'I was pushing the boundaries. I wanted my parents to realise we'd gone; I wanted them to find out what we'd been doing. It would've meant they gave a toss.'

'Do you and your mum talk about how things were for you back then?'

'Have I been honest with her?' Lise closed the last of the diaries. 'I've tried to be, although at the same time, I wanted to move things on, to make a new relationship with her. I see now that perhaps she did her best. And after being with Xavier, I can see how easy it is to fall into a life, be almost under a spell. Being with him has given me a certain amount of empathy for Mum. And as for Dad's part in it all, well, he's not here to ask.'

'Does that make you angry?'

'Not any more. I think if I let it, it might, the same way that if I let what Xavier did really get to me, it might just bowl me over completely. It wasn't fair. Lives were altered with his omission of the truth. I suppose these days, I'm trying to think of the past as being that: the past. I'm more inclined to think about what I can do for the future. With mum, with Maisie, with you.'

Emma didn't respond because they both looked up when they heard the front door go.

'That's Maisie,' said Lise.

'And Naomi by the sounds of it.'

The girls' voices, giggling away about some boy or another, travelled along the hallway all the way to the kitchen.

Maisie and Naomi clearly hadn't expected to see both of their mothers here either, and certainly not together.

'What's going on?' Maisie asked. 'Are we in trouble?'

'Don't automatically assume it's that.' Lise gestured to the two chairs opposite. 'But I think the both of you had better sit down.'

'No time like the present,' Emma murmured, her nerves likely in the same place as Lise's.

'Mum...' Naomi sounded nervous.

In fact, both girls looked terrified.

And it was time for Lise and Emma to tell them both about their friendship, what happened in Paris, their falling-out.

It was time to tell them everything.

28

NOW: 2023

Lise

Maisie looked at Naomi and Naomi looked at Maisie as they took in the news that their mums had once been good friends, best friends, and then they'd had a spectacular falling-out that had lasted for years. Until now.

Maisie's eyes danced. 'The drama club at school could make this story into a production, one that people might actually want to go and see.'

'Don't you dare pitch it to them, Maisie.' Lise wasn't sure whether her daughter was joking or not. 'There's more too...'

Both girls were intrigued and Lise hoped to God this wasn't going to be the worst news of their lives. Maisie had known for so long that Xavier wasn't her biological dad; she'd accepted Lise's explanations and hadn't really asked too much more.

Emma gave Lise a look to urge her to keep going now she'd started. Lise felt skin on skin, Emma's hand clutching hers beneath the table. She felt the years, no matter how many of them they'd spent apart and not talking to each other, all bundled into one and the support of her very best friend in the whole world. And it was all the encouragement she needed.

'Maisie, I told you a few things about your father, your biological father.'

'Thomas...'

Lise took a deep breath. 'That wasn't true. His name was Toby.' She felt Emma's hand clutch hers a little tighter as though she was just as worried about the girls' reaction as Lise was.

'Toby.' She said the name as if it didn't have a relevance whether it was Thomas or Toby but it wasn't long before her gaze moved across to Emma. 'Your brother was Toby.' She looked to Naomi. 'Your uncle was Toby. You both talk about him all the time.'

Lise was waiting for her daughter to explode, but instead, the kitchen was eerily quiet.

'Toby is my dad,' said Maisie as though trying the claim on for size.

After a pause, Naomi looked at her new friend. 'You mean we're cousins? Bloody hell.'

'Language,' Emma reminded her daughter, although there was little power in the reprimand, because the swearing could be forgiven under the circumstances.

'I don't believe it,' said Maisie.

Naomi admitted, 'Neither do I.'

Maisie's eyes filled with tears. 'I'll never get to meet him.'

'Oh, darling.' Lise was at her side in seconds. She'd told Maisie that Thomas passed away suddenly but now, her daughter finding out the real identity of her biological father seemed to ignite new feelings as though it was a fresh loss of what might have been.

Lise knew she had to stay strong and let Maisie work through her emotions, have a say in how all of this went from now on with regards to the Millers, with what she wanted to know. 'Toby would've adored you – I know that much.'

Tears pricked at Maisie's eyes for the overwhelming information shared tonight. 'I wish I had got to know him. He sounds…'

Lise, tears in her eyes, told Maisie: 'Kind, handsome, funny, loving.'

When Emma sniffed, she apologised.

When Lise looked at Naomi, she'd started crying too.

Before long, their tears turned to laughter, laughter amongst the four females sat in the kitchen in Honeybee Place balling their eyes out in shock, in happiness.

'You know Toby would have a field day with this.' Emma blew her nose so loudly, her daughter rolled her eyes. 'He'd ask if we were all right but he'd tease us for unleashing our emotions once he knew we were.'

'I still can't believe we're cousins.' Naomi looked at Maisie and smiled; already they were good friends. 'What if instead of meeting and being friends, we'd hated each other?'

'Thank goodness that never happened,' said Lise.

'It's kind of cool,' Maisie said.

Naomi clearly thought so too. 'Mum, do you think Grandad's heart can take it if we go and tell him?'

Emma held up a hand. 'Hold on, not yet.' But when she looked at Lise, Lise shrugged.

'Might be nice to do it all tonight, get everything out in the open. As long as you think he's all right to hear it all.'

'He's not that fragile.' She didn't think much longer before she stood up. 'Okay then, let's go. But you two stay here, give Lise and I half an hour to give him the news.'

'I want to see his reaction,' Naomi complained.

'This is too big, Naomi. Let us do this, the two of us.'

* * *

At number four Honeybee Place, Brendan's face filled with joy, his eyes glistened, not only at seeing the girls together after all this time but when Lise delivered the news that Toby was Maisie's father.

'I can't believe it,' he said for about the fifth time.

Lise had wondered whether he'd be upset she hadn't come clean before now, whether he'd call her out on the fact she'd kept this news to herself for so long. They briefly explained that paternity hadn't been questioned at the start, not until well after Toby died, without having to give all the details.

For now, Brendan only seemed focused on the fact he had another granddaughter and that was more than what Lise could've hoped for.

'My Toby.' He shook his head still in disbelief. 'He would've made a great dad.'

'I think we're all in agreement over that one, Mr Miller.' Lise sat next to him on the ottoman that positioned her lower down than him and made her feel like a youngster all over again.

'You know you really should call me Brendan,' he said. 'You're not a sixteen-year-old girl come to tell me you're in trouble – you're a grown woman, Lise, part of this family even before I knew that Maisie was Toby's.'

Lise gulped back the emotion. 'Thank you.'

'When you two came in here together tonight, it filled my heart with so much joy, I didn't think it was possible to feel more until you told me about Maisie.' He looked over at Emma. 'Have you two talked properly? About everything?'

Emma came to his side, crouched down on the floor next to him. 'We're talking; we're working it out.'

'Your mother would be proud of you, Emma.'

Lise knew in that moment that had Toby had the chance to be a parent, he would've been just like Brendan Miller. He'd see his children, be there for them without question, make them feel as though they were his entire world.

When they heard the door go and the girls' footsteps coming downstairs, Lise would never forget the look on Brendan's face when he clapped eyes on Maisie. It was one of pure joy. It didn't matter that he'd seen her before in passing – this was different. This was a new normal he was welcoming with open arms.

'Maisie...' His voice faltered.

It wasn't often a sixteen-year-old showed so much emotion in front of the adults but Maisie looked about to fall apart and welcomed the hug Brendan offered her.

Brendan held his granddaughter for the first time until he gingerly lowered himself back down into his chair. 'You look like my Toby when you smile.'

'Will you tell me about him?' Maisie asked.

Lise got up from the ottoman. 'Maisie, it's late—'

'I don't mind in the slightest,' Brendan interrupted. 'It's not like I have to be awake early in the morning unless I have an appointment you've not told me about, Emma?'

Emma shook her head and Lise noticed she couldn't stop watching the interaction between these two relative strangers who had so much to catch up on.

'Make yourself comfortable, Maisie,' Brendan began, 'and I'll tell you all about your dad.'

Naomi gave Maisie a wave goodbye, hugged Emma and went on up to her room.

'I'll be up soon,' Emma called after her before tilting her head for Lise to follow her up the stairs. 'Want me to walk Maisie home when she's done?'

'I get the feeling it might be a while. But thanks, although it's not far.'

'I know.' Emma smiled. 'I remember.' There were plenty of

times each of them had run from one front door to the other under the cover of darkness, in the snow, in the pouring rain.

Lise headed for the front door and opened it to a chilly wind that made her wish she'd brought her coat. They'd done that too, back in the day, gone door to door in very little when the temperatures required more layers, in their pyjamas sometimes.

Emma leaned against the door frame after Lise opened up the door to number four and stepped outside. 'You've brought a part of Toby back to Dad, to all of us, with Maisie. And for that, I don't think I can ever thank you enough, Lise.'

Lise barely hesitated before she threw her arms around her friend as the wind whipped up behind her. The chill of the night draped its blanket over Honeybee Place and the rest of the city of Bath as the hug endured and two best friends spun back in time to their school days, back to the start of their friendship with their whole lives ahead of them.

29

NOW: 2023

Emma

'I still can't believe we're doing this.' Emma sat next to Lise on the Eurostar, on their way to Paris, the way they'd done all those years ago except back then, it left from Waterloo rather than St Pancras. A few weeks ago, they'd been hugging goodbye at the front door after reshaping their family with the addition of Maisie; now they were leaving the country in search of answers.

The day after the whole truth had come out and been shared with the girls, Lise had come to see Emma in the café.

'Dad is besotted with your daughter,' Emma told her as Tara held the fort and she took a pile of dishes out to the kitchen.

'Besotted with your niece, you mean.'

'Yeah, that too.' And it felt so good to say it. That morning, she'd woken up wondering whether it had all been a dream. She was wholeheartedly glad that it wasn't. 'Mum would've loved her; she would've spoiled her rotten.'

'I know.'

'I'm sorry, I'm making you feel guilty.'

'I'll feel guilty no matter what you say.'

'It's Xavier who is to blame, Lise. If he'd mentioned back then about his infertility, if you'd known Maisie wasn't his, if he hadn't wanted you so badly he'd do anything...'

'If, if, if,' said Lise. 'It's no use thinking that way. We'll slowly drive ourselves crazy doing that; believe me, I've tried it.'

The cutlery clattered against the pile of crockery Emma set down ready to load the pieces into the dishwasher.

'I've just been to see your dad,' said Lise.

'That's nice. With Maisie?'

'Oh Maisie is there all right, not sure she'll come home much now she's getting to know her grandad. She never had much to do with Xavier's parents, mum was always far away but did her best – making up for the way she was with me, I think – but your dad is right here a few doors away. And besides, she's lapping up tales of Toby's escapades.'

'I'll bet Dad is loving every minute of that.'

Before Emma could lead the way out into the café again, Lise stopped her. 'I have something I need to tell you.'

'There's more?' She smiled.

'I spoke to your dad about something earlier. Now don't flip out. But I told him I wanted to do something to make things right between us.' She paused. 'What I want to do... what I *need* to do is take you back to Paris.'

Emma burst out laughing before she realised Lise was entirely serious.

'You never got closure,' Lise went on, 'you never got to hear from Gabriel that you were through, why he did what he did with the drugs, why he ended your relationship just like that.'

'I think the time has passed, Lise.'

'No, it hasn't. And so in a few weeks, we're going. I have two tickets booked on the Eurostar. And I have Brendan's approval too.'

'And I have this place.'

Lise nodded. 'I know that but this counts as an emergency and so closing your doors for two days won't be the end of the world. People will understand.'

And deep down, Emma had realised she was right. She'd never been back to Paris and perhaps that was what she needed to do to move on fully, to feel entirely at peace, or at least as at peace as she ever could be when she'd left Paris completely undone. Sam had tried to tell her the same thing, hadn't he? And here was Lise doing it too, the woman who had often known Emma better than she knew herself.

Now, here they were on the Eurostar, having gone through the tunnel and out the other side, in France after all this time. Maisie had moved into the Millers' for forty-eight hours in a bid to get to know her grandad even more as well as spend time with her cousin and not be home alone.

They disembarked, grateful of the foresight to bring backpacks not suitcases for such a quick trip given how easy it was to exit the train and navigate their way out of Gard du Nord compared to anyone with extra baggage.

Stepping onto the Paris streets was surreal. After all this time. Traffic was unforgiving, a bus belched as it pulled up close by, a taxi honked its horn at a pedestrian who wandered out in front of them. Conversations and exchanges wrapped around them as they crossed over and headed for their hotel, smoke from a woman in front wafted over her shoulder and they overtook her to avoid it. It was exactly as Emma remembered, as though time had almost stood still.

Everything happened on fast forward after that. They checked into a cute little hotel, filled up on croissants and a coffee each, their next destination on the agenda not getting a mention until it was time. Because their next stop was the café that may or may not give Emma the answers she'd wanted and needed for years.

* * *

'I can't believe we're here.' Emma's nerves were a tangled mess, she felt half her age, as though back there on the first time she'd come here to the café to see Gabriel and wondered whether he was too good to be true. Those nerves back then had eventually been swapped for a sense of safety and belonging in this man's arms, this man she'd loved with her whole heart. And then she'd lost him. Everything had changed. He'd broken off all contact and she'd never seen him again.

Before they left London, Emma and Lise had searched Facebook and found the café, pictures of food, the place, but no evidence of its owners. Social media had come along after she'd returned from Paris and despite curiosity, her life had been filled with Sam, with Naomi, with the café and she'd wondered whether she'd be in more pain if she found out anything about Gabriel and so she'd left it alone. Until now.

In the photos of the café that did exist on social media, none of them showed Gabriel. None of them showed Delphine either and so today was a long shot. But even if they didn't find out anything, at least Emma had returned to Paris. It felt like that might well go some way to helping her process what happened. It wouldn't be the same, but maybe it could be enough.

The café didn't look much different. It was still nestled in the centre of a row of other businesses, the cobbled street out front as uneven as it had always been. The bright-yellow awnings of a shop on the opposite corner had faded somewhat but the stands were still outside hanging with paraphernalia – hats, a mishmash of clothing.

'If it's not owned by Gabriel and his sister any more,' said Lise, 'then the new owners might point us in the right direction.'

They were hovering thirty paces or so from the café frontage. A moped sped past, its crochety engine drowning out conversation for a moment until the air around them settled again.

'I'm so nervous, Lise. It's ridiculous. He's probably well and truly gone.'

'I know this is hard, but it's why I wanted to bring you here.'

'Is it difficult for you?'

Lise smiled gently. 'Not difficult but definitely weird, because you're here. It's a long time since we were those two girls excited to be in Paris, wowed by the City of Lights, ready for an adventure. Real life kind of gave us a huge slap in the face, didn't it?'

'You always did have a unique way of looking at things.'

'At least I've made you smile and dampened the nerves.'

But still her heart thumped so hard, she had to focus on breathing to calm herself down.

Lise urged her to go into the café and find out once and for all whether Gabriel was still there after all this time. 'You won't find anything out otherwise. And not to be dramatic but we've got around twenty-four hours until we have to get back on that Eurostar, so I wouldn't leave it too much longer.'

When Lise tilted her head and it looked like she was about to lead the way, Emma's arm shot out and pulled her back. 'Thank you for coming here with me. I wouldn't have got on the train, never mind coming up here to the café, if it wasn't for you. But this next bit has to be on my own.'

'Are you sure?'

'Yes, completely sure.'

Lise didn't question it again.

'What will *you* do?'

'You want to know if I'm seeing Xavier.' Lise smiled. 'I'm not.

He's in touch with Maisie but I don't need to see him. This trip is about you. I'm happy to have a wander and I have my phone if you need me, okay?'

Emma nodded and Lise left her to it.

She stood there, frozen in time, with no idea what came next. She felt as though she was stuck in the mist looking down at a clearing, as though everything around her was real and yet somehow, she wasn't.

A woman muttered in French, which Emma took to mean get out of the way. A man bullied his way past in the opposite direction, the line of ash on his cigarette suspended in the air until it broke off and fell to the ground.

Emma's gaze was still fixed on the wide mouth of the café with its darker interior and bright exterior, its tables dotted along the cobbles each with a red and white tablecloth. But what got Emma out of her trance was the woman who came to one of those tables. She was laughing with a customer. She hadn't turned around, but she didn't need to because Emma recognised her instantly.

She felt a familiar lurch of dread in her stomach.

Delphine.

Delphine picked up some plates to go back inside and as she turned, Emma caught her breath and her attention.

It seemed Delphine's filthy look hadn't changed in all these years as she clocked Emma. The death stare didn't last long before she turned her back. She wouldn't have had the chance to pass the information on to the man who came into Emma's field of vision next because he was a few tables away.

Gabriel.

Emma felt her legs almost buckle. She wasn't sure whether she was glad to have found him or not. There he was, setting down two glasses of beer from a round tray balanced on his palm. He had a softness about him now. His hair was shot through with silvery strands, but he had the same familiar smile and tip of his head as he spoke to his customers.

A woman came to his side, kissed him once on the lips and waved her goodbyes at the same time as he looked up, ahead and into the street, and he locked eyes with Emma.

Despite the gap of more than seventeen years, he recognised her instantly and as he did, his shock gave way to the pleasant demeanour she remembered from the day he'd first spoken to her in the supermarket. Without him saying a word, she could already conjure up his smooth, French accent, the gentleness of his tone as his personality and his mannerisms all came flooding back to her.

Gabriel disappeared for what felt like ages but was probably less than a minute and then came back outside, minus the tray he'd been holding, minus the half-cloth clung over his shoulder. And when he reached Emma, he said her name softly, as though it would help him make sense of what was happening.

He leaned in and kissed her first on the right cheek, then the left. He'd put on a bit of weight over the years but it suited him. His hair had thinned, his eyes seemed set a little deeper and the crinkles around them spoke of a life led, a wisdom gained from experiences good and bad.

He took her hands in his. 'Emma, you look well.'

She opened her mouth but when no words came out, he looked over her shoulder, then gestured for her to come with him as he led them away from his own café.

They'd only walked a few metres when they stopped at a different venue, the strong smell of rich coffee enough to bring anyone in from the street. Gabriel put a hand to the small of her back, guiding her inside, where he greeted the owner familiarly and uttered something in French that Emma didn't quite catch before going straight to a table.

'I've asked them to bring us some water and then leave us

alone,' he clarified. When she still said nothing, as though she didn't even have a voice, he added, 'Thank you for coming here to Paris after all this time.'

She had no idea what to say, whether to be mad he'd just broken things off between them when he ceased all contact, that he'd never bothered to try to get in touch, that he hadn't even let her see him when she'd tried time and time again.

He reached out and put his hands over hers and his touch wasn't a shock; it was remembered, a comfort. 'It's been a long time.'

She took her hand away when the waiter brought over a bottle and a couple of glasses. He left them to it as Gabriel had requested.

Gabriel poured the water and Emma realised he wasn't as at ease as he'd seemed when he saw her outside the café or as he'd guided her here. Her own nervousness had stopped her from seeing it at first but she could now. He slopped the water with an unsteady hand as he poured, his shoulders were tense, his gaze kept leaving hers, he gripped his wallet now the drinks were sorted as though it was a talisman.

Finally, he looked up at her again, sadness, devastation and shame written all over his face. '*Je suis perdue pour les mots.*' I don't know what to say.

For some reason, hearing it in French mollified Emma. Not that she was angry but she was still hurt even after all this time. It was why she was here: to get the answers she'd never had. After a breath, she told him, 'Neither do I.'

'It's been so many years.' He moved one of the glasses of water towards her when she didn't touch it. 'Are you staying for a long time? In Paris?'

'It's a quick visit. I'm leaving tomorrow.'

He didn't seem surprised. 'I'm not sure how to begin, where to start, how to say how sorry I am. For everything.'

'I'm here for answers rather than an apology.'

'Delphine saw you,' he said with a small smile that Emma matched. 'She's very protective.'

'She always was. And she's family, I understand. I was the same with my own brother.'

'Toby, I remember.'

'He's dead.' She wasn't sure why she said it like that, maybe to shock him, to inflict a pain he might not even feel, to show just how long it had been since they were Gabriel and Emma, involved in a whirlwind love affair she once thought would never end.

'I am so sorry,' he said both in French and English. Even after all this time, he did what he'd done back then, flipping from one language to the other to make it easier for her to both understand and to learn. 'When?' His hand twitched as though he was going to reach out to her again.

She kept her hands around her water glass, leaned back in her seat. 'Less than a year after I last saw you.'

Being here in a French café, the accent didn't feel as strange as it had the first time she and Lise had come to Paris. Back then, it had been alien, an oddity for them – something they knew they needed to get to grips with. Hearing the rise and fall of French voices this time felt nice, like the appearance of the first spring flowers after a cold, cold winter, a flash of colour hinting at brighter days. Emma hadn't spoken French since she left Paris. Even helping Naomi with her French homework had been a source of pain, something she'd resisted doing. Naomi never had understood why someone who'd spent time living in France wouldn't want to show off their prowess with a second language but she hadn't known the truth then of course. She did now. The night Emma and Lise talked to the girls, they'd told them every-thing, including about the cannabis and the police stop. Naomi had wrapped Emma in a hug and told her she was glad her mum had never got in trouble with the police or taken drugs. It was one of those poignant mother-and-daughter moments Emma would never ever forget.

He expressed his condolences about Toby again but keen to move on to the reason she'd taken this trip, she said, 'You cut me out of your life, just like that.'

Gabriel had never been one to hide his emotions and with him, Emma had only really seen love, tenderness, brightness. Now, he hung his head in mortification like a prisoner who knew they were guilty and had to pay the price. 'I'd brought shame to myself, my family. I knew what you experienced with your friend Alison. I knew your opinion on drugs of any sort. I was ashamed, embarrassed, and I brought humiliation to you.'

'You didn't do anything to me.'

'I felt like a criminal. I felt lucky not to have been sent to prison. It was unimaginable. And I couldn't face you after that. I thought the best thing was to walk away. I bought the drugs; nobody made me. I am a proud man, Emma. I didn't expect you to be a part of my world.'

'But I was. And you were a part of mine. At least you were until suddenly, you weren't. I lost my mind when you wouldn't see me. And Delphine made things so much harder for me.'

'She told me the way she behaved and for that, I am truly sorry.'

'I tried to keep working at the café. I wanted to somehow stay attached to you, but she wouldn't have it and I didn't have the energy to fight for a job where I wasn't welcome.'

'You didn't deserve to be treated that way.'

'You both made it impossible for me to stay.'

He didn't deny it.

'I told Xavier what I thought of his part in it all. Lise and I had a big fight – I had no idea how she could stay with a man who could deal in cannabis. Not after what I saw with Alison, the effect it had on my life. I reached a point where I couldn't take it any more, not when I couldn't even see you or speak to you. So I packed up my things and left. I went back to England for good.'

He kept saying he was sorry and she knew he meant it but there was more she wanted to know. 'Did you ever really love me, Gabriel?'

He looked totally distraught she'd even asked the question. His voice soft, he reached for her hand and this time, she let him take it. '*Ma cherie...* I loved you with all my heart. How could you doubt it? And I did come to find you, Emma. It took me a while but six months after my life fell apart, I came to the apartment. Someone else was living there by then.'

'You came to find me?' She'd questioned his love for her, whether what they'd had had been more in her imagination than reality. She wanted to believe it hadn't been but sometimes, it was easier to think that way, less painful. 'I thought because you wouldn't see me...'

'That we were over?' He shook his head. 'Like I say, I am a proud man and what I'd done filled me with shame. I knew I wouldn't be able to look you in the eye. I moved out of the city, in with my mother who needed me. The distance kept me from being tempted to come after you.'

Emma let the information sink in. He'd come for her, and she'd never known. 'I loved it here in Paris.' She looked out towards the street where life in France rushed on by with the sounds of the car trundling past, someone yelling to another person on the opposite side of the street, the whiff of cigarette smoke that drifted their way from the woman hovering beside the lamppost outside. 'But without you, it all felt different.' The streets full of adventure and promise became dirty, dreary. She'd noticed the crime, the darker edges of the City of Lights, which had faded as the desperate longing for her family tugged at her soul.

Emma waited for the waiter to pass on by with drinks for the table at the back of the café. She lowered her voice to a whisper. 'I don't understand why you bought the cannabis, Gabriel. That's the bit that I really don't get and don't think I ever will. Did you... did you buy it to impress Xavier?'

He swore in his native tongue. 'Even after all this time, I still remember what sort of man Xavier was. He liked to think he was better than everyone else but he wasn't. I didn't do it to impress him, Emma.'

'Then why?'

'I bought the drugs for my mother.' His eyes welled up. 'She's dead now.'

'Shit.'

'*Merde*,' he corrected with a smile that took her back years.

'*Merde*,' she repeated with a smile back at the man who'd once been hers. 'I'm so sorry.'

'My mother was sick for a long time. I never shared the details because it wasn't what she wanted. She was a proud woman. It runs in the family, and she kept her illness hidden. She didn't want to tell everyone her diagnosis and that went for a lot of family except Delphine and I.'

The story poured out, how his mother had been diagnosed with multiple sclerosis, the years that followed, the better times and the hard times. When they were together, Emma had seen Gabriel's mother on a couple of occasions but the visits had been fleeting, she'd never picked up on anything, or perhaps she'd been too blind to anything other than the man she loved.

'When I met you, Emma, she was in a lot of pain every single day. I hated to see her that way. One day, I overheard her talking to someone she met in a support group and they were berating the government for not legalising medicinal cannabis. This friend and my mother had been to Amsterdam several times, before neither of them was able to travel any more, and I listened to them talking about how much it had reduced their pain. They were joking together but I could still hear the desperation in their voices.

'I never intended to do anything about it. I never mentioned to my mum that I'd heard her, but that night at dinner, when Xavier smoked the joint, I found myself wanting so badly to put a smile on my mother's face again, to see her without her pain, to hear her laugh, see her smile. I didn't think about consequences. As a son, I couldn't let her suffer if there was something, anything that I could do. I spoke with Xavier without you or your friend knowing and at first, he said no. He told me he wasn't a dealer, that he didn't want to do anything too risky. But I wouldn't take no for an answer and I persuaded him to get me a decent amount. I thought better to get it all at once than risk having to visit a drug dealer over and over again to get small quantities each time. I didn't think at all about what could happen. Xavier must have – that's why he didn't want to do it.'

'So he was trying to help you?'

'He was. I'm pretty sure he appreciated the money when I bought the cannabis. It didn't come cheap, and I think he'd have liked me asking him for a favour. He was the type of man who would feel power in that way.'

'Why didn't you tell me any of this?'

'I bought the drugs. I got caught. It was my mistake, my shame. Delphine knew about the police stop. I had to tell her with my commitments at the café, and she blamed you because without you, I would never have met Xavier. As far as she's concerned, I would never have been able to get my hands on any drugs.'

Emma understood why he'd done it but she hated that he hadn't told her, that he hadn't trusted her to stand by him.

'I will always be sorry, Emma, for everything,' he said with a look of such hurt in his eyes, she saw the man he was now and the man back then, one with the biggest heart who wanted what was best for those he loved.

Gabriel signalled to the waiter and ordered a coffee for each of them.

'Did your friend go back to England with you?' he asked while they waited.

'Lise? No, she stayed. With Xavier.'

He raised his eyebrows. 'I liked her. I thought she could do better.'

'So did I, but she stayed with him. They got married. Then divorced and now she's back in England. We recently reconnected.'

'I'm glad.'

She told him about the café she ran in England. They joked about the work experience she'd got here being key to her success now. Gabriel talked about a recent offer from a chain to buy his café, which he'd flatly refused.

'It was Lise who persuaded me to come here now,' she told him. 'I don't think I would have otherwise.'

'I'm glad you did.' With a sigh, he said, 'It must feel like another world here after all this time.'

'It does, and yet in some ways, it's like it was only yesterday.'

'You look well, really well.' His gaze dipped to her left hand.

She knew what he was thinking. She'd worn her wedding ring for a couple of years after Sam died but now it was in a box in her bedside table drawer at the back. Now and then, she took it out and slipped it on, but she'd never worn it properly again.

'I hope you've been happy, Emma.' It was more of a question than a statement.

'I have been. And I was married. I met a wonderful man – Sam.

But he died.' Her eyes glistened. 'So many people have died. I hate it.'

'Me too.' He took her hands, both of them, this time. 'But please tell me you still have a lot of love in your life, Emma. You deserve it.'

A smile formed. 'I have a daughter – Naomi.' She took her hands away and pulled out her phone from her bag to show him a picture of her with Naomi taken last summer in Honeybee Place by the railings with the garden behind them an abundance of colour.

'She is beautiful. Like her mother.'

'Thank you.' She thought of Naomi getting to know her cousin, keeping her grandad company, probably desperate to know what was happening in Paris right this very minute as her mum returned to reconnect with the former love of her life. 'And you? Do you have children? Are you married?'

He nodded. 'I have two boys and I'm married to Yvette. She was at the café before. She went to pick up the boys from her parents'. I told her about you, about everything that happened.'

'I'm glad. Secrets are no good in a marriage.' She asked, 'Do you still paint?'

He smiled. 'Whenever I can.'

'I'm glad – you always loved it.'

'I still have the portrait I did of you. Would you like me to send it?'

She briefly considered it but thought twice. 'You keep it.' Having it now wouldn't change anything; it wouldn't bring back what they'd had and lost. They'd both got on with their lives.

After they settled the bill, they emerged onto the street. Neither of them needed to say that this would be the last time they would see each other.

'I'll always be glad we met,' said Gabriel. 'Be happy, Emma.'

He didn't kiss her on the cheek; instead, he wrapped her in a hug that was years too late and the final stamp on their relationship.

And as she walked to meet Lise after texting her to find out where she was, she felt a sense of departure from everything she'd held on to for years, an embrace of what was still to come.

30

NOW: 2023

Lise

'You look nervous.' Emma stood behind Lise as they looked into the full-length mirror at Lise's outfit. Back in Honeybee Place after a whistle-stop trip to Paris, Lise had a dinner to get ready for.

'Do I look like I'm trying too hard?' With the both of them standing here, it reminded Lise of all those times they'd got ready for nights out, throwing outfits on the bed, getting another from the wardrobe, swapping outfits where they could, mixing and matching, trying to find the perfect combination.

'Of course you don't.'

'Maybe I should put jeans on instead of a dress. I mean, who wears a dress when they're entertaining at home?'

Their gazes met in the mirror as Lise said, 'My mother' at the same time as Emma announced, 'Your mother.'

Over the weeks since their return from Paris, they'd fallen back into their friendship gradually and tentatively. They'd talked about the men in their lives past and present. They'd talked about Toby a lot, with Emma sharing as much as she could with his daughter.

They'd talked about Sam a lot too. He had no graveside to visit – he hadn't wanted that. Naomi and Emma and his parents had scattered his ashes at sea. Maisie had gone with them to the cemetery to visit Toby. They'd left her alone for a while but Lise knew her daughter was unlikely to have said anything out loud. Slowly but surely, Maisie was getting to know the father she would've absolutely adored – Lise had no doubt about that.

Lise unzipped her dress. 'I just want this to go well. Maisie has met Max but having dinner all together officially feels a bit more serious.' Tonight, there would be five of them – Lise, Emma, Max, Maisie and Naomi. Brendan had been asked along too but he'd turned down the invitation and would instead be having a few games of cards with Max's father William. Lise had a sneaky suspicion Brendan might want to shout it from the rooftops that Maisie was a part of his family, and William would be a good place to start.

'It's serious because you've said the magic three words,' Emma teased before floating around the room grinning. 'I love you, Max. Technically that's four but you know what I mean.'

'Stop!' But Lise was giggling like a teenager all over again.

'I'm so happy for the both of you,' said Emma sitting down on the bed. 'Max has been like another brother to me since losing Toby. He's a part of the family.'

'That's what worries me.' She paused mid removing her dress. 'You're all close to him. What if it doesn't work out and then I can't show my face at the Millers'? Again.'

'Lise, would you stop worrying and hurry up and decide what to wear.'

She grunted and shimmied off the dress. Her red, Victoria's Secret underwear earned her a whistle from Emma.

'Since when could you whistle?' Lise burst out laughing.

'Sam taught me.'

Lise found a pair of jeans she loved with flowers embroidered on the rear pockets and took out a black, silk top with a flattering V-neckline. She pulled them on and reassessed.

'Perfect,' said Emma. 'And the red underwear, pretty hot. The question is, will Max be a fan of red lace?'

'Ew,' came a voice behind them.

'Maisie,' groaned Lise. 'Haven't you heard it's rude to creep up on unsuspecting parents who may or may not be getting ready for a date?'

'You're wearing sex underwear.' Maisie cringed.

'Is it so terrible to imagine a forty-four-year-old woman – who, I might add, is in the prime of her life – being intimate with a man?'

'Yes! When it's her mother! Imagine Nanna.'

Lise pulled her daughter into a playful hug and ruffled her hair. 'Now that really is ew. But you've made your point.'

Maisie straightened herself up. 'You do look sexy, Mum.'

'Why thank you.' Lise nodded to Emma. 'That's top approval from a teen.'

'How about you, Auntie Emma?' Maisie sat next to Emma on Lise's bed. 'When are you going to start dating?'

'Me? No, I don't have time for dating.'

'I beg to differ,' Lise chipped in while she applied siren-red lipstick to her lips. 'And that guy in the café yesterday was definitely interested.'

'Which guy?' Maisie leapt in.

'His name is Liam,' Lise told her. 'He was watching Emma yesterday, couldn't take his eyes off her in fact.'

'I need to know more!' Maisie's eyes danced.

'Nothing to tell,' Emma insisted. But Lise knew that look: the slight coyness, the almost undetectable blush. It meant that Emma would very much like there to be.

When the doorbell went, Lise requested five minutes to say hello to Max before the others came downstairs and called back over her shoulder, 'I heard that,' when Maisie said something about kissing.

'Wow,' was the first word out of Max's mouth when Lise opened the door. He leaned in and kissed her passionately, uncaring that he got lipstick on his own lips. 'I'm not sure anyone could pull off jeans and a shirt so well.' He held up a bottle of wine. 'Where should I put this?'

'Let me take it for you.' She led the way to the kitchen.

'Something smells good. I think my stomach just groaned.'

With a laugh, she told him what was on the menu. 'Piri-piri chicken with buttered corn on the side.' It was almost a one-pot dish, save the corn, and had allowed her to do all the prep earlier then have it out the way so she could get ready.

She offered him a glass of wine. It was weird having him here because Emma was right: things felt as though they had shifted since they'd said 'I love you' to each other a couple of nights ago. She only hoped they hadn't ruined what was turning out to be a good thing by rushing it. She didn't think so but maybe Max did and the uncertainty was something Lise hadn't had to face for a long time, not since before Paris.

Lise and Max had been walking through Royal Victoria Park and for a moment, she'd got the feeling he was trying to pluck up the courage to end things with her. He was quieter than usual. She heard him clear his throat. Whenever she turned to look at him, his gaze was down at the pavement.

'Max, what is it?' she demanded, walking into his path and stopping him with a hand to his chest so he could walk no further. 'There's something you're not telling me and this is torture. Look, if you want to break up with me, just do it, just get it over with. No hard feelings – we can be friends. I won't hold it again—'

He pulled her into a kiss that took her breath away and earned them a yell from the other side of the road from two schoolkids who instructed them to, 'Get a room!'

'What was that for?' He still had his hands on her upper arms, holding her there when he pulled away.

'It's to make you shut up.'

'Well, charming.'

'I do have something to say to you.' Another nervous swallow, a hesitation preceded: 'Lise, I love you. There, I said it. Now you might not say it back, but I'm prepare—'

This time, it was Lise who silenced him. She stood on her tiptoes, her arms around his neck and went in for more than a firm kiss; it was a kiss that lasted and lasted and had them laughing and heading over to a tree so they would be out of view of anyone else.

She barely let a gap form between their mouths when she breathed, 'You know I love you too, right?'

He looked down at her, his gaze on her mouth but darting to her eyes. 'Well I do now.'

They'd walked home with their arms around each other but Max had had to rush off to pick up his dad when he called to say he'd missed the bus and then the day after that, Max had a commitment with work, Lise had an outing with Maisie and a dinner at the Millers'. This was the first night they'd seen one another since they'd both admitted their feelings.

In the kitchen now, Max poked his head out the door, had a quick check the coast was clear and then pulled her into his arms. 'No offence to Maisie, Emma and Naomi, but I can't wait to get you all to myself later.'

She kissed him again. 'I can't wait either.' The last man she'd admitted to being in love with had been Xavier and there hadn't been anyone serious since. There'd barely been anyone at all. Max was unexpected but in a totally different way to Xavier. Xavier had swept her off her feet with his attention, his compliments. Max and Lise getting together had been without much drama, a gentle falling for each other, the slow burn that had the power to last. In some ways, it was fuelled with more passion than the way she'd fallen for Xavier. Max was gentle, considerate and tender-hearted and she didn't feel she needed to look for his attention, she was looking for a match, someone to talk with and laugh with and someone who made her toes curl when they kissed. Max ticked every single one of those boxes.

Maisie interrupted. 'You should leave a review,' she said from behind Max.

'Maisie, stop sneaking up on people,' Lise reprimanded.

'To be fair, I heard someone coming,' Max admitted and when Maisie went to answer the next knock at the door, wondered, 'What does she mean about the review?'

Voices came along the hallway and Maisie, Emma and Naomi piled into the kitchen – Naomi with a cheesecake Emma had made earlier which Emma expertly transferred straight to the fridge.

Maisie leaned back against the counter next to Max and told him, 'What I meant was that you could leave a review of Victoria's Secret.'

Poor Max still looked confused. Emma was laughing and Lise thought she might well have to have a word with Maisie about boundaries no matter whether it was amusing or not. She ushered the four of them out of the way while she cooked the sweetcorn and readied the plates for dishing up the piri-piri chicken casserole that had been cooking in the slow cooker for hours and smelled delicious.

As Lise waited for the corn to cook, she surreptitiously watched her guests sitting at the kitchen island. Emma was explaining to Maisie how she'd made the Seville orange marmalade cheesecake for dessert and Max and Naomi were debating the merits of sport for all ages. The scene here now was a relaxed affair compared to anything she'd witnessed in this same kitchen growing up with two parents who had no idea to give her what she needed.

The evening went on in much the same way as it started – with a healthy level of chatter, of laughter, reminders of the past, the present and the future.

Max, inexperienced with teenagers and the way they grasped hold of threads of information, rendering it impossible to sweep what you'd said underneath the carpet, happened to mention Liam and Naomi was onto it.

'Are you going to date him, Mum?' She put her cutlery together on her plate.

'I don't know.' Emma shot Max a look and he mouthed the words *I'm sorry* in return. 'Would you mind if I did? Not that I'm saying that I will.'

'As long as he's not a complete tool,' Naomi said with such seriousness, they all laughed. 'I mean it. There's a girl at school and her mum is on her fourth boyfriend and they've all been weird so far.'

'Okay,' Emma agreed, 'I promise not to date any weirdos.'

Lise told her niece, 'He's got that sexy professor vibe going on with those glasses.'

Maisie and Naomi sniggered and Naomi said, 'I've seen him in the café. I guess he's good-looking for an older man.'

Emma shook her head. 'Enough analysing a man I'm not even dating. Why don't you let me be in charge of my own life. If he asks me out, you lot better back off a bit.'

'Never.' Lise grinned, earning a lively agreement from Naomi and Maisie.

They all agreed to put the dessert on hold for a bit and talk turned to travelling. Maisie and Naomi floated the idea about going somewhere the summer after they finished their A levels and by the sounds of it, it wasn't their first conversation about it.

'We were thinking of backpacking.' Maisie tested the waters alongside her cousin.

'We'd have to save up first,' said Naomi.

'We could do it without working if we save enough,' said Maisie, 'six months of seeing Europe, no parents, no responsibilities. Go interrailing – I know a couple of girls from badminton who did it last year. Let's ask them.'

Lise and Emma exchanged a look.

'We could start in Paris,' Naomi went on, their excitement rising. 'It's an easy trip on the Eurostar.'

'Girls, are you sure about this?' Lise interrupted.

They both chorused, 'yes' and Lise looked at Emma, who shrugged.

And as the girls went on to plan the city after Paris, the next and the next, Lise resigned herself to the fact that her daughter wanted to spread her wings. The difference with Maisie and the way she'd been, however, was that Lise had wanted and needed to get away and, unlike Lise, Maisie would always know that there was a place for her with her mum who loved her more than life itself.

When Lise took the plates to the dishwasher and insisted her guests stay seated, it wasn't long until Emma came over.

But Lise wouldn't let her help. 'You do enough of this at work. Sit down, Emma.'

'Not until you tell me what you're thinking.' Emma stubbornly hovered next to the dishwasher.

Lise rested her hands on the edge of the sink. 'I'm thinking that I don't want to lose this,' she said softly, barely able to meet her friend's eye. 'Any of this.'

'You mean us?'

'No... at least I hope not. We're in a good place now, aren't we?' She braved a look at Emma.

A lively conversation continued around them, with Max recalling his rugby days with Toby, keeping the girls more than entertained.

'I'm not going anywhere, Lise,' said Emma. 'I promise you.'

'No, but I am.' She looked around the kitchen, its warmth all wrapped up within its walls now that it was full of people, of noise. 'This place – I have a buyer. A very keen buyer.' She looked at Emma, who momentarily froze but not for long. 'You don't seem surprised, or bothered.' And that saddened her because it meant that perhaps they wouldn't ever be those two best friends again.

'I'm not surprised as it's a gorgeous house,' said Emma. 'You know how sought after Honeybee Place is.'

Lise had to wonder whether Emma was happy with the development or whether she was trying to be positive for Lise's sake.

'Emma, why aren't you sad that I'll be leaving?'

'Because *you're* not. I know you, Lise. I've known you for decades. I knew you then, and I know you now. *Then,* you were a different person, not entirely happy here, unsure of yourself, looking for what you thought your life should be. *Now,* you're this gorgeous, glamorous and successful woman and an even bigger part of my family than you were. *Now,* you know what you want.'

'Do I? What if I don't want to leave?'

'Only you can make that decision. I know what I'm hoping for but this isn't about me, it's about you. And that's okay.' Emma put one arm around her friend and squeezed tight. And she went back over to the others without adding anything more.

Lise batted away more offers to help clean up and once the dishwasher was chugging away and the worst of the pots soaking in the sink, she took another bottle of wine over to her guests and sat next to Max as he looped an arm across her shoulders.

When they were all ready for it, the cheesecake went down a treat and eventually, Emma declared it was time to go home given she had a café to run in the morning. The girls decided they'd go see their grandad if he was still awake and even if he wasn't, it was a sleepover at the Millers' tonight. Just like that, Naomi and Maisie could almost be Lise and Emma when they were the same age, sharing their lives on a daily basis.

Lise wrapped her friend in a close hug in the hallway as Maisie came bundling down the stairs with a bag packed, her pyjamas hanging out of the top. 'That cheesecake was something I'm going to have to try again.'

'Plenty left in the fridge.' Emma smiled before turning to Max to hug him goodbye. 'You're all invited to my place next.'

As Emma, Maisie and Naomi left in a gaggle as though they were three teens who hadn't spoken for weeks when they'd exhausted every avenue of conversation tonight it seemed, Lise and Max hovered in the doorway.

Lise sighed. 'I love the end of the day when the city goes to sleep and the stars come out.'

Max wrapped his arms around her from behind. 'Me too. I enjoyed tonight.'

'Maisie likes you.'

'Yeah?' She felt him laugh into her hair. 'I like her too. But I'm secretly glad we have the house to ourselves now.'

'About the house…' She rested her hands on his. 'I had an offer come through this afternoon from the estate agent.'

She felt his body sag. 'That's good I suppose.'

'I don't think I want to leave this place.'

He latched on to the suggestion when he told her, 'So don't.'

She grinned. 'I won't. I just emailed them back. I declined officially. I'm not selling.'

When he spun her around to face him, she looped her arms

around his neck. 'Number twelve is off the market,' she said, 'and so am I.'

'I should hope so too.' He bent his head, found her lips and kissed her with more passion than she'd ever felt before.

And as the door to number twelve, with its gleaming brass knocker, closed, the stars twinkled above the rooftops of Honeybee Place, illuminating the rows of townhouses, shining down on the grass square in the middle.

Lise climbed the stairs with Max in the place she didn't plan on leaving any time soon. Because tonight, number twelve Honeybee Place was no longer a house. Finally, it was a home.

ACKNOWLEDGEMENTS

When I sat down to plan this book, I knew I wanted to write a story focused on the bonds of female friendship. Therefore my biggest thank you this time goes to all the friends who have inspired this novel. Some of you will recognise parts of the book, I'm sure! It's been so much fun to write, emotional at times but I hope what I've given readers is a touching story about the enduring nature of friendships in our lives despite tough times and challenges.

Thank you to my family who are my biggest supporters always, whether it's staying out of my way while I write, being my sounding board or helping me celebrate every publication. (This is book number thirty-one so I'm surprised they haven't had enough yet!)

Thank you to Rachel Faulkner-Willcocks for her editing expertise to help shape this story into a much better version of itself and to the rest of the team at Boldwood Books who work tirelessly to bring our books to readers on publication day in all formats all around the world.

And finally, an enormous thank you to you, my reader, for picking up this book. I hope you love the story as much as I do.

Love Helen x

ABOUT THE AUTHOR

Helen Rolfe is the author of many bestselling contemporary women's fiction titles, set in different locations from the Cotswolds to New York. She lives in Hertfordshire with her husband and children.

Sign up to Helen Rolfe's mailing list for news, competitions and updates on future books.

Visit Helen's website: www.helenjrolfe.com

Follow Helen on social media here:

facebook.com/helenjrolfewriter

x.com/hjrolfe

instagram.com/helen_j_rolfe

ALSO BY HELEN ROLFE

Heritage Cove Series

Coming Home to Heritage Cove

Christmas at the Little Waffle Shack

Winter at Mistletoe Gate Farm

Summer at the Twist and Turn Bakery

Finding Happiness at Heritage View

Christmas Nights at the Star and Lantern

New York Ever After Series

Snowflakes and Mistletoe at the Inglenook Inn

Christmas at the Little Knitting Box

Wedding Bells on Madison Avenue

Christmas Miracles at the Little Log Cabin

Moonlight and Mistletoe at the Christmas Wedding

Christmas Promises at the Garland Street Markets

Family Secrets at the Inglenook Inn

Little Woodville Cottage Series

Christmas at Snowdrop Cottage

Summer at Forget-Me-Not Cottage

Standalones

The Year That Changed Us

LOVE NOTES

LOVE IN EVERY CHAPTER

WHERE ALL YOUR ROMANCE
DREAMS COME TRUE!

THE HOME OF BESTSELLING
ROMANCE AND WOMEN'S
FICTION

 WARNING:
MAY CONTAIN SPICE

SIGN UP TO OUR
NEWSLETTER

https://bit.ly/Lovenotesnews

Boldwood

Boldwood Books is an award-winning fiction publishing company seeking out the best stories from around the world.

Find out more at www.boldwoodbooks.com

Join our reader community for brilliant books, competitions and offers!

Follow us
@BoldwoodBooks
@TheBoldBookClub

Sign up to our weekly
deals newsletter

https://bit.ly/BoldwoodBNewsletter